AND ONLY MAN IS VILE

SUSAN ALEXANDER

Also by the author

The Snowdrop Mysteries:
The Ainswick Orange
The Snowdrop Crusade
A Remittance Man
The Heracles Project
St Margaret's
Beaumatin's Blonde
Hereford Crescent
Wolcum Yole
Gnat
And Only Man is Vile
Jersey Jones and the New World Order

A Woman's Book of Rules

Cover: Daniele da Volterra. The Massacre of the Innocents
(1557)

AND ONLY MAN IS VILE

To Bill, Gosia and William

From Greenland's Icy Mountains

From Greenland's icy mountains, from India's coral strand;
Where Afric's sunny fountains roll down their golden sand:
From many an ancient river, from many a palmy plain,
They call us to deliver their land from error's chain.

What though the spicy breezes blow soft o'er Ceylon's isle;
Though every prospect pleases, and only man is vile?
In vain with lavish kindness the gifts of God are strown;
The heathen in his blindness bows down to wood and stone.

Shall we, whose souls are lighted with wisdom from on high,
Shall we to those benighted the lamp of life deny?
Salvation! O salvation! The joyful sound proclaim,
Till earth's remotest nation has learned Messiah's Name.

Waft, waft, ye winds, His story, and you, ye waters, roll
Till, like a sea of glory, it spreads from pole to pole:
Till o'er our ransomed nature the Lamb for sinners slain,
Redeemer, King, Creator, in bliss returns to reign.

The Right Reverend Reginald Heber
Bishop of Calcutta 1783 - 1826

The Massacre of the Innocents

Then Herod, when he saw that he was deceived by the Wise Men, was exceedingly angry; and he sent forth and put to death all the male children who were in Bethlehem and in all its districts, from two years old and under, according to the time which he had determined from the Wise Men. Then was fulfilled what was spoken by Jeremiah the prophet, saying:

> "A voice was heard in Ramah,
> Lamentation, weeping, and great mourning,
> Rachel weeping for her children,
> Refusing to be comforted,
> Because they are no more."

Gospel of Matthew 2: 16- 18

Chapter 1

"That really was the straw that broke the camel's back," muttered Maggie to herself as she drove away. Although what had happened had not been just a straw. It was more like an entire bale of straw. Maggie assumed that a bale of straw would be quite heavy. Not that she had ever lifted a bale of straw. Though there were certainly enough bales on the estate had she wanted to try.

Earlier that afternoon, William Conyers, who was her husband Thomas' oldest son from his first marriage, and his wife Gweneth had come to visit and Gweneth had happily announced that she was pregnant with a third child. She and William already had a son Harry, aged eight, and a daughter Elizabeth, aged six.

"It—the baby I mean—should be due in November sometime," Gweneth told Maggie.

"That's wonderful, Gweneth," Maggie had said, while she ignored the inner voice that was sniggering, "Step-grandmother? Again?"

Maggie had been married to Thomas for less than a year and was still adjusting. The tall, post-menopausal American with emerald green eyes and unruly auburn curls had been a professor at Oxford's Merrion College when she had improbably met and fallen in love with Thomas, who happened to be the twenty-eighth Baron Raynham. They were living together at Beaumatin, the Raynham estate in the Cotswolds.

Thomas was also pleased by Gweneth's announcement.

"Why don't you stay for dinner?" Thomas asked his daughter-in-law.

"The Ainswicks are coming. And Chloe and David. I'm sure they'll be delighted at the news and you and Chloe can talk babies."

Lord and Lady Ainswick were old friends of Thomas. They lived at nearby Rochford Manor with their daughter Chloe and her husband, David Osborne. Chloe had married David the previous autumn and was expecting a child in July. And Gweneth was Lord Ainswick's niece.

The Ainswicks and Osbornes arrived together. Lady Ainswick—Beatrix—was an energetic woman in her mid-sixties, with long greying hair confined in a bun and sharp blue eyes. Cedric, her husband, was ten years her senior. He stood straight and tall, with a full mane of white hair and distinguished features.

Chloe Osborne was a pretty brunette who resembled her mother at a younger age while David was a good-looking man in his early thirties, with curly brown hair and hazel eyes. A botanist, he had taken on the responsibility of overseeing Rochford Manor's famous snowdrop garden.

The group was chatting and enjoying salmon in a mustard dill sauce prepared by Mrs Cook, the Beaumatin housekeeper, when noises were heard from the hall. The dining room door opened and a young woman entered. She was in her late twenties, blonde and very pretty, but looked tired and dishevelled from travel. It was Thomas' daughter Constance.

"Hello everybody. I've come home," she announced.

Her proclamation was greeted by stunned silence.

Mrs Cook entered behind her. In her fifties, she was pleasingly plump, had curly grey hair and had spent the last quarter century managing the Raynham household.

"Miss Constance, where would you like me to put your luggage?" the housekeeper asked somewhat anxiously.

"In my usual room, please, Mrs Cook. But first, I'd love some dinner."

While Beatrix moved over to make a place for Constance beside her father, Mrs Cook hurriedly put out an extra place setting.

Thomas, who had stood, along with the other men, sat down again and said, "Constance? This is a surprise. What brings you here?"

Constance daintily ate a bite of salmon.

"I've left Nils and quit my job. I'm moving back home," she said complacently

"What?" William exclaimed and Maggie tried hard not to show how horrified she felt.

Constance hated Maggie and made no attempt to hide her feelings. Her wedding at Beaumatin, which had taken place just before Christmas three months before, had nearly wrecked Maggie's marriage.

Everyone was staring at Constance in varying degrees of disbelief.

"I'm pregnant. Nils was unhappy about that. Having a baby so soon after the wedding. I didn't care for his attitude so... Here I am."

"Good God," said Thomas.

"And you think you're going to move back to Beaumatin? To live?" Maggie spoke before she thought.

"Why yes. Of course. Where else would I go? Beaumatin is my home. More mine than yours, certainly."

"But…"

"You're just jealous, you barren bitch," Constance snapped.

There was a moment of shocked silence. Then…

"I say, Constance," Cedric remonstrated.

"Really, Constance," protested Beatrix.

"Shut up, Constance," ordered William.

Maggie waited for Thomas.

"That will be enough, Constance," he spoke repressively.

Constance subsided, but not before she smirked triumphantly down the table at Maggie.

That will be enough was not enough, thought Maggie. No way would she tolerate sharing a house with this spoiled, toxic girl. Especially since, for whatever reason, Thomas seemed disinclined to address her bad behaviour.

So while people were enjoying coffee and cognac in the drawing room, Maggie excused herself. She went to her room, put some clothes and toiletries in a bag, packed up her laptop and took off in the Land Rover Thomas had given her for her birthday. Her right arm was still in a cast from having been broken two weeks before, but she could just about manage to drive. That she could use her left hand to shift made it possible.

She would go to Oxford. It was March. Hilary term was over and Trinity term would not start until well into April. She decided she would not go to the elegant townhouse on Hereford Crescent. Part of the Raynham real estate portfolio, the house had been fixed up by Thomas so they would have a place to stay while she was at Merrion and he could get away from the demands of Beaumatin. Instead, she would stay in her own rooms at the college.

But what to do with the car? Parking near the University was notoriously difficult, not to say impossible. And she was avoiding Hereford Crescent. Maggie decided to call Stephen Draycott, a colleague who had a home not far from the college. His wife had died the previous autumn and he had moved into his rooms at Merrion while he prepared to sell the house with its memories.

"Stephen? It's Maggie. I'm making an unexpected trip to Oxford and wondered if I could park my car at your place?"

Stephen graciously said of course. Maggie promised she would call him as soon as she arrived at Merrion and they could meet for a drink.

Maggie climbed the flight of stairs to her rooms and dumped her bags on the floor. She looked around at the oak-panelled room with its large wooden refectory table surrounded by eight ladder-backed wooden chairs she used for seminars, a pair of comfortable leather club chairs in front of a fireplace and an old-fashioned wooden desk. The walls were lined with bookcases. An adjoining room that she almost never used had a Victorian brass bed covered with an antique quilt, another arm chair, an old wooden chest of drawers and a small bathroom.

The rooms were comfortable and functional. Meant to welcome rather than to impress. There were no great halls, no ancestral portraits, no Aubusson carpets, no ornately plastered ceilings, no inlaid floors, no tapestries, no crystal chandeliers, no eight hundred years of Beaumatin's baronial grandeur. But it was her space and, bruised as she was feeling, she needed to be someplace that was her very own.

Her broken arm was aching badly after the drive, so she took a painkiller before calling Stephen. She was sorry her closest friend on the faculty, Chitta Kazi, was not there. Chitta had rooms directly over Maggie's and knew about her friend's problems with Constance. But Chitta was away on her own honeymoon in Costa Rica and would not be back for another week.

Maggie called Stephen to tell him she had arrived and then turned off her mobile.

Stephen appeared bearing a bottle of Bollinger champagne. A handsome man of fifty, with long dark hair he wore combed back and chocolate brown eyes, he was dressed casually in jeans, a dress shirt and a tweed jacket. He stopped abruptly when he saw Maggie's cast.

"Good God. What happened?"

"A stupid accident. Too boring to recount."

"And your right arm. Hand. Must be inconvenient."

"You have no idea."

"Thomas around?"

"No."

"And you're staying here?"

"Yes."

"Not at Hereford Crescent?"

"No."

Maggie sighed.

Stephen began to open the Bolly.

"Thomas' daughter? Constance? Hates me. Would love to dance on my grave. She got married at Beaumatin just before Christmas, which was its own nightmare. But I thought she was safely back in Switzerland with her new husband and life could go on.

"Then suddenly tonight she showed up at Beaumatin during dinner, announced she had quit her job—a good one, too, as an epidemiologist at the World Health Organisation in Geneva—left her husband and was moving back home. Because she was pregnant. Apparently Nils was less than thrilled at the prospect of becoming a father so soon after the wedding.

"She's never bothered to hide her feelings for me and, for whatever reason, Thomas just ignores her bad behaviour. So it gets worse and worse. I certainly don't want to put him in a position of having to choose between us. But tonight, when I voiced my concern about her moving back to Beaumatin—can you imagine what meals would be like? — she said I was jealous and called me a 'barren bitch.' In front of the Ainswicks. And their daughter and her husband. And William and Gweneth. And Thomas' reaction? He just tsked tsked. I found that... inadequate. So I left and came here."

Stephen handed her a glass of champagne. He looked shocked.

"But I thought his lordship was a stickler for proper behaviour."

"Apparently Constance is the exception that proves the rule. Anyhow I decided I needed to get away. Create some space. Maybe it will be easier for Thomas to deal with Constance if I'm not around. If not…"

Maggie shrugged and took a large sip of her champagne.

"But enough of my problems. What have you been up to?"

"Finalising arrangements for Liu Zhengyu to come here as a visiting professor for Trinity term. He's a distinguished scholar. Professor of International Relations at Renmin University in Beijing. But you wouldn't believe the paperwork that's involved. In the meantime, we've already started working on the book on China we'll be producing for your Global Press series."

Maggie nodded. That was good news. Maggie was going to be the editor of a series of books called "The Developing World."

"And we have the first in a string of retirement bashes for Alastair on Friday," Stephen reminded her.

Alastair Carrington, the Master of Merrion College, was leaving after two distinguished decades at the helm of the institution. A festive reception between terms to which senior faculty and their spouses were invited was the first of a series of commemorative events.

"And have you heard anything about his replacement?"

"No. Although rumours abound. And Alastair hinted that I should be hopeful."

Stephen aspired to be the college's next master.

"That would be wonderful, Stephen. I certainly would be quite pleased."

"I also heard that they have chosen a new Appleton fellow."

Maggie had been the Appleton fellow for eight years when she had married Thomas, but had found trying to balance her work at Oxford and life with her new husband difficult. She had accepted another position, the Weingarten chair, whose demands could be primarily fulfilled at Beaumatin. Although that might no longer be an issue, she reminded herself.

"Do you know who it is?"

"Only more rumours. Some Islamic scholar. Possibly chosen to counterbalance your views," Stephen teased.

Maggie wrote about immigration and cultural integration. And her view was, if you immigrate to Britain in search of a better life, you should be prepared to integrate culturally and leave the niqab at home. Her research indicated immigrants who did integrate were more successful, especially when it came to their children. The liberals hated her positions and the conservatives thought she was anti-immigration. Both thought she was anti-Muslim, which she was not. But neither side seemed to actually read her work before they praised or condemned.

Maggie suddenly found she could hardly keep her eyes open. She remembered it was probably not a good idea to combine alcohol with the painkiller.

"I'm sorry, Stephen, but I'm exhausted. Let's talk more tomorrow."

Maggie collapsed fully clothed on her bed. Her mobile lay on her desk, turned off.

Chapter 2

Thomas did not appear until six o'clock the following evening.

Maggie had been working and heard a knock at her door. She assumed it was Stephen, whom she had arranged to meet for dinner, although he would be early.

"Come in."

Thomas burst through the door. For a brief instant he looked relieved. Then relief was replaced by anger.

"So here you are. Anne didn't know where you were. Beatrix didn't know. Malcolm didn't know. You hadn't been to Hereford Crescent. And your phone is shut off. If you hadn't been here I would have thought about trying to find you in Scarborough. Or Boston."

Maggie looked at her husband without expression.

"I'm taking you home."

"Home?" Maggie sounded incredulous.

Thomas was taken aback, but persisted.

"Yes. Home."

"No. Absolutely not. Certainly not if things are as they were when I left."

"Yes. You left. Without saying a word. To anyone."

"I didn't think there was anyone to tell. And I had already been humiliated enough, thank you."

Thomas flushed. Both Beatrix and William had not hesitated to let him know exactly what they thought about Constance's behaviour. And his not sticking up for Maggie.

"Really, Father. You have to do something. Constance is getting worse and worse. What she said was inexcusable and I suspect even Maggie has her limits."

William was irate.

"I'm genuinely shocked, Thomas. That wedding was bad enough. The position Constance put Maggie in. And if that girl thinks she can say such things in the presence of others… Obviously you've given her the impression that you'll tolerate any amount of bad behaviour. And William is right. If you don't do something, you'll lose Maggie. I'm assuming you would rather not have that happen," Beatrix scolded.

Then William had gone to tell Constance she could not stay at Beaumatin. She could come home with him and Gweneth if she wanted until other arrangements could be made. Constance pouted but finally consented to go with her brother.

Meanwhile, Thomas had gone in search of Maggie. He had combed the entire house and become increasingly frantic when he failed to find her. Finally he realised her laptop was gone. As well as the Land Rover. Were William and Beatrix right?

Maggie continued.

"Actions should have consequences, Thomas. But you seem to have given Constance an exemption certificate. Wasn't her wedding enough for you?"

When Thomas had remonstrated with Constance about what had happened at that event, his daughter had said that she wished the murderer who had killed one of the wedding guests had killed Maggie as well.

"I have always treated Constance with courtesy. And tried to turn the other cheek. But you never... You never..."

Maggie stood. She turned to go into the back room. She needed a tissue.

"Maggie..."

"No." She was blinking back tears.

Thomas caught her arm.

"Maggie. I'm sorry."

"Sorry's not enough."

She tried to pull away, but he grabbed her other arm as well.

"Maggie, you promised. You promised you would never leave, no matter what I said, no matter what I did..."

"It wasn't what you said or did. It was what she said. And what you didn't do. It was just... intolerable."

Maggie pulled away and went into the other room. Where was that box of tissues?

She sat on the edge of the bed and swiped at her eyes with the back of her hand.

Thomas sat down beside her and handed her his handkerchief, a perfectly pressed, pristine white cotton square.

Maggie wiped her eyes and blew her nose.

"Constance is staying at William's until she's, er, straightened out. If she doesn't go back to Nils she can stay in one of the Raynham flats in Cheltenham. Or London."

"There are no Raynham holdings in Ulan Bator?"

"I'm afraid not, Papillon. But I promise Beaumatin is not an option. And I will speak to her. I doubt she'd want her allowance withheld."

Maggie looked stricken. "Truly, Thomas. I don't want to…"

"No. You're right. Her behaviour is completely unacceptable. I've been too tolerant. Or perhaps, if I'm honest, just hoping to avoid unpleasantness. I'm sorry, Maggie."

He pulled her up.

"Come."

She shook her head.

"Maggie?"

Thomas' voice held the beginnings of panic.

"Constance was right when she said Beaumatin was more her home than mine. I keep feeling like my presence there is provisional. Subject to approval. Your approval. It makes it hard for me to feel like Beaumatin is home. That any Raynham property is home. So I've decided…"

"What?" Thomas' voice was strained.

"That I need my own space. Someplace not part of the Raynham, er, empire. That's not provisional. So I decided.

When I'm in Oxford. And you're not here. That I am going to stay here. In my rooms. At Merrion. And not at Hereford Crescent. When you're not here."

Maggie was regarding Thomas nervously.

Thomas felt a rush of relief. Then became coolly calculating. He knew the reason Maggie felt like she no longer had her own space was that he had manoeuvred her into giving up her comfortable Oxford flat and moving into the Hereford Crescent townhouse.

He had told her at the time that her flat was too small for the two of them and that he wanted to be able to come and stay in Oxford when she was there, although his motives were, in fact, more complicated.

However, with her new position, which limited the hours she needed to be physically present at Merrion, he figured the amount of time when his wife would be at Oxford without him would be small.

So he responded mildly, "As you wish, my dear."

Maggie, who had not realised she had been holding her breath, exhaled.

Thomas put out his hand, "So, as I am here, shall we go?"

"I, um, told Stephen that I'd have dinner with him. I'm sure he'd be pleased if you joined us."

Thomas looked unenthusiastic.

"It will be simple. A gastro-pub probably. I expect him around seven-thirty."

Thomas hesitated,

"I'm sure they'll have some sort of pie," Maggie added encouragingly.

Thomas checked his watch. Reached a decision.

"All right. We have an hour, then. I wonder what we could do?"

And he pulled Maggie to him, wrapped his hands in her curls, and kissed her.

Chapter 3

Someone was calling.

"Maggie? Maggie?"

Stephen was early.

Thomas stuck his head out of the bedroom. He was still buttoning his shirt and his hair was mussed.

"Draycott?"

"Oh. So you're here, Thomas. Is Maggie…"

"I'll be with you in a moment, Stephen," Maggie called.

Not at all embarrassed, Stephen grinned.

"I'll wait. I have news."

Maggie came out a couple of minutes later, dressed, but with her hair in turmoil. Thomas followed, holding a hair clip.

"Hello, Stephen. So what's this news?"

"I know who the new Appleton fellow is."

"Yes? Really? Who is it?"

"Shall I keep you in suspense? Or make you guess? No. It's too good not to tell."

Stephen made motions like a magician about to pull a rabbit out of a hat.

"Faisal bin Abdulaziz," he announced and waited for Maggie's reaction.

"Faisal bin Abdulaziz?" echoed Maggie incredulously. "You must be joking."

"I'd heard a rumour and, when I saw Alastair a while ago, he confirmed it."

"Faisal bin Abdulaziz? What were the Appleton people thinking?" Maggie was outraged.

"Perhaps that they could establish another fellowship using the proceeds from ticket sales when you two sit at the high table at the same time. Or happen to meet crossing the quad."

"Who's Faisal bin Abdul-whatever?" Thomas demanded.

"He's Maggie's arch enemy. Her Nemesis. Her Moriarty," Stephen explained.

"Oh, it's not that bad," Maggie protested.

"It isn't? You could have fooled me."

He turned back to Thomas.

"Bin Abdulaziz is Saudi. Some connection to the royal family. Of course, so are a lot of people. A conservative of the 'Women shouldn't be allowed to drive' variety, although not quite a Mutaween. You know, their religious police. I don't think he'd let schoolgirls burn up in a fire for not being properly attired. Or I would hope not. And he's not a supporter of al Qaeda or any other terrorist group. Well, I guess he couldn't be if he's getting a visa. But definitely of the 'Keep 'em veiled and pregnant' school of gender relations.

"I've heard he has three wives, although I'm not sure he'll be able to get visas for all of them. I guess they'll have to visit in turn," Stephen grinned.

"Anyhow, he's famous for a book he wrote called *The New Crusaders*, which is a critique of western policy vis à vis the Arab world. Borders on being a polemic. And whenever Maggie writes a new book, the *Guardian* or one of the other liberal rags gets him to write a scathing review. Does the talk shows as well. In fact, he's become a bit of a celebrity for being the anti-Maggie. Did I mention all the wives wear niqabs? So maybe there aren't three. How could you tell?

"He has degrees from Princeton. And Yale. Had a distinguished academic reputation before the Iraq war. Then he became more radical. Left a professorship at Columbia and went to the Emirates. He's against any Western presence on Arab soil. Sees it as a desecration as well as being a neo-colonial grab for oil. But thinks the removal should be done through political policy, not violence. Well, as I said, he'd hardly be given a visa if that were the case. And whatever you do, don't mention Israel when he's around."

"What were the Appleton people thinking?" said Maggie again. "Is this their revenge for my resigning their position?"

"Maybe they thought it would be fun. Or that now no one can accuse them of bias," Stephen suggested.

"Fun?"

"What's the line from that Simon Gray play? *Butley*? 'Trouble for you, fun for me.'" Stephen teased.

"Eurgh!" Maggie threw her hands in the air and her curls became even more out of control.

"Maggie, sit down," ordered Thomas.

She did and he deftly pulled her hair back and put in her hair clip.

"Well, I think this calls for a drink. And dinner," Stephen announced.

"I won't argue with that," agreed Thomas.

"I could certainly use a drink. Probably two," said Maggie.

They walked to a nearby pub known for its good British food and, while pie was not on the menu that evening, the men were happy to settle for steak.

Maggie, who realised she hadn't eaten since she'd left Beaumatin the night before, had pasta with asparagus and drank Sauvignon blanc.

"You know, you won't be the only person who'll be unhappy about bin Abdulaziz's appointment," Stephen pointed out as he enjoyed some Rioja.

"No? Whom do you mean?"

"Eunice."

Eunice Enderby was another colleague and an expert on colonialism. And post-colonialism. She was also disliked by the liberals for insisting that not all aspects of colonialism were bad and that more than one nation had not done especially well in its aftermath, with "one man, one vote, once," being a good example.

But, to put it kindly, the cameras were not flattering to Eunice, a tall, bony, horse-faced woman in her forties who shopped at Oxfam and was known for being parsimonious.

She also had no sense of humour. Or of the media's need for sound bites. In all fairness, she had absolutely no resentment of the public attention Maggie received and was respected by both Maggie and Stephen.

"Like several of his other positions, bin Abdulaziz believes somewhat simplistically that 'colonialism bad, independence, good.' If Eunice had a higher media profile, he'd be all over her like, what do you Yanks like to say?"

"Like white on rice. Or like a bad suit," Maggie supplied.

"Quite," said Stephen.

"Well, this should make for some interesting faculty meetings," said Maggie.

"I thought you didn't have to attend those anymore," protested Thomas.

"Most. But not the one where we elect Stephen as the next Master of Merrion College," Maggie said.

"Oh. Really? I hadn't known. Congratulations, Stephen."

"Let's not count our chickens before they're hatched," Stephen cautioned.

"I know I have Alastair's support. And Maggie's. And Chitta's and Eunice's. And probably Laurence's as well. I don't think he's interested."

Laurence Brooks was a colleague and the husband of Maggie's good friend Anne.

"He's not," said Maggie reassuringly.

"But then there's Gordon. And Andrew."

27

Gordon Ross and Andrew Kittredge were two other senior fellows. Maggie was not especially close to either, although Thomas had met both at a party at the Brooks' the previous summer.

"I don't think Gordon has aspirations, but Andrew might. And Gordon would support him."

Stephen considered this, then continued. "At least bin Abdulaziz can't vote."

"He can't?" Thomas asked.

"The election is just before his formal start as a senior faculty member."

Thomas shook his head.

"Anyhow, enough Merrion politics. Have you been following the cricket, Thomas?"

Both men were fans and Maggie tuned out.

Over coffee and, for the men, whisky, Stephen said, "So Thomas, I'll see you at the bash for Alastair on Friday night?"

Thomas grimaced and looked at Maggie.

"I did tell you. And sent you an email." Maggie decided she would not be too apologetic.

"It's the first in a series of events marking Alastair's retirement. This one is senior faculty, present and future. Liu Zhengyu will have just arrived and is attending. Bin Abdulaziz may be there too."

"Do you think he'll wear his robes? And I don't mean his academic ones," Maggie wondered.

Stephen laughed, while Thomas asked, "Do they have formal robes in Saudi Arabia that would be the equivalent of a tuxedo?"

"I have no idea. But I guess we're about to find out," said Stephen.

SUSAN ALEXANDER

Chapter 4

Outside the pub, Thomas said, "So we'll see you at Merrion Friday night, then."

Stephen nodded.

Thomas took Maggie's arm and turned away from the direction of Merrion, towards Hereford Crescent.

"Well, the agreement was, I'd stay at Merrion when he isn't here and at Hereford Crescent when he is. And he is here," Maggie reminded herself.

Aloud she said, "Good night, Stephen."

They walked quietly for a few minutes. Then Thomas suddenly asked, "How much of a problem is this bin Abdulaziz chap going to be for you?"

"A problem? Hard to say. We won't be the first two fellows at one of the colleges to have professional disagreements. As for his attacks on my work, Malcolm says they only increase book sales. In fact, maybe he'd like to write one of the books for the new Developing World series."

"Well, if he's going to be unpleasant, it's fortunate you'll be spending most of your time at Beaumatin."

Maggie fleetingly wondered which place would be more unpleasant if Constance were going to be in the neighbourhood.

They had reached Hereford Crescent. Maggie sighed inwardly.

It was a beautiful townhouse, one in a row that reminded Maggie of a scaled down version of the Royal

Crescent in Bath. Thomas had fixed it up for them and had said he was excited about their having a home of their own. And it was true that Maggie did tend to refer to Beaumatin as an ancestral museum. And was pleased that Thomas was happy about the house. And had even been able to pick out drapery fabric.

However, even without Beaumatin's galleries of baronial portraits, she found the house with its plaster-festooned ceilings and inlaid floors and crystal chandeliers a bit too grand for her. She did not feel as comfortable there as she had in her old flat and feared it was not simply a matter of time before she adjusted.

And she did not have the same alliance with their housekeeper, Mrs Royce, which she had with Mrs Cook, her Beaumatin counterpart. She suspected the woman gossiped. However, Mrs Royce, who had an apartment on the building's garden level she shared with her husband, was the sister of Ned Thatcher, Thomas' estate foreman and sidekick. So Maggie had made her peace with the arrangement.

Maggie was in her bedroom getting ready for bed when Thomas came in. He was wearing his blue paisley silk bathroom and her stomach did the fluttery thing it frequently did when she saw Thomas. However, it stopped abruptly when she sensed his mood.

Thomas was still angry and Maggie did not do well with anger. Especially Thomas'. And especially when it was directed at her. Mostly Maggie knew he was angry when he became cold and withdrawn. Maggie had given names to its various degrees. Jack Frost. Sub Zero. And the worst, Absolute Zero, when she expected to see ice crystals covering the walls and to make clouds when she exhaled.

Thomas was somewhere between Sub Zero and Absolute Zero. Oh dear. What was the matter now?

"Thomas?"

Maggie was sitting at a dressing table. Thomas took her arm and pulled her up and turned her so she faced him. He had both hands on her shoulders and his bright blue eyes, which were one of the things Maggie normally loved best about him, were glacial.

"I just want to make sure we're clear."

"Clear?"

"That you'll never leave Beaumatin again without letting me know. Without telling me first."

Did he mean she was supposed to ask permission?

"I assume it's all right if I tell Mrs Cook I'm going to Waitrose when you're out with Ned," she said tartly.

"Telling Mrs Cook..." Thomas began and then decided he was not going to be diverted.

"That's not what I mean and you know it. I want your promise. Do I have it?" he pressed and his grip tightened.

And Maggie knew she had a problem. And had no idea what to do about it.

She sighed, which Thomas took for acquiescence.

"I was frantic, Papillon. I was afraid... I was afraid I had lost you. I never want to feel that way again. Can you understand?"

Twice in the ten months they had been married, Thomas had told her the relationship was over and to get out. She knew what that felt like. But was that the same way Thomas felt?

Again he took her silence for agreement.

"Good. We're clear. Well, then,"

And he hoisted her over his shoulder and carted her off to his bed.

Chapter 5

Maggie was getting ready for Alastair Carrington's retirement party. She had a large collection of what she considered to be her "professional" outfits, tailored and conservative, in black and grey and navy. They emphasised her natural reserve and made her appear even more aloof than she normally did.

Since she had married Thomas, however, Maggie had decided she needed to loosen up a bit, as she had told her friend Anne. In addition, slender to begin with, Maggie had lost even more weight since her wedding so that many of her old clothes were loose and hung unattractively. Life with Thomas had tended to have a roller coaster quality and when Maggie was upset, she lost her appetite and neglected to eat.

So Maggie had done some clothes shopping and had decided to wear one of her newer dresses that night. It was the antithesis of a niqab and Maggie figured that if bin Abdulaziz were going to be there, she would be throwing down the gauntlet. In fashion terms, so to speak.

The dress was the one she had worn to the wedding of Chloe Osborne the previous September. It was made of heavy cotton lace in deep green and was strapless. The top just covered her breasts—not that their size made that a challenge—and the back began beneath her shoulder blades. The bodice fitted her like a glove and the skirt flared out at her hips until it stopped at the bottom of her knees. She loved how it fit and how it made her feel. Which was like she could eat bin Abdulaziz for lunch.

The dress had a matching bolero jacket but it did not fit over her cast and there was still a month or more before her fractures healed fully. So Maggie had gotten a pashima wrap in the exact same shade of green as the dress. She could use to avoid goose bumps—it remained unseasonably chilly—or drape over her arm. She had caught up her hair except for some tendrils that insisted on escaping and she wore a pair of emerald earrings Thomas had given her as a wedding gift.

Bring it on, bin Abdulaziz.

Thomas was waiting in the hall, pacing. Maggie was a few minutes late, which was unlike her, and he watched Maggie coming down the stairs.

"Are you sure you'll be warm enough?" His mouth twitched.

"I find the rooms at Merrion tend to be overheated," she said, while admiring Thomas in his tuxedo. Thomas in a tuxedo made her feel like she was about to melt into a large puddle on the inlaid marble floor. Thomas in tails and she had to remind herself to breathe.

Thomas turned her around. "Well, at least there's some fabric back there. I wasn't sure."

Given the impossibility of parking, Thomas had ordered a taxi.

Cocktails were being served in the Senior Common Room. There was already a good-sized crowd. And a receiving line. First was Lady Crista, Alastair's wife. Lady Crista, who was the daughter of an earl, was a thin, faded woman who wore a conservative black cocktail dress with pearls. Her greying hair was pulled back in a bun. She liked Maggie and smiled warmly when she saw her and Thomas.

Next was Carrington himself. Alastair was also grey and thin and, with a long, pointed nose, a balding pate and a slight slouch, had always reminded Maggie of a stock. He was

36

a terrible old snob and had been beside himself when Maggie had married the twenty-eighth Baron Raynham and invited him and Lady Crista to Beaumatin. Maggie hoped he would make the honours list soon. He had been an able Master and certainly deserved it.

He turned to introduce the man standing beside him but did not really need to tell Maggie who he was.

Faisal bin Abdulaziz was wearing traditional Saudi dress, starting with a white men's robe, called a thobe. Over it he had a mishtah, a black cloak trimmed in gold. On his head he wore the red and white checked gutra, held in place with double black cords called igal. Maggie knew the terms for the clothing from her consulting work in the Gulf.

Bin Abdulaziz was in his early forties. He was tall, dark-eyed, and, with a neatly trimmed moustache, handsome and regal. Maggie decided he would be the object of quite a few crushes if he taught any undergraduate seminars.

"Dr bin Abdulaziz, may I present Professor Eliot," Alastair intoned.

Maggie was aware that the whole room had become quiet and people were waiting to see what happened next.

"Dr bin Abdulaziz, it is a pleasure to meet you. Congratulations on your appointment."

She smiled and extended her hand.

Abdulaziz did not extend his. He scowled, looked her up and down, frowned even more deeply as he took in her bare shoulders and said in a baritone voice that carried, "In my country, a woman like you would be stoned. Or given one hundred lashes."

Someone gasped audibly and Maggie was painfully aware she needed to respond with an appropriate rejoinder or she was toast. Where were her script writers? She was also aware that Thomas had gone stiff beside her. She hoped he was not about to throw a punch at bin Abdulaziz.

But she did not flinch or blink. Her formidable Great Aunt Margaret, who had taught Greek at a women's college and after whom she had been named, would have been proud.

She laughed and said in a clear voice, "But we are not in your country. We are in Britain, where women like me are honoured by being awarded prestigious fellowships at great universities."

Maggie heard someone applauding faintly. She continued to smile and moved on to Stephen, who was standing next in line with his Chinese colleague.

Behind her, Alastair, who was a stickler for propriety, was saying in a strangled voice, "Lord Raynham, may I present Dr bin Abdulaziz."

Thomas' eyes were glinting dangerously, but he was also a stickler for propriety and disliked scenes, so he too extended his hand, which bin Abdulaziz touched briefly.

"And sir, in my country, a husband is expected to control his wife."

Alastair's felt compelled to murmur, "It is my lord, not sir. He is addressed as my lord," which caused both men to look at him.

Thomas replied, "Quite possibly, Dr bin Abdulaziz. As I am sure you would know. But, as Lady Raynham already pointed out, we are not in your country, a fact for which I am sure everyone here, except possibly yourself, is most thankful."

To murmurs of "Hear, hear," Thomas moved on and said to Stephen, "Stephen, good to see you. Is this your new colleague from Beijing?"

Dr Liu Zhengyu was also in his forties, of medium height and stocky, with a round face and cheerful eyes behind thick, black-framed glasses. His hair was short in a kind of buzz cut and he wore a rumpled grey suit. Maggie guessed that events at Renmin University did not often require a dinner jacket. Perhaps he could rent one for his stay.

Introductions were made and Dr Liu was wished well for the coming term. Stephen murmured "That was well played. I'll catch up with you later," and Maggie, followed by Thomas, headed to where she saw Anne and Laurence Brooks standing with Eunice and David Enderby.

"Well, if that were a case of 'Begin as you mean to go on,' things are going to be quite interesting," Maggie announced.

"What a dreadful man." Anne was indignant.

"I'm sure Alastair will have a word with him." Eunice was trying to be optimistic.

"What were the Appleton people thinking?" asked Laurence, not for the first time.

Laurence was a tall, good looking man in his fifties and, along with Stephen, Thomas and Alastair himself, one of the best-dressed men in the room. He ran the Institute for Global Development at the University.

Given their overlapping interests, Maggie had been introduced to Laurence as soon as she had arrived at Merrion and had also met his wife Anne, a pretty woman with brown eyes and short, artfully highlighted hair. Anne was a model academic wife and had raised three sons. Now that the boys were successfully launched, she busied herself with her church, her garden, gourmet cooking and a range of local community groups.

She had been extremely supportive of Maggie when she had first arrived at Oxford and it had been when Anne had dragged Maggie along with her to a snowdrop weekend at Rochford Manor that Maggie had met Thomas.

Thomas noticed Laurence's whisky and Anne's flute of champagne, in addition to the Enderbys' more traditional glasses of sherry.

"It seems Alastair is treating this like a grand event. Should I see if there is some white wine?" he asked Maggie.

"Please. And if not, some champagne will be fine."

Maggie turned to Eunice.

"Well, Eunice, what do you think of our newest colleague?" Maggie asked.

"I assume you are not referring to Dr Liu," she said grimly.

"I think we're going to have to do something," Eunice said finally. "I'm just not sure what. If I expressed similar sentiments that were anti-Muslim rather than anti-female, I would be out of here in days, if not hours."

"The curse of political correctness," agreed David, her husband. David was a few inches shorter and a few stone heavier than his wife. He worked as an accountant and gave the impression of being perpetually anxious.

"Perhaps it's just first night jitters. It must not be easy, meeting our group," Laurence tried to rationalise.

"He obviously never heard the one about 'You only get one chance to make a first impression,'" said Anne, who was less tolerant.

She turned to Maggie. "Interesting choice of outfit."

"Do you think it's too dressy?"

Anne considered her friend. "The dress itself is fabulous. But I assume you mostly wore it to provoke our new resident misogynist."

"Guilty as charged, I'm afraid. And it was successful. I was able to find out he's not even going to try to be collegial."

"Or perhaps only selectively collegial," commented Anne. The receiving line had disbanded and bin Abdulaziz, holding a glass of orange juice, was chatting with Andrew Kittredge and his wife Claire.

Maggie called the couple to herself "Dumpy" and "Frumpy" which, however apt, she had never shared with anyone, not even Anne, given how gossip travelled in college circles.

Andrew was an economist and specialised in the often inaccurate and misleading economic figures of developing nations. If someone wanted to have an idea of the GDP of Burkina Faso, he called Andrew. Callers included the United Nations, the African Development Bank, the CIA and Burkina Faso itself.

Maggie assumed Andrew received the same generous fees for this extracurricular work as she did when she consulted with governments on issues relating to immigration. However, if he did, it was not evident in his or his wife's appearance. Both Andrew and Claire came close to rivalling the Enderbys in achieving that authentic Oxfam look.

Maggie noticed that the Rosses had joined the Kittredges and bin Abdulaziz. Gordon Ross was a Glaswegian and his work focussed on poverty, its causes and cures. He carried his working class, council estate origins like a badge of honour, although Maggie always found it a bit ridiculous that an Oxford don should still consider himself a member of the oppressed proletariat.

Standing next to Gordon was Mrs Ross Number Three. She was also drinking orange juice instead of the sherry which she normally preferred. The professor had dumped Mrs Ross Number One in favour of a younger model and subsequently dumped her as well when he had met the current Mrs Ross. Deirdre was a pretty blonde at least twenty-five years younger than her husband. Ross' romance with one of his graduate students had created quite a scandal until he had finalised his divorce and Deirdre had married her mentor and abandoned academia to become a housewife.

If Alastair reminded Maggie of a stork, Ross was a cock and Maggie had always found his manner towards Deirdre a bit cavalier, even though Deirdre obviously adored the older man. The young woman was wearing a modest blue silk shirtwaist dress with discrete mother-of-pearl buttons. Maggie wondered if she would have gotten a different reaction from bin Abdulaziz had she been similarly attired, then decided probably not. Bin Abdulaziz's attitude towards her had been firmly fixed long before they had actually met.

Alastair was making the rounds and, from his flushed face and unusually animated manner, had obviously had more than the glass of sherry he currently carried. He came over to

Maggie, the Enderbys and the Brooks' at the same time Thomas returned with some white wine for Maggie and some whisky for himself.

"Maggie, I really must apologize for bin Abdulaziz's deplorable behaviour. And to you as well, Thomas. I know the selection committee questioned him extensively about whether he would feel comfortable working with women and particularly with you, my dear, given his critical attitude towards your work. I'm afraid he may have misled them."

"Don't worry, Alastair. I am sure Merrion can survive some collegial controversy and, as you can see, I remain unscathed."

She glanced at her cast.

"Well, at least any scathing I have suffered was not because of bin Abdulaziz."

"Yes, I was going to ask. How are you getting along?"

"Progress, slow but steady. At least I can wiggle my fingers, which means I can use both hands to type. And use my mouse."

Alastair nodded. He emptied his glass. A member of the catering staff, a young man with hair dyed black and gelled into permanent disorder, was passing with a tray that had one remaining glass of sherry and an assortment of used glasses. Alastair stopped the boy, took the glass and replaced it with his empty one.

The waiter, who looked like he could be a student, was taken aback.

"I'd be happy to bring you a fresh one, Master," he said anxiously.

"No, no. This will be fine, my boy. Thank you."

The young man hurried off and Alastair turned back to Maggie.

"And are you ready to assume your duties as the Weingarten fellow?"

"Yes. We've made progress on getting the Developing World book series launched. I believe Stephen and Dr Liu have already begun to work together and Eunice is also going to contribute a volume."

"It's an interesting experience. Summarising my work and trying to make it accessible to a non-expert reader," Eunice commented.

"I would think it would be."

Alastair took a sip of sherry, then made a face, looked at his glass, took another sip and shook his head.

"Can sherry be corked?" he asked no one in particular. He took a third sip, turned away and then stiffened.

"Arrr..."

"Alastair?"

Anne was concerned and put her hand on the Master's arm.

"Urrr..." Alastair clutched at his throat.

There was something wrong with Alastair.

"Alastair?" Maggie was now alarmed as well.

Alastair jerked, then collapsed and writhed on the floor. There was foam at the corners of his mouth.

"Alastair?" Laurence knelt down beside Carrington.

"Alastair! Can you talk? What's wrong?"

Carrington was breathing rapidly. He looked terrified.

"Is he having a stroke?" asked David,

"He's not epileptic," said Anne.

"Errr." He tried to speak but failed. His face was pink.

"Is it his heart?" Eunice wondered.

Alastair shuddered, then lay still.

Anne pulled her mobile out of her purse and dialled emergency and Maggie suddenly thought how ironic it was that, in a room full of people with doctorate degrees, not one was an actual doctor. She also knelt down beside Alastair. She tried to find a pulse. Nothing. She looked up at Thomas and shook her head.

Lady Crista had noticed and rushed over.

"Alastair?"

Eunice put her arm around the woman.

"Alastair? What's wrong? Alastair?"

Lady Crista wobbled and Eunice caught her before she fell.

Maggie remembered that she had witnessed the same thing happening before.

"Anne, I think Alastair was poisoned. We should call the police."

Anne nodded and dialled.

SUSAN ALEXANDER

Chapter 6

The next half hour was chaotic.

People stood in small groups, talking quietly and keeping well away from the corpse. Maggie had draped her shawl over the dead Master. Eunice had taken Lady Crista back to the Master's Lodge.

There had been a confrontation between Stephen and bin Abdulaziz when the latter had tried to leave.

"This has nothing to do with me," the Saudi had protested.

"Nevertheless, the police will want to question everyone who is here," Stephen said.

He added, "If you leave, it will only make you look suspicious."

"Suspicious?" bin Abdulaziz was incredulous. "But Carrington was old. Surely he had a heart attack. Or a stroke. Unfortunate, but these things happen at his age."

"Alastair was only sixty-eight and in perfect health," Stephen insisted. "And while I'm no expert, it looks to me like he was poisoned."

Stephen went and said something to Liu Zhengyu in Chinese, then joined Maggie, Thomas and Laurence.

"I think we should move people out of here. As it's between terms, the Junior Common Room should be empty. Or near enough. What do you think?"

Maggie agreed.

Stephen encouraged everyone to move into the Junior Common Room. As Stephen had predicted, it was vacant. The pathologist arrived with the SOCO unit. Stephen showed them where Carrington was lying, then went to join his colleagues. A few minutes later, a pair of police constables posted themselves beside the door of the JCR.

Finally, two men in suits appeared. The older was in his early forties. He kept his salt and pepper hair cut short and his brown eyes, which gleamed fiercely behind black-rimmed glasses, reminded Maggie of a terrier. He was overweight and developing jowls. The second man was probably twenty years younger. He had carrot-coloured hair he wore in the style of some footballer, stuck up on the top with gel to produce a woodpecker effect. He had light green eyes and freckles and seemed to be intimidated by his superior.

The older man called the room to attention.

"I am Detective Inspector Moss and this is Detective Sergeant Bixby. We'll want to talk to each of you individually about this unfortunate incident."

Moss looked like he was not thrilled at this prospect.

"Morse?" murmured Stephen to Maggie.

"No. Moss," she answered repressively. But had to admit that the death of the Master of an Oxford college in the Senior Common Room could certainly form the plot of one of the famous mystery series.

One of the PCs began to circulate and take down names and contact information. When everyone's details had been collected, he left and, a few minutes later, DS Bixby started to summon people for questioning.

Thomas had identified Maggie and himself to the police as "Lord and Lady Raynham," even though she would have preferred to call herself Professor Eliot. However, since they were among the first called, she had to conclude that it had not been a bad strategy. She imagined Moss looking at the list, frowning and saying to his sergeant, "Let's see these toffs and get it over with."

Maggie and Thomas went in to see the inspector together. They found he had commandeered some space in Merrion's dining hall. He was sitting at the end of one of the long dining tables and looked disgruntled.

"Here is Lord and Lady Raynham, sir," said DS Bixby.

Moss scowled. He indicated they should sit opposite him.

Thomas pulled out a chair for Maggie and then sat down beside her. Moss' scowl deepened.

"So Lord Raynham. What brought you to an Oxford faculty party?" he snapped.

Thomas was about to tell the detective that he did not care for his tone, but thought better of it. Instead he said neutrally, "My wife is a professor at Merrion and spouses were invited to the reception."

Moss looked at Maggie as though he had forgotten she was there, then turned back to Thomas.

"And what can you tell me about this unfortunate incident?"

Thomas glanced at his wife, then said, "We were talking with Carrington. A waiter passed by with a tray. There was a glass of sherry on it as well as some empty ones.

Carrington had finished his sherry, so he put his glass on the tray and picked up the full one. He took a sip, a second sip, then began to... He clutched his throat. Fell to the floor. He was dead within seconds."

Moss nodded while Bixby scribbled notes on a pad.

"And did you notice anything suspicious? Did you see anyone put something into Carrington's drink?"

"No."

Moss frowned, then asked, "How well did you know Carrington?"

Thomas was surprised the question had not been directed to Maggie.

"Only casually, really. Through various Merrion social events. And he visited our home in Gloucestershire once."

"So you don't know if he had any enemies."

"No. Or at least none of whom I am aware. He was well respected."

"And you didn't notice anyone putting anything into his drink?"

"No."

"Did you, er, Lady Raynham?"

"No."

"Humpf."

Maggie waited for Moss to ask her another question. Instead he said, "Well, Lord Raynham, that will be all for now. I may have some additional queries once the pathologist has determined the cause of death. Carrington was not a young man. It could have been natural causes—a heart attack for instance—rather than what we like to call a 'suspicious death.' In the meantime, please remain in Oxford for the next few days."

"But..." Maggie began to protest but Thomas interrupted.

"Very well." He stood, then pulled out Maggie's chair. When Maggie rose as well Thomas took her arm and walked with her out of the room.

As soon as Sergeant Bixby had passed them on his way to fetch someone else to interview, Maggie turned to Thomas and said indignantly, "That Moss is a complete pig!"

"Perhaps. But at least we're done for now."

"All right. Fine. Then just let me tell Stephen..."

"No." Thomas was firm.

"But..."

"If you went to see Draycott we could be detained I don't know how much longer. Send him a text if you must. But I want a whisky. And my bed."

As they left the college for Hereford Crescent, Maggie said, "That Moss. He really made me appreciate Inspector Willis."

The Gloucestershire homicide detective was well known to both Maggie and Thomas.

"I can't believe I'm saying this, but I'm inclined to agree."

Susan Alexander

Chapter 7

Over dinner at Hereford Crescent the following evening, Thomas announced, "Ritchie called today with some interesting news."

"Ritchie?"

"Yes. My agent in Oxford. The one who handled the rental of your apartment."

"Oh." Maggie had been reluctant to leave her cosy flat for the much grander Hereford Crescent townhouse and had neither met the man nor learned his name. Thomas had acted as an intermediary.

"It seems we will have a new neighbour. Here on Hereford Crescent. Not immediately next door. Three houses away in fact."

"Oh."

Pause.

"How did Ritchie find out?"

"He arranged the rental."

"Ritchie is an estate agent?"

Thomas put down his fork.

"The Raynhams own Hereford Crescent. The townhouses, to be precise. And the land, of course. Among our other Oxford holdings."

"Really?" Maggie was startled. Oxford had some of the country's most expensive housing outside of London.

"You knew we owned real estate in Oxford," Thomas pointed out.

Maggie assumed Thomas was employing the royal "we."

"I knew you owned this house. Not the entire row."

"We can thank the sixteenth baron. Apparently he won it in a card game."

"Really? Anyhow, who is this new neighbour?"

Thomas took a swallow of Haut Brion and then stated, "Your new colleague. Bin Abdulaziz."

"Faisal bin Abdulaziz?"

"Yes."

"Your Mr Ritchie couldn't have found something further away? And found another tenant for the house?"

"Bin Abdulaziz wanted at least six bedrooms. Within walking distance to the college. And shops."

Maggie looked troubled.

"He has excellent credit. He is quite well-to-do in fact. Well, he'd need some means to afford the rent. Suitable tenants are not all that common."

"Is he aware that we're three doors down?"

"I don't know. I doubt Ritchie would have mentioned it. And the name Raynham would not appear in the lease."

"Oh."

"I thought you should know. In case you saw niqabs in the neighbourhood."

"Niqabs. Yes. Thank you."

Maggie drank some white wine.

"At least as the Weingarten fellow, you'll be spending more time at Beaumatin than in Oxford anyway," Thomas pointed out.

Maggie suppressed a sigh.

Chapter 8

At the urging of the University Vice-Chancellor, Merrion's senior faculty had moved up the election of their new Master. Gordon Ross and Andrew Kittredge did the math and, as a result, Stephen ran unopposed and was elected unanimously.

Maggie congratulated Stephen over some celebratory champagne.

"Thank you. I just wish the circumstances were different."

"Yes. Poor Alastair."

They sipped some bubbly.

"Have you heard anything about the police investigation?"

"Only that they seem to be stymied. The cause of death was definitely cyanide."

"Poor Alastair," Maggie said again.

"And they aren't even sure whether it was Alastair who was the intended victim. Anyone could have taken that glass of sherry."

"You mean the victim was random? Aimed at the college faculty generally? That's a disturbing thought."

"But it makes some sense. Who would want to kill Alastair? He had no enemies, at least none of whom I know, and he was leaving in a few months."

"Yes. He does seem an improbable victim."

"So the police are looking at who might have had a grudge against the college. Has Moss asked you if you know anyone who thought they deserved a first but got a second instead?"

"No."

"Well, I'm sure he will. Or that sergeant of his."

"The one who looks like Woody Woodpecker?"

"That's the one. Bixby, I think his name is."

"Bixby. Right."

"That detective. Moss. I can't say he inspires much confidence'

"And he's unpleasant as well," Maggie agreed.

"Yes. And I keep having to stop myself from calling him 'Morse.'"

Maggie laughed. "That's funny. So do I."

"I much preferred your Inspector Willis. Even when he thought I might be a murderer."

Inspector Willis had investigated the death of Stephen's wife the previous autumn.

"Oxford is out of his jurisdiction, unfortunately."

"Quite."

"I understand there was a time when the police were not allowed onto University premises at all and the colleges used their own internal security forces to deal with wrongdoing."

"I read that as well. But I also suspect there was more covering up of crimes than actually solving them. And less bringing the perpetrators to justice. Depending on who was involved."

"You're probably right about that," Maggie agreed.

"Um, Stephen. I was thinking. I'd like to organise a reception. At Hereford Crescent. A multi-purpose event. In honour of your election. And in memory of Alastair. And to celebrate Chitta's wedding. What do you think?"

"I think it's an excellent idea. Not that I especially want to be feted. But I'm sure something would be arranged anyway. And Hereford Crescent would make a nice change. I'm not sure people would feel comfortable in the Senior Common Room so soon after Alastair's death. His lordship won't mind?"

"I don't see why he should."

"Let me check with Mrs Steeples, then, and we can discuss a date."

Mrs Steeples served as the Master's secretary and was a Merrion institution in her own right.

"All right."

"Now I had better go mingle."

"Yes. You have expectations you need to meet."

"Indeed."

SUSAN ALEXANDER

Chapter 9

It was the next day that Maggie saw the figure in the niqab for the first time.

Having met with Mrs Steeples to set a date for the reception at Hereford Crescent, Maggie had been crossing the quadrangle on her way back to her rooms. Along one side of the square ran a cloister. Rounded arches rested atop pairs of Corinthian columns that sheltered a walkway.

Deep in thought, Maggie caught a flicker of something dark out of the corner of her eye.

She paused and turned and saw a figure shrouded in black pass from one set of columns to the next.

That's strange, she thought.

As she watched, the figure moved between two more sets of columns.

Black fabric fluttered.

Not a ninja, then. But no face was visible. Could it be a niqab?

But who wore a niqab at Merrion?

There was no further sign of the mysterious figure. And Maggie remembered that bin Abdulaziz's rooms were in that hall. Had one of the wives come to visit? But then, she thought a wife could not go out on her own. Not without a male relative.

Maggie arrived at her rooms, then paused and went up to the floor above.

Chitta Kazi had returned from her honeymoon that morning. The beautiful Bangladeshi scholar had married Maggie's friend Stanley Einhorn, the famous American hi-tech venture capitalist. Chitta had met Stanley the previous summer when she had worked with Maggie on a proposal for the foundation Stanley was establishing.

Maggie knocked on Chitta's door.

"Come."

Maggie entered and was greeted by chaos. Never tidy at the best of times, Chitta had been unpacking and books, items of clothing, bottles of shampoo and conditioner, flip flops and a flock of gaily coloured papier-mâché parrots were among the items strewn on top of every available surface.

Maggie paused to absorb the mess.

"My goodness."

"I know. I'm just hopeless. Anyhow, here. I brought you back a souvenir."

Chitta thrust a strident green bird at her friend.

"Thank you."

Maggie had already welcomed back Chitta earlier that day so she came right to the point.

"I just had an odd experience."

"Yes?"

"I thought I saw someone wearing a niqab walking in the quad."

"Really?"

"Yes. In the cloister. Which is why I only think I saw her. The pillars obstructed my view. But does anyone at Merrion wear a niqab, do you know?"

"No. No. Not that I know of."

"Then she—I assume it was a she, but how can you tell—disappeared. She must have gone inside. Into one of the stairwells. And that is the hall where bin Abdulaziz has his rooms."

Chitta had yet to meet the new Appleton fellow but had heard all about him from Maggie.

"Do you think it was one of his wives?"

"Maybe. Except I thought they're not allowed to go out alone. And I'm sure it was just the one. Person. In a niqab. If that's what it was. Although it certainly looked like one."

Chitta thought.

"You could ask Higgins."

Roger Higgins was the porter on duty.

"You mean if he let in someone wearing a niqab?"

"He would certainly remember."

"And have quite a bit to say about it too," Maggie smiled.

Chitta looked around and sighed.

"I need a break. Would you like some tea?"

"No, thank you," said coffee-drinker Maggie.

Chita made herself a cup and sat.

"So how is it? Being married again?" Maggie asked.

When she had met Stanley, Chitta had been a widow. Her first husband Salman, a molecular biologist, had been killed in an accident three years before.

"It's nice. Of course it's early days, but Stanley is attentive. Chivalrous. Hardly lets me lift a finger. In fact, sometimes it's surreal. The effect of all that money. We never have to wait in a queue. Or carry a parcel. Or use public transportation. Even first class. I'm thinking of insisting he take out the garbage. And gather his laundry. And do the occasional grocery shopping. Just so he doesn't lose complete touch with ordinary reality. Ordinary life."

Maggie nodded.

"How was Costa Rico?"

"Awesome. You know it has coasts on both the Atlantic and the Pacific. And rain forests. It's very eco. I did end up eating a lot of rice and beans, though. With the inevitable after-effects. Poor Stanley," Chitta laughed.

Chitta was a vegetarian.

"Oh and I have some other news."

"Yes?"

"But you have to promise not to say anything. To anyone. Especially at Merrion."

"All right. I promise. But you've certainly made me curious. What is it? Your news? And please don't say that you're resigning to take a position at Stanford."

"No. My staying at Oxford was part of my deal with Stanley."

Chitta paused. Blushed.

I'm… I'm pregnant."

Maggie knew that Salman had had what Chitta referred to as a "plumbing problem" and her parents had been unhappy that the marriage had produced no grandchildren.

"Chitta, that's wonderful! Congratulations. You parents must be thrilled."

"Um. They don't know. Yet."

"Oh?"

"Well, it's better if I wait. For a couple of months."

"Hm. How far along are you?" asked Maggie shrewdly.

"Three months."

"I see."

"Er, yes. Better they don't do the math just yet. And think the baby is a bit early."

"And Stanley?" asked Maggie, thinking of Nils' reaction to Constance's pregnancy.

"He's completely thrilled. Over the moon. He'd already be buying Baby iPads but figures the technology will be outdated before the birth. So he's having to wait."

"Any clue about whether it's a boy or girl?"

"Not quite yet."

"Do you want to find out?"

Maggie knew some people preferred to be surprised.

"Oh yes."

"Are you going to continue at Merrion? Sorry if this is sounding like an interrogation."

"Yes, I'm going to continue and no, don't worry. I'm glad to talk to someone about all this. But, like I said, I don't want it to be generally known. College gossip being what it is. Of course, at some point it will be impossible to hide."

Chitta rubbed her belly.

"May I tell Thomas?"

"Of course."

"Is Stanley here?"

"No. He had to go to the US. Some company board meetings. In New York. And Boston."

"You must miss him."

"Yes. And I'm sure he misses me. But that's all right. I even enjoy missing him. And looking forward to him returning."

Maggie reflected how different this was from Thomas' reaction when she had had to spend three or four days a week at Merrion, away from Beaumatin. She had resigned her position as the Appleton Fellow and accepted the Weingarten chair Stanley had endowed so she would not need to be away so much from her increasingly unhappy husband.

"Oh. Speaking of your wedding…"

Maggie explained about the event she was planning and the date.

"Will you and Stanley be here?"

Chitta checked a calendar on her smart phone.

"It looks like it. I'll let Stanley know. But you really don't have to do anything."

"I'd like to. Anne keeps reminding me we never did have a housewarming last autumn. And I also want to do something to celebrate Stephen's election. And in memory of Alastair."

Chitta looked sombre. "Poor Lady Crista. And poor Alastair. Why would anyone want to kill Alastair?"

SUSAN ALEXANDER

Chapter 10

Back at Beaumatin, Maggie walked into Thomas' study and somewhat nervously decided to come right to the point.

"Thomas. I'm organising… I guess what you'd call a 'do.' At Hereford Crescent. At the end of next week. To celebrate Stephen's election as Master. And Chitta's wedding. And as a kind of memorial to Alastair. And we never did have a housewarming last fall because… Well, you know why. And Anne said she'd help. So I thought you might want to mark your calendar. I checked with your social secretary and she said you had nothing special planned."

Thomas leaned back, narrowed his eyes and steepled his fingers.

Maggie continued. "It won't be the first faculty party I've done. Just the first since… since we've been married."

"I see." Thomas was inscrutable.

"It will be black tie. The default attire for any Merrion social event. And Anne knows these excellent caterers, so Mrs Royce won't be under pressure except for housekeeping."

Mrs Royce who would doubtless want to prepare a plethora of pies. Shepherd's pie. And chicken pie. And fish pie. And… Maggie thought but did not say.

"It will be cocktails. Hors d'oeuvres. I talked to my trusted wine merchant, so there'll be no depredations on the Beaumatin wine cellar. Or the Hereford Crescent one for that matter. And I'll probably have some music. Not rock and roll. I've seen our faculty dancing and it's not pretty. Especially once people have had a few drinks."

"But you've been improving so nicely," said Thomas with a straight face.

Maggie was hopeless at ballroom dancing but had been trying hard to learn to foxtrot to please Thomas.

Maggie glared and Thomas' mouth twitched.

"Well, my dear, it seems you have things well in hand. Let me know if there's anything you need me to do besides be present," said Thomas mildly.

Then he thought. Frowned.

"Will our new neighbour be there, do you know?" he asked.

"Bin Abdulaziz? He's certainly been invited. I can't imagine he'll come, though. And niqabs or not, I don't think the wives attend social events. Or any events, for that matter.

"I've asked some of the University bigwigs. As a courtesy. But I doubt that any of them will come either. Although the invitations looked impressive."

"Invitations?"

"Well, email seemed a bit casual. And Alastair was such a stickler. If something were being done in his memory. So they were engraved. On heavy cream stock. With computers etching the plates rather than someone doing it by hand, it's so much faster than it used to be."

"I see."

Thomas thought.

"And in whose name are these invitations?"

"Well, Anne and I debated that one. I would have preferred to use my own name, er, I mean, my professional name," Maggie quickly corrected herself as she saw Thomas' expression.

"But it turned out, the proper thing to do, etiquette-wise, was to use our names. Um, both our names. I hope you don't mind." Maggie was becoming increasingly flustered.

"You mean…"

"Um, Lord and Lady Raynham."

Thomas knew Maggie was ambivalent about her title and there was a time when she used to physically flinch when called "Lady Raynham." Now the flinching tended to take the form of the faintest flicker behind her eyes.

"If you wanted to impress the bigwigs, it's too bad you didn't use our coat of arms. You know, it's embossed at the top of the paper," said Thomas, feeling like a cat toying with a mouse.

"Um, Mrs Cook knew where the die was from Constance's wedding invitations and she gave it to me," said Maggie with the same expression she would have if she were confessing to mass murder.

Thomas already knew this, as the housekeeper had mentioned it casually in passing.

Thomas got up, crossed to one of the chairs in front of the fireplace, sat down and pulled Maggie onto his lap.

"Mon pauvre papillon. Of course you needed to do what's proper. And I look forward to an entertaining evening. Although hopefully without anyone dying."

"Isn't there an expression about lightning not striking twice?"

"And also to see what you will wear."

"It will depend on what the weather is like," said Maggie, who had already decided exactly what she would wear.

Chapter 11

Maggie was crossing the quad on her way to her rooms when she noticed the figure in black again. Only this time there seemed to be two figures. Wearing niqabs. Walking in the cloister.

Maggie stopped. Stared. The figures continued walking. Then, when they came to the end of the walk, they paused. And turned. And, although Maggie could not be sure, seemed to look directly at her before disappearing around a corner.

Maggie started after them but when she reached the end of the cloister, the figures were nowhere to be seen.

Hm. Strange. And it made her feel vaguely uneasy.

Maggie went to talk to Stephen, but first she had to get past Mrs Steeples. A brittle, champagne blonde around her own age, the secretary treated visitors strictly according to their status. Mrs Steeples had been polite but formal when Maggie was the Appleton fellow. When she had married Thomas and become Lady Raynham, her manner bordered on warmth. Actual warmth was reserved solely for the Master.

Mrs Steeples let Maggie know how fortunate she was that the Master had a spare ten minutes in which he could see her.

Stephen looked up from some paperwork when she entered his office. Packing boxes were stacked against walls and several stood open, half-full of books.

Maggie looked around.

"Alastair's things?"

Stephan nodded solemnly.

"And the police still have no idea…"

"Apparently not. Moss is increasingly dour."

Maggie shook her head.

"Anyhow, that's not why I came by. And thanks for taking the time."

"I welcome the distraction."

Stephen indicated the piles of papers stacked on his desk.

"Oh. Well. It's just that I have a rather strange question. Are there any students who wear niqabs at Merrion?"

"Niqabs? Students? No. None of whom I'm aware. I'm not even sure what our policy is on niqabs. After all that kerfuffle about cross-dressing last autumn. Why?"

"Well, twice now, I've been crossing the quad. On my way to my rooms. And I've seen first one and just now two figures wearing niqabs walking along the cloister."

"Really?"

Stephen considered.

"That building is where bin Abdulaziz has his rooms."

"I thought of that. And the first time, the figure might have gone into his staircase. But today, just now, the two Niqabis—I can't tell if they're actually women under those things—they kept on to the end of the cloister and then just, er, disappeared."

"His wives?"

"Maybe. Although I thought Saudi women didn't go out unaccompanied. By some male or other."

"You probably know more about that than I do."

"And I asked Higgins, the porter, and he says he had certainly not let anyone wearing a niqab into the college. I won't repeat what he said at the suggestion."

"I can imagine," Stephan grinned.

"So I thought I'd ask you."

"Well, as I said. No Niqabis—I like the term—to my knowledge."

He paused.

"Although I know you have positioned yourself as the 'anti-Niqabi'..."

"I have nothing against the women, just the garment. And the attitude toward women it represents," Maggie protested.

"Quite. But why do you care?"

"I know it sounds silly, but it seemed to me that their presence was deliberate. That it was somehow... personal."

"Personal?"

"Well, you know. Seeing a niqab in the quad once might be serendipity. But now twice? I think it's not just a coincidence."

"You think you're being stalked?"

"I don't know. It does seem improbable, I agree. Perhaps I'm a bit sensitive because of bin Abdulaziz. But I thought I'd ask. And let you know. In case…"

"In case the next time there are three?"

"Um, yes. Although I certainly hope there won't be a next time."

"As do I."

Stephen paused. "You know. Faisal has started a Quran study group."

"He has?"

"Yes. He even asked if it would be all right. Of course I said yes."

"But isn't there an Oxford Islamic Society? At Pembroke? And quite a few mosques?"

"Yes, but he seemed quite keen and I could hardly refuse. But perhaps that would explain your Niqabis."

"Perhaps. Anyway, now you know. And I am sure my ten minutes granted by Mrs Steeples are up. So I had better go before I am rousted."

"The woman is a force unto herself. But invaluable. Now that I'm on this side of that door."

Maggie laughed.

Chapter 12

It was the evening of the reception. Everything was ready at Hereford Crescent. Anne and Laurence had come early and helped with overseeing the caterers set up bars in the drawing room and library and a bar and buffet in the dining room. Anne and Maggie knew their faculty. The Brooks' were spending the night and, when things were safely in the hands of the caterers, had retired to dress.

Maggie had been surprised by the response to her event. Everyone had accepted—even the University bigwigs, as she called them—except for bin Abdulaziz, who had failed to respond at all to the RSVP. Maggie hoped that meant he was not coming. Otherwise she had to assume that titles and embossed coats of arms had more cachet than a mere Professor Eliot and she reflected on the shallowness of human nature.

"O tempora, o mores," Maggie said to herself. Then she remembered that Thomas would tell her she was being naïve if she thought otherwise. And perhaps she was. Naïve. But naïveté had allowed her to have a more positive view of the human condition. And she really did not want to be cynical. She was not a lesser woman and only a lesser woman would assume the worst about people.

However, it was time to get ready.

Maggie was wearing a dress she had worn to a party at William's the previous fall. It was a bit dressy, so she had told Anne and Chitta they should "dress to the hilt" and that they should get the word out to the other women who were coming. Not that that would make much difference to Eunice Enderby. Or Claire Kittredge. Or Lady Crista, who had said she would stop by, but not stay long.

Maggie's dress was sleeveless and deeply V-necked, which would have shown cleavage had she had any. It had a swirly bit of flounce around the hem that ended at the tops of her knees. It fit her torso like a second skin and its fine, silky fabric was completely covered with small, delicate sequins that gradually went from a pale smoky taupe at the bottom to the palest blush at the top. It shimmered when she moved.

The fineness of the fabric meant underwear was a challenge. Any underwear. Having a VPL—visible panty line—was unthinkable. So the amount of coverage Maggie had on under the dress would not have been enough to make a bikini for a guinea pig. Not that she imagined guinea pigs wore bikinis.

Maggie came down to find Thomas already waiting in the hall. He looked magnificent in his tuxedo.

He eyed his wife, then leaned over and murmured in her ear, "Remember. If I see a hint, even the slightest hint, of a nipple showing, it won't be only in Saudi Arabia that they flog women for indecency."

Maggie, who was distracted by Thomas' citrusy-spicy aftershave, smiled vaguely.

A chime sounded. Thomas shook his head and went to open the door. It was Stephen Draycott with Dr Liu. Since the last reception, Liu had been provided with the proper attire but looked uncomfortable in the unfamiliar clothing. He ran his finger under his collar as though it were too tight.

"I know you wanted me to come a bit early. And I brought Dr Liu, so he didn't get lost. I hope that's all right."

"Of course," said Maggie, meaning it, and was echoed by Thomas.

Anne and Laurence appeared. Anne was wearing a sleeveless sheath of teal satin shimmering with abstract swirls of silver and black sequins. Maggie thought she looked fabulous.

Anne exclaimed over Maggie's dress.

"But what do you have on underneath that?" she whispered.

"Thomas wondered the same thing," replied Maggie, giving nothing away.

With the exception of Dr Liu, who had already wandered off to find some whisky, the group had divided the evening's labour. Anne would supervise the caterers and Laurence would make sure drinks were flowing at the bars. Thomas and Maggie and Stephen would greet people as they arrived. Afterwards, Stephen and Thomas would attend to the University bigwigs and Maggie would circulate as hostess to make sure everyone was enjoying himself.

The invitation stated the evening was from six to eight, with the assumption that people would come for drinks and nibbles and then go on for a more substantial dinner. However, given her experience with Oxford parties, Maggie knew some people would come early and stay late and either drink their dinners or have enough hors d'oeuvres not to need further sustenance.

Maggie was not surprised when Eunice and David Enderby were the first to arrive. Eunice was wearing a new Oxfam find—a sheath of fuchsia satin that was a challenging colour for her and at odds with her personality. The sleeves of David's dinner jacket needed shortening and, from an assortment of faint spots on his lapels, would have benefitted from a trip to the cleaners. However, Eunice was an ally and Maggie was glad to see her.

Next to arrive were the Kittredges, who looked around at the elegant townhouse with expressions of equal parts disapproval and envy. After that, people began to appear with greater frequency and Maggie lost track of who had arrived, with the exception of Lady Crista, dressed in grey silk and looking like she had aged ten years since Maggie had last seen her. Anne appeared and took charge of the widow.

In the drawing room, Stephen called the group to order by banging a spoon on his tumbler of whisky. Thomas welcomed the guests, then asked the biggest of the bigwigs to say a few words. The bigwig, warned in advance, said a great many words, as fewer would not have been worthy of an Oxford bigwig.

Then Stephen thanked the bigwigs for their presence, gave a brief eulogy for Carrington, offered his sympathies to Lady Crista, assured her she would always be part of the Merrion family and expressed his intent to be a worthy successor to the dead Master.

The formalities over, the guests went back to the main business of the evening which was drinking, eating and gossip. Of a more or less vicious nature. Maggie was aware she would be the subject of quite a few of the conversations, but that was nothing new. Social Oxford ran on alcohol and gossip. Not unlike the Cotswolds, Maggie reminded herself.

Maggie had just had her glass of white wine refilled by a barman when she inadvertently backed up into another guest. A male from his size and feel.

She turned around.

"I'm so sorry," she began, then realised it was bin Abdulaziz, properly attired in black tie.

80

He looked her over. Maggie could imagine what he was thinking about her dress.

However, she was the hostess, so she smiled and said, "You came. Welcome. And I understand that we are now neighbours."

To Maggie's surprise, bin Abdulaziz merely nodded.

Help appeared unexpectedly as Chitta walked over.

"Maggie?" Chitta looked from her friend to bin Abdulaziz.

"Hello, Chitta. Have you met our new Appleton fellow, Professor bin Abdulaziz? Dr bin Abdulaziz, may I present Professor Kazi?"

Chitta was also wearing the same dress she had worn to William's party. It was black lace, high necked, long sleeved and modest except that, with her beauty, Chitta would make a plastic garbage bag look extraordinary.

"Kazi. Is that Pakistani?" bin Abdulaziz asked.

"Bangladeshi," said Chitta.

Bin Abdulaziz nodded and looked down at the glass of orange juice Chitta was holding. Maggie imagined he was thinking that at least there was one person here who was not an infidel.

Stanley Einhorn came over. In his early forties, the billionaire was slight and of medium height, with thinning brown hair cut short and nearly colourless eyes.

"Hi Maggie. Nice party."

"Thank you, Stanley. Stanley, this is our new colleague, Professor bin Abdulaziz. Professor bin Abdulaziz, this is Professor Kazi's husband, Stanley Einhorn. Tonight's reception is partly in honour of their recent wedding."

Frown lines had appeared on bin Abdulaziz's forehead. Maggie imagined him wondering if Einhorn were a Jewish name.

"In fact, Stanley has recently established a foundation. He and Chitta are going to head it. Its first project is going to be establishing schools—free schools—for young women in the developing world. The first school is going to be in Dhaka and the second in Palestine."

"Palestine?"

"Yes."

"And just for girls? Not, er, co-ed?"

"Yes. Just for girls."

Maggie saw bin Abdulaziz considering whether Einhorn might possibly be a German name. Or perhaps Dutch. She continued.

"And in parallel to the foundation's work, The Global Press, the publishers, are launching a new series of books called The Developing World. Several of our Merrion faculty are contributing. Stephen Draycott is collaborating with Dr Liu on a book about China, for instance. And I have been wanting to ask whether you might be interested in producing a volume as well."

Bin Abdulaziz's eyes slid past Maggie and Chitta and settled on Stanley.

"Yes. I might be. We should talk," he said.

"That's great, Faisal," said Stanley. "But Maggie is the one you need to speak to. She's the editor in charge."

Maggie wanted to give Stanley a hug. Possibly a kiss as well. But she had caught a faint whiff of citrusy-spicy aftershave and knew that, while Chitta would not care about Maggie's expression of affection, Thomas certainly would.

She drew Thomas into the circle.

"Thomas, you've met our new neighbour, Professor bin Abdulaziz. I've been telling him about Stanley's foundation and Malcolm's Developing World Series and he is going to consider contributing a volume."

Thomas nodded and smiled tentatively. He looked around at the apparently pleasant faces and abruptly realised he was standing on a minefield and would have to tread very carefully.

Stephen had drawn the same conclusion and walked over.

"Hello, Chitta. Stanley. Faisal, have you been introduced to our newlyweds?"

"Yes."

"And Stephen, er, Faisal said he might consider contributing to the Developing World volumes." Maggie couldn't resist.

"Really? That could certainly be interesting."

Bin Abdulaziz looked at Maggie, who gazed back at him calmly with her deep green eyes. He still would like to have her stoned. Or flogged. Or flogged and then, if she were still alive, stoned. He imagined her crying. Pleading. Begging for mercy.

He wondered whether she could be lured to Saudi Arabia to lecture or consult with the government and he could arrange for her arrest. And punishment. He would enjoy that. Whatever international furore such an event would cause, it would soon die down. The world had a short attention span.

Meanwhile, he realised he did not fully understand the dynamics of the situation and needed to be cautious. After his missteps at the previous reception, where Carrington had died, he had been called into the offices of one of the bigwigs and sternly reprimanded. Threatened with the loss of his position. And he noticed the same bigwig was standing not far away and watching him closely.

Maggie also had an intuitive flash that, even though bin Abdulaziz was being more collegial, his basic attitude towards her had not changed. He was her enemy. He might even be dangerous. She should not forget that.

Bin Abdulaziz asked Maggie, "So you resigned the Appleton fellowship to become the Weingarten fellow. What kind of name is Weingarten?"

Oh good grief, Maggie thought. Aloud she said, "American."

"American?" It was clearly not the answer Bin Abdulaziz was expecting.

"Edna Weingarten was my mother. I established the chair in her memory," Stanley explained.

"She and my father were killed in an accident. A big truck lost control in the rain. Crossed the highway and hit them head on. She wasn't even fifty. I was still at Stanford, studying computer engineering.

"My mother loved England. And all things English. I think she would have been thrilled to have a chair at Oxford named after her."

"I see," said bin Abdulaziz.

"My mother taught Latin. And Greek. She insisted I learn both languages. And I must say it's been more useful than I expected. Timeo danaos et dona ferentes," he turned to Maggie.

I fear the Greeks and the gifts that they bring, Maggie translated silently to herself and assumed Stanley was referring to bin Abdulaziz's change in attitude.

"Virgil. *The Aeneid.* Book 2," said Stephen, showing off.

Thomas had also studied Latin and glanced at Stanley, who nodded back.

"Do they teach Latin in Saudi Arabia?" Maggie asked bin Abdulaziz.

"They teach the words of the Prophet," he snapped, then remembered he was supposed to be conciliatory. He turned and indicated a painting over the fireplace-

"Your ancestors?" he asked Thomas.

It was a picture of a family posed under some trees. An elegantly dressed man loomed benevolently over a seated woman who was holding a baby. Four other children were gathered around their parents, along with a spaniel.

"Er, yes," Thomas replied simply, but Maggie could not resist expanding.

"The fifteenth Baron Raynham. Early seventeen hundreds. With Mrs Baron Number Two. Number One died in childbirth. The oldest son pictured here died as well soon after this was painted. Typhus. So his brother became Baron Number Sixteen." Maggie pointed.

"Unfortunately, Baron Number Sixteen was profligate. Drank. Gambled. Womanised. Fortunately, he drowned trying to win a bet before he could completely bankrupt the estate and the third son who was more responsible became Baron Number Seventeen." She indicated the youngest boy in the picture.

"You're making that up," Stephen said accusingly, while Thomas looked pained.

Maggie smiled enigmatically.

"Isn't it strange how the children all look like little adults?" Chitta observed.

"That's because that's how they thought of children. The Georgians. They even dressed them like small adults, as you can see. They had no idea of developmental psychology. Even though it must have been obvious that children lacked certain adult capacities. And vice versa, I guess. Or maybe they didn't notice, with the children kept segregated in a nursery," Maggie said thoughtfully.

"Lady Raynham, have you no respect for our noble lineage?" Thomas asked, only half joking.

He saw bin Abdulaziz looking at him sympathetically, clearing communicating, "In my country, we know how to deal with a woman like this."

Thomas smiled ruefully in agreement. The first time he had seen Maggie in the dress she was wearing that night, he had suddenly understood why a man would want his wife to wear a niqab. Or a burqa.

Maggie caught the wordless exchange between the men. She saw that Chitta had noticed it as well. She took a deep breath.

You are not a lesser woman, she reminded herself. Only a lesser woman would lose her composure in public because her husband was busy bonding with her enemy.

So instead she said, "It looks like one of our honoured guests is preparing to leave. Please excuse me."

She walked away, her dress shimmering as she moved. Bin Abdulaziz, Stephen and Stanley watched her. Thomas watched the men watching his wife and Chitta took in the moment.

Chitta wished she had Maggie's perfect posture and elegant walk. Maggie had once confessed to her that her mother had made her practice balancing a book on her head while she walked down a straight line every day until she had left for college.

Chitta also attracted her share of masculine attention and Stanley was proud that she did. His attitude was, "Yes, she's brilliant and beautiful, and I'm the man she chose to marry."

Thomas' attitude was different. Chitta suspected he would have preferred Maggie attracted no masculine attention at all. Except his, of course. Perhaps he and bin Abdulaziz had more in common than looking good in their respective tuxedos.

Stephen said, "Chitta, Stanley, have you met Dr Liu, our visiting professor from Renmin University? Let me introduce you."

They left Thomas and bin Abdulaziz standing together. The men talked quietly.

The bigwig was thanked for his presence and sent on his way, Maggie returned to the drawing room and saw Chitta chatting with Deirdre Ross. Maggie thought the young woman looked unusually pretty. Her eyes sparkled and her complexion glowed. Maggie also noticed that she was drinking orange juice again. Maggie knew Deirdre liked her sherry. And wine. And gin and tonic. Perhaps it helped support her role as sycophant to Gordon's pontiff. She joined the women.

Chitta and Deirdre were talking in low tones. Conspiratorially. Maggie looked at the two women, with their glasses of orange juice and their general appearance, and came to a conclusion.

"Deirdre, please don't think me impertinent, but are you pregnant?" she asked.

Deirdre blushed.

"Oh dear. Is it that obvious? Chitta guessed right away. Well, she told me her own good news. Anyway, please don't say anything. Gordon doesn't know. I have a doctor's appointment in a few days and, if that goes well, then I'll tell him."

Deirdre looked nervous.

"I'm sure you'll be fine and Gordon will be delighted."

Deirdre grimaced. "I hope so. Gordon was fairly adamant that he didn't want any children. And I did try to take precautions, but, well, you know they're not always completely reliable. And I really would like…"

"I'm sure he'll be pleased when he finds out. And you're young. Of course you'd want children," Chitta was reassuring.

"I hope so."

Deirdre looked like she wanted to believe Chitta but was not sure.

"Anyhow, let us know what the doctor says," Chitta continued.

As the women continued to discuss the minutiae of pregnancy, Maggie went off to see how Anne was faring. A musical trio had set up in the hall. The violin, viola and pianist—he had brought an electronic keyboard—were playing Cole Porter. Rogers and Hammerstein. George Gershwin. Thomas-compliant music. Maggie hoped he would be pleased.

Anne was talking with the Enderbys and the Kittredges, who were enjoying the buffet.

"So it looks like bin Abdulaziz has decided to be more conciliatory," Anne remarked.

"Perhaps. Although I suspect it's all an act. After he had his head handed to him at a very high level. Although his bonding with Thomas seems to be genuine."

"Oh dear."

"My sentiments exactly," Maggie agreed.

She continued, "Anyhow, Eunice, it looks like bin Abdulaziz may also contribute a volume to the Developing World series. Although he looked less than thrilled when Stanley told him he would have to deal with me. A real horns of a dilemma for him."

"Scylla and Charybdis," said Eunice.

"Do you think so? Faisal seems like a good enough chap to me. Just having to get used to a different culture. Integration doesn't happen instantly, you know," Andrew reminded Maggie.

Maggie decided if bin Abdulaziz could be conciliatory, so could she and responded, "You're right, of course, Andrew."

"You certainly have a good turn out," said Claire Kittredge unexpectedly.

Everyone looked at the woman in surprise. Claire— "Frumpy" —was known for never uttering a word at social events.

"I know. My, er, daughter-in-law, Gweneth, would call it a complete scrum." Maggie wanted to be encouraging.

Claire nodded. "And you have such a lovely home. And the food is delicious."

"It certainly is good," said David, who was working his way through an overflowing plate from the buffet. From his shining face, Maggie suspected it was not his first.

"You must thank Anne for that. She recommended the caterers," Maggie admitted.

Maggie continued to circulate and had no further close encounters with bin Abdulaziz.

At last people were beginning to leave. It was approaching midnight and Maggie congratulated herself on seriously over-ordering food and drink and warning the caterers that they might need to stay late. But apparently they were used to Oxford faculty parties and were prepared. And would charge her accordingly.

Finally, it was just Anne, Laurence, Stephen, Thomas and herself. Stephen was saying goodnight when Anne appeared from the library and announced, "You have to see this."

Dr Liu was sitting upright in a chair with a tumbler and an empty bottle of whisky on a table beside him. He had untied his bow tie. He was smiling and his eyes were open, but glazed.

"Dr Liu?" Stephen asked, but got no response.

He waved his hand in front of his colleague's eyes but there was no reaction.

"Bloody hell. Well, I guess we'll need to get a taxi. I'll get him back to Merrion," said Stephen, half irritated, half amused.

"I'll call," Thomas offered.

After Stephen had managed to bundle Liu into a cab, and Anne and Laurence had gone to their room, Thomas turned to Maggie and said, "Well, Lady Raynham."

They were in Thomas' bedroom.

"I don't need Beatrix to tell me that you have outdone yourself. Again."

He untied his tie and circled around her.

"Although I was surprised at the extent of your knowledge of Raynham family history."

"You did give me that book your grandfather wrote about the Raynhams," Maggie reminded him.

"Yes. I did."

He slipped off his jacket.

"And I am almost disappointed that, despite my expectations, you did not reveal any more of yourself than you were already. How did you manage that, I wonder? As I am quite convinced that under that wonderful dress, you are wearing absolutely nothing at all. I believe bin Abdulaziz thought so as well."

From behind her, he bent, took hold of the hem of her dress and, in one fluid movement, slipped it over her head.

He stood still. From the back it did indeed seem that Maggie was quite naked. He turned her around.

He realised Maggie had on the smallest thong he had ever seen. Flesh toned. Hardly visible. And on her breasts, just covering her nipples, there were two flesh-toned cups. Unattached. Gravity-defying.

"Not quite nothing, as you can see. In fact, made to be worn under a dress like this."

Thomas continued to regard her in bemusement.

"They're made of silicon. And they use adhesive," she explained.

"Really? Are they hard to remove?" he asked.

"I don't know. I guess you could try to find out." Maggie smiled.

Chapter 13

After a long day of working at Merrion, Maggie returned to Hereford Crescent to have Mrs Royce inform her that Thomas had gone out to dinner and would be back later.

Maggie was surprised. This was unusual Thomas behaviour. Unprecedented, in fact. At least in the thirteen months that she had known him. Which was not all that long, she had to admit. Perhaps he had met some old college chum from Balliol.

She politely declined Mrs Royce's offer of some chicken pie and decided she would be fine with a glass of white wine. Maybe two glasses. Something from the south of France.

Had she known Thomas would be out, she would have stayed in her rooms. Gotten some more work done. But it was a half-hour walk back to Merrion and it was drizzling, so she decided to stay at Hereford Crescent.

What to do?

She found some journals she had yet to read in her study and took them down to the library and settled on the sofa. She read for an hour, then felt her attention wandering. Perhaps some television.

Hercule Poirot. David Suchet. Wonderful acting. Wonderful settings. And cars. And costumes. Everyone dressing for dinner. Who cared if sometimes the plots were thin?

The programme ended. The murderer was exposed, thanks to Hercule's little grey cells. Taken away for trial. Eventually to be hanged. Or was it hung? Either way, grim.

Maggie was glad they no longer executed people. At least not in Britain.

Thomas was still out. Maggie was not the sort of wife, no, make that person, who would call. Or text. Or wait up like an anxious parent. The wine had made her sleepy. She would get ready for bed. Thomas would get back when he got back.

Maggie was sitting at her dressing table in her nightgown, a little slip of sea green silk that fell to just above her knees. She was contemplating a small bottle of serum that promised to "increase the renewal and regeneration of the skin for a luminous, youthful glow, diminish fine lines, wrinkles and skin roughness, restore an even skin tone, provide an intensive lifting and firming effect" and other miraculous benefits. Whether it performed as advertised or not, she liked the way her skin felt when she used it. Which was almost every night. Well, most nights, anyway.

She heard footsteps in the hall. Her door opened. Thomas had returned.

Oh dear.

A glance showed that, while not completely drunk, Thomas was far from completely sober.

"Thomas?"

"I'm back."

"So I see."

"Come. Let me tell you."

He was carrying a large, white rectangular box under one arm. With his free hand, he took her arm and led her across the hall to his room.

Maggie sat on the bed, cross-legged. Thomas took off his jacket and collapsed in a chair. Maggie admired his braces. They were proper braces with leather fasteners that attached to buttons inside his trousers. She found them incredibly... masculine.

Thomas loosened his tie and announced, "I had dinner with Faisal bin Abdulaziz."

"Really?"

Maggie was surprised.

"He invited me. A bit short notice. But I thought it would be interesting."

"And was it? Interesting?"

"Oh yes."

"Did you meet the wives?"

"No. The wives are completely off limits. Out of sight. Apparently you only get to see them if you're a male relative. Which I am not. Faisal explained."

"But there are wives. More than one?"

"There are three."

"Three?"

"Yes. Number One was arranged by Faisal's father. When Faisal was around twenty-two. Newly graduated from Princeton. A nice young woman from another prominent Saudi family. Number Two came a few years later. Also arranged by his father. But young. Well younger than Wife Number One was by that time. And Faisal himself.

95

"Number Three Faisal arranged. Apparently all marriages are arranged. You don't get to go out on dates first. She was really young. Seventeen. Pretty. But spoiled, according to Faisal. Needed some discipline Administered by himself and Wife Number One."

Maggie felt herself starting to get angry, but Thomas continued.

"However, it's been five years and Wife Number Three has redeemed herself by producing three sons. Wife Number One gave Faisal one son, but three daughters. Wife Number Two has produced one son but again, two daughters."

Maggie did the math. "That's ten children."

"Yes, but only five sons."

"Good grief."

Now Maggie was angry.

Thomas went on, oblivious to Maggie's mood. "To continue. Wife Number One stayed back in Saudi to look after the household. And most of the children. Wives Numbers Two and Three are here. Wife Number Three's youngest son who is still nursing is here. Don't ask me about visas.

"Dinner was laid out when I arrived. Some sort of chicken with tomatoes. Spices, And rice. I forget what he called it. But it was very tasty.

"Faisal said he had decided that, as long as he was not in Saudi Arabia, he would forego the prohibition against alcohol. The Princes do, so he thought he would as well. He had some very fine whisky. And some nice Lebanese wine with the chicken.

"And he's looking for Wife Number Four. Not a Saudi. Possibly Syrian. Apparently Syrian girls are highly valued for their looks and culinary skills. Now that Wife Number Three is under control…"

Thomas noticed Maggie's expression.

"Those were his words, not mine," he added hurriedly.

"Faisal thought four wives would be enough. His father has six. Twenty-one children. Faisal was his third son. But his mother was his father's favourite wife, which gave him certain advantages. Like getting to study at Princeton. And Yale."

Maggie was speechless.

"He used Gordon Ross as an example. Of the problem with our western ways. Our so-called monogamy. Gordon has had three wives. Sequentially. What's happened to Mrs Ross Numbers One and Two? Who knows? Faisal said he takes good care of his wives. He is a caring and indulgent husband. And father."

"Thomas. He has two women… sequestered in that house. They can't even come downstairs when you're there. And they're used like, like brood mares. For sons. I assume the daughters get traded away like camels. If they're pretty enough. If there's nothing wrong with them. And, of course, they'd have to be virgins."

Thomas looked exasperated. Like Maggie was being very dim.

"Men want sons," he said simply.

"Yes. So there can be a twenty-ninth baron."

"Well, yes. Of course."

"What would you have done if William and James had been girls?"

"I don't know. The question never arose."

Maggie was always surprised by Thomas' lack of introspection.

"Lady Crista is the third of five girls. Fortunately, the sixth child was a boy. He's now the current earl," Thomas pointed out.

Maggie realised she was feeling the way she had one night when she had been in Amsterdam for a conference. A group had decided to walk over to De Wallen, the red light district. Its streets were filled with packs of men, many drunk, checking out the girls on display in their windows. They made lewd gestures and shouted out comments that, even though most were in languages Maggie did not know, she recognised as being obscene. She became so upset that she left after just a few minutes and made her way back to the hotel on her own.

She felt a fundamental outrage at men treating women like chattel. As less than fully human. Not that some women didn't treat men like objects as well. Desirable for their position and wealth. And with divorce settlements regarded like the spoils of war. But bin Abdulaziz's assumptions about women and how they should be used. And treated. And Thomas' nonchalance about this. She found it appalling.

Finally Maggie said in acid tones, "Well I guess it was fortunate for me that, when we met, needing sons was not one of your considerations."

"Yes. When it came to you, my considerations were different."

He noticed the box that was lying on the bed.

"Oh. Faisal gave me this. For you. He said something in Arabic. I think your Yank equivalent would be, 'Don't knock it until you've tried it.'"

"For me?"

"Open it," Thomas urged.

Maggie lifted the lid. Inside folds of tissue paper was fabric. Black fabric.

She looked at Thomas.

"Egyptian cotton."

"Yes. But…"

He lifted the material. It was a robe. Long-sleeved. Stark.

"It's an abaya." Maggie recognised the garment.

There was more.

"What's this?"

It was a niqab.

"Good grief."

"Try it on."

"You must be joking."

"You're always going on about them. Have you ever put one on?"

"No."

"Why not?"

"There are some things you don't need to try to know they're wrong. Heroin comes to mind."

"Come on. I'm curious to see…"

Thomas picked up the abaya and put it over Maggie's head. He pulled her arms through the sleeves. Her cast just fit. He pulled her up.

"And now…"

He threw the niqab over Maggie's head. Adjusted it.

The niqab was long. It fell down in the front and back almost to her knees. Two green eyes glared from the slit.

The clothing fit perfectly. Maggie wondered how bin Abdulaziz had managed that.

"Your eyes give you away," Thomas commented.

He walked around her. "Interesting. Sort of elegant. Suggestive. Try moving."

Maggie figured the sooner she humoured Thomas, the sooner she could get out of the garments.

The niqab restricted her vision. She took two steps. On the third her foot caught on a chair leg and she crashed to the floor.

"Ow." Her broken arm hurt.

"Maggie! Let me help."

Thomas helped her up.

"All right. That's enough."

"No. Come on. Try again."

"No." She started to remove the restrictive clothing.

"No. Don't. Leave them on." Thomas wrapped his arms around her.

Maggie suddenly felt claustrophobic. And suffocated. She couldn't breathe properly under the niqab. She started to panic.

"Thomas!" Muffled.

He still had hold of her arms.

Maggie felt like she was being smothered. Had bin Abdulaziz impregnated the fabric with some toxic substance?

She could not move. So she took as deep a breath as she could and screamed.

It was the sound of a mortally wounded animal.

Thomas dropped his hold. Maggie tore off the niqab and bolted out of the room, across the hall and into her own bedroom. She slammed the door shut behind her, pulled off the abaya and threw it on the floor.

The Royces had heard the scream and came racing up the stairs. George Royce carried a handgun.

"What's wrong?" George asked Thomas.

"Nothing. I'm sorry. It was nothing. It was... Lady Raynham tripped. Hurt herself. Her broken arm. Sorry to cause alarm."

The Royces exchanged glances but knew not to argue. They returned to their flat.

Thomas paused outside of Maggie's door. It was quiet inside. He opened it.

Maggie was huddled on the bed, knees up, head resting on her knees.

"Maggie..."

"I couldn't breathe."

"I didn't realise…"

"I panicked. Sorry about the drama."

"I guess breathing under a niqab is an acquired competence," Thomas tried to joke.

"Not one that I'm going to acquire."

"Apparently not."

"And you can't see properly."

"Quite."

Maggie drew a shaky breath.

Thomas sat down beside her. She smelled citrusy-spicy aftershave. And whisky.

"I was afraid I was being poisoned. That bin Abdulaziz had put something on the fabric…"

"Faisal wouldn't do something like that. He's quite a good fellow, once you get to know him."

Maggie mentally bit her tongue to keep from saying what she thought about that.

Thomas put his arms around her.

"I am sorry."

Maggie was silent.

"And now I intend to show you what my considerations were."

"Considerations?"

"The ones I had when I married you. And which had nothing whatsoever to do with sons."

Chapter 14

The next morning Maggie was drinking coffee in the kitchen when Thomas came in. He kissed her and poured himself a cup.

"I think I forgot to mention last night..."

"Yes?"

"I invited Faisal to Beaumatin for the weekend."

Maggie was speechless. Finally she managed, "You invited Faisal?"

"Yes. He seemed interested. In the barons. And the estate. And the sheep."

"Is he bringing his wives? Or is he coming alone?"

"Alone. It's that thing about women only being allowed with male relatives."

"And you're not one."

"No. I'm not."

"Do you want me to be there?"

"Want you to be there? Of course I do."

"Even though Faisal isn't one of my male relatives? Neither is he one of Mrs Cook."

"Oh I think he'll put up with our infidel ways. I told you he's decided it's all right for him to drink."

"Drink. Right."

Maggie thought.

"So what are you going to do? Play Boys' Own together?"

"He rides. I can show him the estate. And he shoots. Perhaps William can organise something at his club. You could go along as well. And I thought you could invite some people around for dinner."

Maggie stifled a sigh.

"It's a bit short notice. I'll see what I can arrange."

"Beatrix and Cedric would come."

"And perhaps the Nesbitts. I know Beatrix is not that fond of Thalia, but to meet a Prince of Arabia…"

Maggie suggested the Nesbitts in the belief that Lady Nesbitt could take on bin Abdulaziz and not even break a sweat.

"And maybe Malcolm would like to come. If Faisal is going to write a book for his series."

"I knew I could rely on you," Thomas said and kissed her again.

"Well, yes. Of course you can."

Chapter 15

When she arrived at Merrion, Maggie went straight to Chitta's rooms. Fortunately, her friend was free. The room was still in its usual chaotic state, but the clothing had been put away and there was no sign of the parrots.

"You won't believe what Thomas did," she began.

She told Chitta about the dinner. And the wives. And the niqab.

Chitta was just as outraged as Maggie had been.

"My first marriage was arranged, as you know. But I had met Salman several times and I did not have to agree to marry him. I could have said no and my parents would have looked for someone else for me. And Salman was a wonderful husband. But I never had to be confined to some harem. Or share Salman with other wives. Or wear a veil when I went out."

"And now Thomas thinks bin Abdulaziz is a fine fellow. And he's invited him to Beaumatin for the weekend."

"What?"

"I'm afraid so. And I wondered. Well, if you didn't have any plans. If you might like to come. Well, maybe not so much like to come. But I could really use some backup."

Chitta thought.

"Stanley is getting back from the US Saturday morning. I guess I could come down on Friday. Give you some support. And I'll ask Stanley if he'd like to join on Saturday. If he's not too jet lagged. And we could go back to

Pemberley after your dinner. I assume you're organising some sort of dinner?"

Pemberley was an estate Stanley had bought that was a few miles from Beaumatin.

"Oh yes. That would be great. If you could come. And Stanley. And I'll ask Stephen. And Anne and Laurence. And Malcolm. And the Ainswicks. And the Nesbitts. And William and Gweneth. Thomas is going to ask William to take bin Abdulaziz shooting."

Maggie paused as an unwelcome thought occurred.

"And Constance is still around. She's staying with William and Gweneth. So she'll need to be invited as well. She shares bin Abdulaziz's views on niqabs, by the way. They should get along famously. And apparently Faisal's decided that, as long as he's at Oxford, it is all right if he drinks. When in Rome and all that.

"And I also wondered. Well, I'm not sure Mrs Cook's culinary repertoire is up for this. No pork sausages and bacon at breakfast, certainly. And with my arm, cooking a dinner all by myself is going to be difficult. Chopping. Mixing. So I wondered. Would you help me fix dinner Friday? Maybe Punjabi? Curry? And do you know where there's a halal butcher in Oxford?"

"Halal?" Chitta frowned at her friend.

"I'm trying to go the second mile. It's something Jesus said. About if someone wants you to go with him one mile, go with him two. If falls under loving your enemy."

"Your enemy. Well at least you've got that part right. And of course you can count on me. And I do know a good butcher, although I hardly use him since Salman...

"And there's a shop where we can get spices and the other ingredients we'll need. That they may not have in Cirencester."

"Chitta, thank you so much."

"Well, I expect to be well entertained for my efforts. And I'll ask Stanley if he can join us when he calls later today," she smiled.

They discussed menu options. Then there was a gentle tapping at the door.

"Come."

It was Deirdre, looking radiant.

"Oh. You're here too, Maggie. That's good. I wanted to tell you both. I've just been to see Dr Bennett. And I am. Pregnant."

"That's wonderful, Deirdre," Chitta enthused.

"Congratulations, Deirdre," Maggie said while she thought, another baby? My goodness. I should check with Victoria. Perhaps she is pregnant as well.

Victoria was the wife of James, Thomas' second son.

Deirdre continued. "She even did a sonogram. And gave me a picture. Here. See?"

It was a black and white image. Grainy.

"That's the head. And the heart is here," Deirdre pointed.

"Dr Bennett says in a month we should be able to know the sex. Whether it's a boy or girl."

"That's wonderful, Deirdre. When is your due date?" Chitta asked.

"Late November. You know, they give all sorts of classes at the clinic. One was even on knitting baby clothes. I've always wanted to learn how to knit. Want to join? Baby clothes are so precious. They're so, so small."

Chitta laughed. "Let me think about that."

Then Deirdre became serious.

"Well, I'm going to go tell Gordon."

"I'm sure he'll be thrilled, Deirdre."

"I hope so."

Deirdre did not seem convinced.

"Anyhow, I wanted to share the good news."

She left.

"Well," Chitta said.

"At this point, I think the only person I know who isn't pregnant is Eunice," Maggie declared.

"Eunice?"

"She's only in her forties. Early forties. It could still be possible."

"Eunice pregnant. The mind boggles," said Chitta.

"I think she and David would be good parents," Maggie insisted.

"An Oxfam baby," Chitta mused.

Suddenly they heard shouting from the staircase.

The friends exchanged glances. Chitta went and opened her door

"I told you I didn't want children. No children!"

It was Gordon.

"It wasn't on purpose."

Deirdre was pleading.

"No? I don't believe you."

"Truly, Gordon. Please."

"Once was enough. More than enough. Little pissant…"

Gordon was raving. Deirdre started to cry.

"But Gordon. I want a child. Our child."

"No. You'll have to choose. It or me."

"But Gordon…"

"It or me. So get rid of it. Let me know when it's done."

"No!"

Deirdre was sobbing.

"If I wanted a wife with sagging breasts and a stretched out belly and a slack vagina, I'd still be married to that fat cow Fiona."

"What? How can you…"

"Now stop crying. You're embarrassing me. Just... take care of it."

"Gordon..."

Maggie heard a door slam. Deirdre crying. Then suddenly she shrieked, "No! Don't! No!"

There was a scream, then Deirdre crashed down the stairs and landed in front of Chitta's door.

"Deirdre!"

The women rushed out of the room. Maggie knelt down. Deirdre lay motionless. Her eyes were open and a thin trickle of blood began to ooze out of one nostril.

"Deirdre, are you all right? Deirdre?" Maggie was distraught.

"Chitta? Is she..."

Chitta felt for a pulse. Shook her head.

Deirdre still clutched the picture from the sonogram in one hand.

Gordon appeared at the top of the stairs.

"What's going on? I'm trying to work," he complained. Then he saw Deirdre.

"Deirdre? Bloody hell."

He hurried down the stairs. Maggie stood in his way.

"Don't you go near her! Don't you touch her!"

Maggie was enraged.

"Don't you tell me what to do!"

He tried to push past her.

Maggie was so furious with Ross that she punched him in the stomach as hard as she could with her broken arm. The cast made up in hardness what her arm lacked in strength. When Gordon doubled over, she punched him in the jaw with her left hand. It was a lucky punch. Gordon collapsed.

Two students tore down the stairs and stopped abruptly as their way was blocked by Ross.

"We heard a scream," explained the boy.

"Are you all right, Professor Ross?" asked the girl in concern. Then she saw Deirdre.

"Oh my God, Mikey," she squeaked and abruptly sat down on the stairs.

"What happened?" demanded the boy.

"Mrs Ross, er, fell down the stairs."

"Is she dead?" asked the girl, who had mousy brown hair, a sallow complexion and wore jeans and an Oxford sweatshirt.

I'm afraid so. Did either of you see what happened?" Maggie demanded.

"I didn't. No. Did you, Emma?" asked the boy. He was medium height, skinny, with worn jeans and a shabby green pullover. Dark hair was cut to almost a stubble.

"No," Emma shook her head. She looked like she was about to cry.

"All right. Were you going out?"

"No. We just wanted to see what happened," said Mikey.

"Then perhaps you should return to your rooms," said Maggie firmly.

The pair exchanged glances, then retreated back up the stairs.

Chitta was calling 999.

"Call Stephen. Have him alert the porter," Chitta ordered.

"If I can," said Maggie. She wasn't sure she could move the fingers of either hand, but she managed.

Stephen was the first to arrive.

"Good God," he said when he saw Deirdre's crumpled figure and Gordon sitting on the stairs, head in hands.

"She's dead." Chitta stated the obvious.

"Gordon. This is terrible. I'm so sorry," Stephen began.

"Don't waste your sympathies on him." Maggie was still outraged.

"This is his fault. In fact, I think he pushed her."

"What?" Stephen was startled.

"No I didn't!" Gordon protested.

"We heard you. Arguing with Deirdre. We heard every word you said. Every one," Maggie was scathing.

"And every word that Deirdre said," Chitta added.

"Eavesdropping…"

"It was impossible not to hear. You weren't in your rooms. You were on the landing. You were yelling. Everyone could hear."

The pathologist appeared. He looked at Deirdre's body, then at the stairs and shook his head.

"Did she fall?"

"No. She was pushed," Maggie stated emphatically.

"It was an accident," Gordon insisted.

"Oh. I see. You accidentally pushed her."

Chitta was equally irate.

"She was pushed from there." Chitta gestured up to the next landing.

The pathologist shook his head.

"I'll call the CID," he said finally. "You people…"

"We can wait in my rooms. Chitta, just in case they close off the staircase, pack a bag. You can stay at Hereford Crescent if you have to. You come too, Gordon," Maggie added.

"That's a good idea, Maggie. You go. I'll be right down," Chitta agreed.

Escorted by one of the pathologist's assistants, Maggie, Stephen and Gordon went down to her rooms.

"Stephen, you know where the whisky is. And cognac. And there's some white wine in the refrigerator, if you wouldn't mind opening a bottle."

"Gordon?" Stephen asked.

"Whisky," said the man, who was sitting slumped in an armchair.

Maggie sat down at her laptop and began to type. She wanted to get down every word she and Chitta had heard while they were still fresh in her mind. Not that she would ever forget some of the things that Gordon had said.

Her eyes filled with tears.

Deirdre. So happy. So excited. With that picture of the baby. Wanting to learn to knit baby clothes. Then, in just moments, distraught. Then dead, the picture of the foetus still clutched in her hand.

Gordon's sheer viciousness. How could he say such things? And now wife and child were gone. Well, he had wanted the baby dead.

But what about Deirdre? Had he wanted her dead too, in a moment of rage? Certainly pushing her must have been impulsive. An act of anger, her death an unintended consequence.

Chitta came in carrying a briefcase and a gym bag.

"Chitta, could you take a look at this please?" Maggie asked her friend.

Chitta was about to ask what it was, but Maggie shook her head and glanced at Gordon.

Gordon was holding an empty tumbler of whisky. He seemed oblivious.

"Chitta sat down at Maggie's desk.

"Tea?" Maggie asked.

"Oh. Yes, please."

While Maggie made some tea, Chitta read what Maggie had written and made a few changes.

"I think you got it," she said finally.

Maggie noticed Chitta was also trying not to cry.

Maggie printed out four copies of the document.

The colleagues sat in silence. Then Chitta said, "Well, Stephen, how is it being Master, under the circumstances?"

Stephen glanced at Gordon, who had not reacted.

"I could certainly wish for different circumstances," he said finally.

"How is Lady Crista coping?"

"She's still with one of her sisters. But she sent a note and said she would be back next week to begin packing. She intends to be out of the Master's quarters about half-way through Trinity term."

Maggie thought about what Thomas had once said. That when he died she would also have to leave Beaumatin within a similar time period, as William and his family would be moving into the house.

Maggie looked around at her rooms. She might think of them as her own space but, in reality, they were also just on loan, hers only as long as she held her Oxford fellowship. And while she had a house in Boston, that felt much too far away. She really needed her own space. That was really hers. That was close. Accessible. That nothing short of an invading army could force her to leave. She would need to find a solution to that. Soon.

"Oh, Stephen. This will distract you. Guess who invited Thomas to dinner last night?"

"Wait until you hear this," said Chitta.

Stephen appeared to think, then said, "I give up. Who invited Thomas to dinner last night?"

"Faisal bin Abdulaziz."

"What? Really?"

"Yes."

"Were the wives there?"

"Well, upstairs, I gather. Apparently they can only show themselves to their male relatives."

"Good God."

"There are two who are here. Numbers Two and Three. Number One stayed behind in Saudi Arabia with the children."

"Children?"

"There are ten. Although the youngest is still nursing and is here. He's Wife Number Three's. That leaves the other nine, of whom five are girls and four are boys. Girls don't count for much, though.

"And bin Abdulaziz is looking for a Wife Number Four. Thomas says his father has six."

"Six wives? Really?" Stephen was fascinated.

"And he sent Thomas home with a niqab. For me."

"You're joking."

"No. And Thomas insisted I try it on."

"Are there pictures?"

"No. Although I'm not sure how you'd tell it was me and not just anyone. Anyhow, I found it an unpleasant experience. One I won't repeat anytime soon."

"I would think not."

"But the result is, Thomas has concluded that Faisal is a fine fellow, I think is how he put it. Although I suspect that Faisal's deciding to forego the prohibition on alcohol, at least while he's at Oxford, had something to do with it. Both whisky and wine were reportedly superior."

Stephen shook his head.

"Which brings me to my point. Which is that, in return, Thomas has invited bin Abdulaziz to Beaumatin for the weekend. And while Faisal won't be bringing his wives, the presence of this wife is required. So I'm looking for backup. Chitta is coming for Friday and hopefully Stanley will be able to join when he returns from the US on Saturday. Do you think you could come as well?"

"I wouldn't miss it. And would love to stay for the whole show, but I'll need to be back here by Saturday. I have a lunch. And you wouldn't believe the paperwork that's piled up. I think the contents of my in-box breed in the night.

"And Chitta, I'd be happy to offer you a ride down."

"Thank you, Stephen."

There was a knock at the door.

"Come in," Maggie said.

It was a pair of police constables.

"You're the ones who were there when the accident happened?" one asked.

"Yes. Except for Professor Draycott, who is here because he is the Master of Merrion College," Maggie explained.

"We've been asked to wait with you until our guv arrives," the other said.

"Very well. Please, um, sit down. Make yourselves comfortable. Would you like some tea? Coffee? Water? Juice?"

"No thank you, ma'am. And we'll stand."

And one positioned himself by the door and the other against one of the walls.

Maggie sighed. And thought that she had too much to do to just sit around in silence because of some PCs.

So she said, "As long as we have to wait, Chitta, how about we draw up a menu plan?"

Chitta glanced at Gordon Ross, who was still sitting slumped in his chair and appeared to be unaware of his surroundings.

"All right. And I'll make a shopping list."

Half an hour later, Inspector Moss entered, followed by Sergeant Bixby. Moss scowled at the group.

"So it's you lot again. I understand some of you think this was a suspicious death and not a tragic accident?"

"Not just think," Chitta said.

Maggie realised Chitta had not yet had the pleasure of making Moss' acquaintance.

"Um, Chitta, this is Detective Inspector Moss and Detective Sergeant Bixby. They are also the ones who are investigating Alastair's death. Inspector Moss, Sergeant Bixby, this is Professor Kazi. Her rooms are directly above mine. We were together when Deirdre was pushed down the stairs. We heard everything that happened."

Moss, who had brightened when Maggie had introduced Chitta, scowled again.

"Heard? You didn't actually see anything, then."

"No. But it was all quite clear. Here. We even wrote out what happened. Exactly what we heard. While it was still fresh in our minds."

Chitta handed Moss one of the printouts.

Moss skimmed through the pages and handed them to Bixby.

"Yes. Well, you'll still need to be interviewed. Separately. Professor Draycott, is there a room where we could talk to people?"

"There's the Senior Common Room. As long as you don't need... I assume it is only Professors Eliot, Kazi and Ross you need to interview?"

"For now," Moss agreed grudgingly.

"And Gordon, considering the allegations, do you want me to call a solicitor for you?" Stephen asked.

Gordon, who was still sitting slumped, straightened. "No. Why would I need a solicitor? Blood-sucking parasites.

I didn't do anything. No matter what they say," he glowered at Maggie and Chitta.

Maggie pressed her lips together.

"You lot wait here, then. You'll be called. And Bixby, when we're done, you'll need to question everyone else in the building. See if they heard or saw anything."

Moss left with Stephen, followed by the sergeant.

Chapter 16

Thomas had spent the afternoon with Arthur Ritchie, the agent who managed the Raynham holdings in Oxford, and had invited the man for a drink at the Randolph before returning to Hereford Crescent. He was surprised to find Maggie, Chitta and Stephen sitting in the library, Stephen with whisky, Chitta with apple juice and Maggie with a half-empty bottle of white wine.

"Well, hello. This is a surprise. Or did I miss an entry in my social calendar?" he asked Maggie.

Then he noticed the mood of the group.

"Maggie? What is it?"

"Deirdre Ross is dead. She fell down the stairs. Our stairs. At Merrion. And landed right in front of Chitta's door. While we were standing there. Except we think she was pushed. By Gordon. They were having a horrible fight. Deirdre was pregnant. Gordon told her to get an abortion or she'd have to choose between him and the baby."

"Good God."

Thomas was shocked.

"I'm sorry. It was awful. Since the staircase is blocked off, I told Chitta she could stay here. Stephen is providing moral support."

"And the good Detective Inspector Moss is investigating," Stephen added.

Thomas grimaced.

"And Maggie punched Gordon. To keep him away from Deirdre. Er, her body. Once in the stomach and once in the jaw. It was impressive. Wham! Pow!" Chitta demonstrated.

"I guess I should be thankful you weren't armed. With a gun, I mean," Thomas clarified.

"Yes. The cast is like having a set of brass knuckles," Maggie admitted, while she unconsciously rubbed her arm.

She stood.

"I'm sorry. I really need to… Chitta, you know where your room is. And Mrs Royce has some cheese and bread and salad and Stephen, please consider staying for supper. I'm sure Thomas would enjoy your company. He can tell you both more about his adventure with bin Abdulaziz. But I need to…" she gestured and walked out.

The others were left staring.

Maggie went to her room. Her broken arm ached and throbbed, but as she could wiggle her fingers and make a fist she hoped nothing too dire was wrong. Her left hand also hurt. Two fingers were swollen and the joints were sore. But she could wiggle and bend those fingers as well.

She got out the bottle of painkillers. She had not taken one of the pills since the night she had driven up to Oxford from Beaumatin. She considered taking two, which would ensure oblivion for the night, but then reminded herself that she had been drinking and, also, the pills were opiates and were no way to deal with her feelings. She took one.

She thought about Deirdre. She could not get the image out of her head of Deirdre's fist clutching the picture from the sonogram. The little head. The heart. The unborn child now dead as well. Despite her resolve, she began to cry.

She blamed herself. She and Chitta should have intervened. Confronted Ross. If he had seen they were watching, he would never have pushed Deirdre down those stairs. They could have comforted her. Deirdre would have needed comforting.

Thomas had once asked her if she had ever wanted children. And she had answered quite honestly that, as she had never married, well, never before Thomas, she had not really obsessed about it. She had her niece and nephews. Her life was full without a child.

She knew women who had gone to great lengths to have children, using hormonal regimes, sperm donors, in vitro fertilisation, surrogates, whatever was necessary to have a baby. Several had adopted, with mixed outcomes. And while she had sympathised with their obsession, she had never empathised.

But if she were honest, she also had to admit that she enjoyed the simplicity, the, all right, she would use the word, the freedom, of being on her own. Of having only herself to consider. Did that make her selfish? She wondered if the reason she was feeling the lack of her own space so acutely was really because she was experiencing a loss of freedom.

She had no doubt at all of her love for Thomas, but she also had to admit that she occasionally found the relationship confining. The times Thomas seemed most content were when they were together at Beaumatin and his day consisted of riding out with Ned in the morning, accounting in the afternoon, a supper of pie accompanied by a discussion of sheep and snowdrops, followed by the History Channel, Laphroaig and bed. Thomas enjoyed his life as lord of the manor and a routine that included the presence of a wife.

While Maggie also enjoyed being at Beaumatin with Thomas, she knew she would go mad if being a wife were all she had to do. Did that mean there was something wrong with her? Was it evidence of a character failing on her part? She had no idea. But the pill had started to work and she drifted off to sleep.

Thomas found Maggie fully clothed, curled up into a ball on her bed, asleep. He saw the bottle of painkillers on her dressing table and pressed his lips together. Chitta had told him a more complete version of what had happened at Merrion.

"And you really think Ross pushed her?" Thomas asked sceptically.

"Well, one moment he was yelling at Deirdre. Then we heard her cry 'No! Don't!' She screamed and then fell."

"And I thought the main problem I'd have as Master was bin Abdulaziz," Stephen commented.

"Oh he's not a bad chap, once you get to know him," Thomas assured him.

Stephen and Chitta exchanged glances.

"Yes. Maggie said you'd had dinner with him," Stephen said.

"But not the wives," added Chitta.

"No. Apparently the only males with whom they get to socialise are relatives."

"And do they have any male relatives here except for bin Abdulaziz?" Chitta demanded.

"I don't know," Thomas shrugged.

"And Maggie has invited us down for your bin Abdulaziz weekend," Stephen said.

"You'll come?"

"I can come down Friday but I need to get back here on Saturday. Work. And now this whole thing with Deirdre Ross. And Gordon," said Stephen.

"And I'm coming early on Friday and helping Maggie cook dinner. Because of her arm," Chitta added as Thomas looked surprised.

"Her arm? Oh yes. Of course. Quite."

Thomas looked down at Maggie's arm, encased in its cast. Her hand did not seem to be swollen, so he hoped she had not injured herself when she had punched Ross.

At least she did not look worn out and exhausted, like she had during Michaelmas term. That had prompted him to form an alliance with Stanley to set up the Weingarten fellowship, which would relieve Maggie of most of the college's bureaucratic demands and allow her to undertake more of her work at Beaumatin.

At the moment, though, it seemed she was still spending three days each week at Oxford, but perhaps that was because she was organising the work for her new position and catching up from having missed Hilary term. And then there was this nonsense about staying in her rooms when he was not in town, rather than at the house here. About needing her own space. Even though she had her own space here. Her study. Her bedroom. As well as her study and bedroom at Beaumatin. Which she had fixed up the way she had wanted. At no small expense.

He knew Constance had upset her. And he admitted that some of that was his own fault. Well, he would give Maggie some time to get over it. And if she didn't... What was Faisal's phrase? About men controlling their wives? Not that he wanted to control Maggie. Well, if he were honest, perhaps just a little.

He left, then returned in a few minutes in his blue silk paisley robe. He lay down on the bed beside his wife and enfolded her in his arms.

Chapter 17

Later it seemed to Maggie that she had spent most of the following day on the telephone inviting people to dinner. At the end she had managed to assemble two groups. The first was what she called "Family Night." Attending would be William and Gweneth, Gweneth's mother Muriel Stonor who was Lord Ainswick's sister and visiting her daughter. Constance, the Ainswicks, Chloe and David Osborne, Simon Peevey, a London solicitor employed by both Thomas and the Ainswicks and two people she considered to be her own "family," Chitta and Stephen.

Saturday evening was a smaller party consisting of Sir John and Lady Nesbitt, Stanley and Chitta, Malcolm Fortescue-Smythe, who owned the Global Press, and an unspecified "guest." Unfortunately, Anne had to decline Maggie's invitation as she and Laurence were going to visit one of their sons in London.

Maggie called Mrs Cook to alert her about the descent of a weekend house party and the two dinners. The housekeeper took the news in stride and said she would ask Mrs Griggs and Mrs Bateson, two local women who helped maintain the huge house, to come and assist.

Maggie was amazed at Mrs Cook's equanimity, then wondered if the woman was enjoying having guests to entertain at Beaumatin. There would not have been house parties during the final illness of Harriet, Thomas' first wife, and she knew her husband had been a virtual recluse following Harriet's death until he had met Maggie four years later.

Well the weekend would certainly give Mrs Cook scope for her talents. Maggie explained that Professor bin Abdulaziz was Muslim and ate no pork and that she and

Chitta would be bringing food with them for Friday night's meal which Chitta would cook with their assistance. Saturday they decided to have roast duck with a port wine sauce, Jersey Royals and peas, with a smoked haddock tart to start and one of Mrs Cook's rich desserts to finish. Mrs Cook promised to fix some additional items for vegetarian Chitta.

Maggie and Chitta shopped on Friday morning and arrived at Beaumatin in time for a late lunch. Thomas had agreed to drive down with the guest of honour later that afternoon.

Under Chitta's guidance, the women spent the next four hours chopping, mixing, cooking and washing up. With her cast, Maggie was relegated to stirring large pots of fragrant curries.

"Chitta, I'm impressed. I had no idea about your cooking skills," Maggie commented.

"Blame my grandmother. My father's mother. She insisted I show her I could cook before I had permission to go to university. And of course I cooked for Salman."

"And Stanley?"

"Sometimes. His tastes are still largely undergraduate. Pizza. Hamburgers. Sushi of course. I consider it a triumph when he eats a vegetable."

Maggie shook her head.

At last everything was ready. Thomas had called to say he and bin Abdulaziz were nearly there. Maggie and Chitta retired to dress for dinner.

Much as she loved seeing Thomas in evening dress, Maggie was glad the days when men wore tuxedos and women cocktail or evening dresses for dinner were over.

However, even though times were less formal, she certainly could not wear the over-sized sweater and jeans she had on, even if her cast limited her wardrobe choices.

In the end, she decided to wear a little teal silk t-shirt dress she had bought the previous summer. The hem stopped just above her knees and she knew Thomas thought it a bit short, but tough tuna. She hoped the little bits of light turquoise lace that constituted a bra, thong and garter belt would diffuse any criticism later.

She put on the impossibly long strand of the Raynham pearls which she was able to wrap three times around her neck, spritzed herself with her perfume and was ready.

She found Thomas was already downstairs in the hall. He was wearing a perfectly cut dark blue suit with an immaculate white cotton shirt and silk tie in a geometric weave of light grey and royal blue. His shirt cuffs, which extended a perfect inch below his sleeves, showed gold cufflinks engraved with the Raynham coat of arms.

The sight of her husband made Maggie feel light-headed and she wondered if he would always have this effect on her. Then she noticed that bin Abdulaziz was also in the hall, examining a portrait of one of the barons. The twenty-third, she thought. Thomas was giving Faisal a tour.

Maggie greeted her guest with a gracious smile.

"Hello, Faisal. Welcome to Beaumatin. Hello, Thomas. You made good time."

"Traffic was flowing. I'm glad I wasn't driving into Oxford," Thomas reported.

Faisal looked good in a deep grey pinstripe suit. Maggie briefly wondered if Thomas had introduced Faisal to his tailor, then decided there would not have been enough time to have had a suit custom made.

"You've met Mrs Cook and she's shown you your room? If there's anything you need, you have only to ask."

Maggie went on to explain to Thomas that Chitta had prepared the evening's menu and that he needed to serve wines which would complement the aromatic curries.

Thomas looked surprised.

"Cooking is awkward with my cast," she reminded him.

"And the meat is halal," she told Faisal.

The man nodded impassively.

Thomas, who had been frowning as he regarded Maggie's dress, turned to Faisal.

"Let me show you our wine cellar. We have some interesting vintages."

The men walked off and Maggie reminded herself that she really needed to visit the wine cellar herself someday. Although to do that, she would have to ask Mrs Cook how to get to it.

Chitta appeared. Both she and Stephen were spending the night and Stephen would drop her off at Pemberley on his way back to Oxford the next morning. Chitta looked lovely in a simple knit dress in her favourite red.

"Faisal and Thomas have arrived. Thomas has taken Faisal off to see the wine cellar. Thomas' default wine is usually some sort of Bordeaux so it will be interesting to see what he finds to go with curry,"

"I won't be able to drink it, whatever it is. Nor will three of your other dinner guests."

"Yes. You'll certainly have company," Maggie agreed.

"Too bad husbands don't have to abstain along with their wives," she added.

"Oh I think husbands have enough to put up with when their wives are pregnant," Chitta laughed.

They went back to the kitchen to confer with Mrs Cook. On the way, Maggie checked the dining room and saw that the housekeeper had used the guest list Maggie had provided and made place cards.

Satisfied everything was ready, the women went to the drawing room to wait. Maggie got Chitta a glass of pineapple juice and poured herself a glass of champagne.

Thomas and Faisal had just returned from the Beaumatin cellar when William and Gweneth arrived, accompanied by Constance and Muriel Stonor.

Gweneth's mother was in her late sixties. She was thin and held herself stiffly. With hair a mixture of grey and faded blonde, blue eyes and pale, finely-lined skin, she greeted Maggie coolly, as though it was something she had to do for politeness and would have avoided if she could.

Constance ignored Maggie completely and went to greet her father and be introduced to Faisal.

Shortly afterward, the Ainswicks arrived. They had driven over with David and Chloe Osborne. They were followed by Simon Peevey, who had politely declined an invitation to spend the night on the grounds that he had an early morning appointment in London. The new arrivals were introduced to bin Abdulaziz.

Last to arrive was Stephen, who apologized and said something had come up at the last minute to detain him. When he had gotten Maggie and Chitta discretely out of earshot of the others, he explained that he had been about to leave when Moss, Bixby and a dozen constables had arrived with a search warrant to go through the rooms of everyone who had been in the Senior Common Room when Alastair had died.

"I got the impression they were looking for cyanide," he said grimly.

"Then they won't search my room, as I wasn't there. And even if they do, they can hardly leave it any messier than it is already," Chitta said optimistically.

For herself, Maggie just hoped the culprit hadn't chosen her rooms to hide a vial of poison. It would be a very foolish murderer who hung on to the murder weapon. In his position, she would certainly try to throw the blame on someone else, if not destroy the evidence altogether.

Then it was time to go in to dinner. Thomas took his place at one end of the long, elaborately laid out table, with Beatrix sitting on his right and Muriel on his left. At the other end of the table, Maggie had Cedric on her right and Faisal on her left. Constance sat next to Faisal while Gweneth sat next to her uncle. While Maggie could not fault Mrs Cook's seating arrangement in terms of correctness, she wished both Faisal and Constance could have been further away. However, she was the hostess and she had certainly presided over more difficult situations.

Because Chitta had cooked a great many dishes, it had been decided to set them out on the sideboard and let people help themselves, as was done at breakfast when they entertained. First came the appetizers. There were onion bhajis and pakoras, fritters of gram flour mixed with bits of vegetables. There were also sheik kebabs, spiced ground lamb moulded into sausage shapes and grilled on sewers, and tandoori shrimp. On the table were bowls with chutney and chili-hot pickles and mint-flaked yogurt sauce.

Thomas had chosen two wines from Alsace. A light red Pinot noir and a white Gewürztraminer, complex and somewhat sweet. For the pregnant ladies and designated drivers there were pitchers of tropical fruit juices and a selection of waters.

The main course was rojan josh, a hearty lamb curry, dark with tomatoes and spices. It was accompanied by dal—lentils—a saffron basmati rice studded with almonds and raisins and white basmati rice mixed with peas and mushrooms. Vegetarian Chitta had also fixed aubergine, cauliflower and sag aloo, or spinach with potatoes.

Everyone went back for seconds and complimented Chitta, who beamed modestly. Cedric asked Faisal many questions about agriculture and land use in Saudi Arabia and Maggie realised she knew very little about the kingdom of the Sauds. Polygamy and niqabs were not mentioned. Talk turned to horses—apparently Faisal kept a stable of Arabians—then China. The men dominated the conversation. Maggie nodded and smiled.

Dessert was sherbet and Mrs Cook's excellent biscuits. Coffee and cognac were served in the drawing room. Beatrix joined Maggie and Chitta.

"Cedric certainly enjoyed talking to your new colleague," she commented.

"Yes. Thomas has apparently decided that Faisal is a fine fellow," Maggie said.

"But he's not?" asked Beatrix shrewdly.

Maggie sighed.

"Beatrix, the man has three wives and is looking for a fourth. He keeps the two he's brought with him to Oxford in seclusion. The first time we met he told me in his country I would be flogged or stoned. I suspect he still holds that opinion."

"I see."

"Well, I suppose I should be glad that Thomas is making friends among the Merrion faculty. And that Faisal is also making some connections."

Beatrix glanced at Maggie sharply but remained silent.

Chapter 18

Mrs Cook prepared one of her usual extravagant breakfasts the next morning with fried, boiled and scrambled eggs, bacon, three types of sausage, mushrooms, tomatoes, smoked salmon, white and whole meal toast and an assortment of homemade jams and marmalade. A separate chaffing dish with a discrete card saying "Halal" had beef sausages.

Thomas and Chitta were already in the dining room when Maggie came in. Maggie was not an early riser but Thomas had propelled her out of his bed by reminding her that they had houseguests. By the time Maggie had helped herself to some scrambled eggs and smoked salmon, Faisal had appeared. Thomas showed him the breakfast options on the sideboard and ascertained that Faisal was a tea drinker.

Stephen, who also liked to sleep late, came in last. He helped himself to eggs, bacon and one of each type of sausage. Stephen, Maggie had learned, had a hearty appetite in the morning.

Thomas was discussing the plans for the day.

"You're taking Chitta to Pemberley, Stephen?" Thomas asked,

Chitta replied for Stephen, who had a mouth full of sausage.

"Yes. Stephen has work awaiting him in Oxford. But Stanley and I will be back for dinner tonight."

"Another curry dinner? Last night's was delicious."

"Thank you. But I believe Mrs Cook is going to prepare something more traditionally British."

Maggie saw Thomas' pleased expression. He was probably anticipating pie, she decided.

"After breakfast, Faisal and I are going out riding. I'm going to show him the estate," Thomas announced.

Faisal nodded.

"As he apparently has a greater interest in sheep than my wife does," Thomas added pointedly.

"But I do take an interest in the snowdrops. And the gardens generally." Maggie was defensive.

Thomas ignored her.

"After lunch, William is coming over to take our guest out shooting."

He noticed Chitta's expression.

"Clay pigeons," he clarified.

"Will you join?" Thomas asked Maggie politely while obviously expecting a negative response.

Maggie was still feeling bruised from Thomas' earlier remark about the sheep.

"Yes," she said

"You shoot?" Faisal asked in surprise.

"Maggie's a crack shot," Chitta assured him.

"She's even shot a few people," Stephen added.

"I've heard the stories," he told Maggie.

Faisal looked taken aback.

"They were bad men. Trying to hurt people I cared about," she explained.

"You saved Stanley without having to shoot anyone," Chitta pointed out.

"Believe me, if I'd had a gun, I would have used it. However, now we have Freya and Loki, our Tibetan mastiffs, so I hope it won't be necessary for me to shoot anyone else."

Maggie noticed Faisal look at Thomas to see his reaction. Thomas shrugged but Maggie saw his mouth twitch.

Chapter 19

William appeared promptly after lunch. Constance accompanied her brother.

"I haven't been shooting for ages and I thought it might be fun to try again," she announced.

Maggie decided she would need to be careful to stay well out of range of Constance.

William had brought his own gun. Maggie got the one from the gunroom she normally used.

Faisal was impressed with the gunroom, its collection of shotguns, rifles and handguns and assortment of hunting trophies. He and William discussed his options before he made a selection. William handed Constance a gun he said he thought would suit her.

The four piled into William's Land Rover and set off to the secluded spot where Ned Thatcher and his son Jamie were waiting with the traps already set up. Thomas' estate foreman was a wiry man in his late forties who reminded Maggie of a cowboy. Jamie was a gangly adolescent who resembled his father.

Everyone took a few practice shots. Maggie knew William was an expert marksman and Faisal also proved he was proficient. Constance had to struggle and Maggie assumed she was a novice. For herself, she was pleasantly surprised to find that her cast did not seem to affect her accuracy.

William proposed they compete to see how many hits in a row each could make. Faisal agreed. Constance pretended to pout, then said she would try but did not expect to make more than a few and that only the men's shots should count. Maggie remained silent.

William went first.

William was the county champion and Maggie had been out shooting with him several times at his club. He made seventeen hits in a row before he missed.

Constance went next. William gave her some advice but still she missed after only four hits. When the others agreed she could try again, she made three.

"I'm done. Faisal, you go next," she smiled prettily.

Faisal smiled back and positioned himself. He looked very much a Prince of Arabia and Maggie pictured him in his robes. Doubtless with a falcon.

Faisal hit nineteen. Constance applauded and William and Maggie offered congratulations.

Then Maggie announced she would also take a turn. Constance walked off and pretended to lose interest. William, who anticipated what was coming, stood nearby. Faisal's expression indicated that he was prepared to humour Maggie for the few shots it would take before she missed.

When Maggie had hit ten in a row, Faisal's expression of polite encouragement had become a frown and Constance had returned from her stroll and was watching with her lips pressed together.

When Maggie reached fifteen she became aware of some hostility simmering beneath Faisal's look of neutral interest and Constance's expression was definitely of the "if looks could kill" variety. She made a quick decision.

Maggie hit the next three and then, making sure it did not appear to be too obvious, deliberately missed the nineteenth.

William looked at her curiously as Maggie congratulated a smirking Faisal.

Constance and Faisal began to walk back to the car and Ned and Jamie began to pack up. William murmured to Maggie, "You missed that last shot on purpose."

Maggie glanced warningly at Faisal. "Shh. Yes, I did. It seemed more tactful not to provoke what was obviously going to be a display of poor sportsmanship. And I don't care if Constance uses it as an opportunity to gloat."

"That's very admirable, I'm sure, but..."

They had reached the car. William and Faisal rode in front and Constance ignored Maggie as she got in beside her.

When they reached the house, Maggie excused herself. Demonstrating her proficiency with a shotgun had probably not been the best idea and her arm was throbbing. She went upstairs to her room, took some aspirin and had a short nap. When she woke up, she showered and began to get ready for dinner.

Maggie was in her closet considering her wardrobe choices when she heard a door open. And close.

"Hello?"

It was Thomas.

In the process of dressing for dinner, he wore pants, a white dress shirt still open at the neck and braces.

"William told me about the shooting," he began.

"Yes. I think our guest of honour enjoyed himself."

Thomas stared at his wife as she sat down on her bed, cross-legged. She was wearing a short, simple slip of creamy satin. Her curls were caught up at the crown of her head except for some tendrils that had escaped and framed her face.

"He said you missed your last shot on purpose. So that Faisal would win your little competition."

Thomas sat down beside his wife on her bed, an eighteenth century four poster in the Chinese style that was topped with a pagoda shaped roof guarded by five gilded dragons rampant. Except for two armchairs and a huge mirror leaning against one wall, it was the only item of furniture in the large room.

Maggie shrugged.

"I did. It seemed the polite thing to do. When it became obvious that Faisal could not abide being beaten by a female. Particularly this female. I suspect in Saudi Arabia, for a woman to beat a man in anything would be a flogging offense. For the female, of course."

Maggie noticed Thomas' expression and decided to change the subject.

"How was your ride?"

"Faisal's an expert rider. He has a stable back home. Arabians. I fear he was not very impressed with Dexter."

Dexter was a black gelding in the Beaumatin stables used by guests.

"Perhaps I should consider getting another thoroughbred. If Faisal becomes a regular visitor."

"He might even know where you could acquire one of those Arabians," Maggie said to hide her feelings at the prospect of Faisal becoming a frequent houseguest.

Thomas decided it might be fun to torment his wife a little.

"He asked... Faisal was curious. Apparently someone had mentioned that I was a widower. Had been a widower. He wanted to know why I hadn't married a younger woman. And had more children."

"More sons?"

"That was doubtless what he meant. I pointed out that I already had two sons and three grandsons, which was probably adequate to secure the Raynham line."

Maggie remained silent. They had had this discussion.

"He also expressed some surprise that I had chosen to marry a woman who wasn't... was not pure was the term he used."

"Not pure? What? Not, um, a virgin?"

"Yes."

"At my age, it would be rather unusual if I were a virgin, don't you think? And I'd imagine that even twenty-year-old virgins are rather thin on the ground in Britain these days."

Maggie's left and right brains began to do an inventory.

Right Brain. There was my first. Adam. A Harvard boy from Eliot House. It was the summer between my junior and senior years in college. In Maine. Neither of us really expected it to last much beyond our return to school in the fall.

Left Brain: That's one.

R.B.: And Hunter. We were both starting as Assistant Professors at Princeton. The relationship provided mutual support and comfort. Once we got our footing, it turned out we really didn't have much in common.

L.B.: That's two.

R.B.: And Joshua, a fellow professor at Harvard. He was completely self-absorbed. And not very big on fidelity.

L.B.: That's three.

R.B.: And finally Thomas.

L.B.: That's four.

R.B.: You certainly jumped into bed with him fast enough.

L.B.: Because I felt the same way about him then that I do now.

R.B.: Does having had relationships with four men in as many decades make me impure?

L.B.: Aren't you forgetting someone?

R.B.: That's wasn't a relationship. That was temporary insanity.

L.B.: If you say so.

R.B. (defensively): Some of my college classmates would have had to have been polydactyl to count their lovers before they even graduated. I have six fingers left.

L.B.: Five.

R.B.: Six.

L.B.: If you say so.

Thomas was watching Maggie do her arithmetic. She unconsciously moved her fingers. He watched them stop at four and his mouth twitched.

Finally she said, "As long as you don't think like Faisal. That you don't regret my not being... pure."

"Mon pauvre papillon. Despite your chequered past, I have always found you to be quite absurdly innocent. It's one of your most endearing qualities."

"Oh."

Thomas ran a finger over the soft, silky surface of her slip. Then he removed her hairclip, tossed it onto the carpet and ran his fingers through her hair. He pushed her back on the bed and kissed her. He slipped off his braces and unbuttoned his shirt while he kissed her again.

A few minutes later the bedroom door creaked. There was a sound of breath suddenly inhaled.

Thomas paused. Looked over his shoulder.

"Faisal? Bloody hell!"

Someone muttered in Arabic. The door closed sharply.

"Faisal?" Maggie was horrified.

"Shh. He's gone."

"Thomas!"

"Shh," he said again and continued with what he was doing.

Chapter 20

Maggie came down to dinner dressed in one of her oldest, most conservative dresses. Navy blue, it had a high neck and the hem came to the bottom of her knees. Short sleeves had just enough room for her cast to fit through. To not feel like a total frump, she wore the Raynham pearls again. It was not just Faisal's remark about her being impure that rankled, and his walking in when she and Thomas had been... But Sir John Nesbitt tended to ogle and his wife, Thalia, was her friend.

Maggie cringed at the thought that Faisal had seen her and Thomas, um, in bed together. No matter what bin Abdulaziz thought, Maggie was painfully shy and self-conscious about her body. Even when she was with Thomas. She never flirted, her hips did not sway when she walked, she never postured suggestively.

Once she and Anne had spent a week at a fashionable spa in France. Many of the staff were men and were matter-of-fact about seeing her naked as she was massaged and scrubbed with Dead Sea salts and wrapped like a mummy after having been covered in slimy, green detoxifying seaweed, then rinsed off. Perhaps it was her Puritan heritage or her critical mother or her lack of curves that made her feel so uncomfortable. For whatever reason, she pretended to be nonchalant to hide her mortification.

So Maggie decided she would adopt the same cool façade and hope that Faisal would feel just as embarrassed as she did and pretend the unfortunate episode had never happened.

Maggie came downstairs to find Constance in the hall. She looked pretty in a light blue suit.

"Hello, Constance," said Maggie, trying to be gracious.

Constance frowned at the pearls, then said, "I told Father I was coming to dinner. I haven't seen the Nesbitts for yonks and they were good friends of my mother."

"You're welcome, of course. Did you tell Mrs Cook?"

"No," said Constance. She walked off to Thomas' study, knocked and went in.

Maggie sighed and went to find the housekeeper, who was in the kitchen.

The air was fragrant with the scent of baking apples and cinnamon.

"Mrs Cook? I just saw Constance and she says she is also going to be at dinner. I hope it doesn't upset your arrangements."

Mrs Cook looked like she wanted to tsk but stopped herself.

"Don't you worry, Lady Raynham. I'll take care of it."

"Thank you. I'm sorry."

"Never you mind." Mrs Cook spoke reassuringly.

Maggie returned to the hall to find that Malcolm Fortescue-Smythe and his guest had arrived. The young woman was thirty at best, which made her more than two decades younger than the publisher. She had dark brown hair that was almost black, dark eyes, pale skin, and was striking rather than pretty. She wore a form-fitting black knit dress and four-inch heels.

"Hello, Maggie. May I present Sophie Falconer? Sophie, this is Lady Raynham."

"Hello, Sophie. Welcome to Beaumatin. And please, it's Maggie," she smiled.

"I told Sophie about the work you're doing. The Developing World series. Sophie works for the *Tatler*. But she's also written her own book."

"I assume it's not a critique of post-crisis austerity policy? Or an analysis of Peronism in twentieth century Argentina?" Maggie teased.

Malcolm laughed.

"No. It's not a candidate for the Global Press. Tell her, Sophie."

"My agent says it's chick lit. I just hope that doesn't mean no one will take it seriously as a work of fiction. Not that I expect to win the Booker Prize. It's about a group of bright young things who've come down to London from University. One of the boys forms a relationship with a woman who's transgender. That's the heart of the story."

Maggie, who knew she was not fully briefed on transgender issues, wanted to ask whether that meant the character had been male or female and was now female or male, but decided she did not want to seem clueless.

"Sounds fascinating. Please let me know when it's published so I can buy a copy. And please come through and have a cocktail. You're the first to arrive."

"Do I know anyone else who is coming?" Malcolm asked.

"Chitta and Stanley. Chitta Kazi, who's a fellow professor at Oxford and Stanley Einhorn. You may have heard of him, He's a very successful high tech venture capitalist," Maggie explained for Sophie's benefit.

"Then there's Sir John and Lady Nesbitt…"

"The Nesbitts? My brother was at school with their son," Sophie said.

Maggie was always surprised by how people in Britain all seemed to know each other.

"And Thomas' daughter, Constance. Constance Conyers. Her married name is von Fersen."

"Von Fersen? I think we covered the wedding," Sophie said thoughtfully.

"And finally Faisal bin Abdulaziz. He's the new Appleton fellow at Merrion. I wanted you to meet him, Malcolm, because he may contribute a book to our new series. Although I am not sure what it would be about.

"Faisal is Saudi. Very conservative. He has three wives although I understand only two are in Britain. He and Thomas have become friends, although I know he is not a fan of my work. And I also suspect he thinks I should be flogged. Or stoned. For indecency. And my attitude generally," Maggie explained to Sophie.

"But Constance likes him. You may too, so don't let me prejudice you," Maggie finished.

"Bin Abdulaziz? Didn't he review your book *Fitting In* for the *Guardian*? Unfavourably? Sounds like it could be an interesting evening," Malcolm commented.

Maggie led them into the drawing room.

Sophie was not looking gobsmacked, like many first-time visitors to Beaumatin, so Maggie assumed that she was herself a bright young thing and used to these sorts of houses.

Next to arrive were the Nesbitts. Sir John was a jolly man in his sixties. His cheerful round face reminded Maggie of a toby jug. Lady Nesbitt—Thalia—was more formidable. Her battleship grey hair was cut short in no particular style. She had a hatchet nose and a full figure she covered with long skirts and blazers. She was the head of the local Church Ladies' Guild, a volunteer group that supported the work of half a dozen small congregations. Maggie had become involved when it became clear that as Lady Raynham her participation was expected. Over time, she had found Thalia's brusque exterior hid a heart of gold and she considered the woman to be a friend.

Maggie made introductions and Sophie and Thalia were soon discussing mutual acquaintances and exchanging gossip.

Malcolm and Sir John were talking rugby when Thomas and Constance came in. Maggie had no sooner finished introducing Constance to Malcolm and Sophie when Chitta and Stanley arrived and more introductions were required.

Faisal was the last to appear. As she did not think Faisal was the kind of person who would wait to make an entrance, Maggie assumed he was either embarrassed about his earlier intrusion or perhaps he had been saying his prayers.

Whatever the reason, Maggie greeted him serenely and introduced him to the company. Not unexpectedly, Sophie found him intriguing. Faisal seemed more interested in talking to Malcolm about getting some of his recent work published.

Maggie joined Thalia, who was looking over the company.

"Well, you certainly have assembled a varied group of guests."

Maggie remembered that Thalia had expressed her reservations about Constance marrying a Swede.

"It's the new Oxford," Maggie explained.

"And I hear that Constance is pregnant and her husband tossed her out. Because he thought it might not be his child."

Maggie was shocked.

"That's just vicious gossip, Thalia. Yes, Constance is pregnant. But Nils is certainly the father. It is true Nils was not happy about having a baby so soon after the wedding. However, it was Constance's decision to come back here. Or at least that's what she says. And I see no reason to doubt her. I hope you will scotch any rumours that suggest otherwise."

"Humpf. This is what comes from not marrying your own kind."

Eek. Did Thalia think that she and Thomas also had a "mixed" marriage?

Thalia correctly interpreted Maggie's expression.

"Don't worry, my dear. I've never agreed with Muriel Stonor about that. I know the Eliots come from good British stock. Even if your ancestors did have some strange notions about religion."

"Thomas did say that two of the earlier barons married American heiresses," Maggie pointed out, while thinking that now perhaps she knew the reason behind Muriel's attitude towards her.

"Yes. A sad necessity. I suppose it will be Russians next. Oligarchs' daughters marrying for a title," she added darkly.

Stanley came up to claim Maggie's attention and Thalia marched off to where Sir John was standing with Malcolm and Sophie.

Stanley looked over his shoulder to make sure Thomas was nowhere close by. His host was chatting with Chitta and Faisal.

"We need to talk," said Stanley in a low voice.

"We are talking, Stanley," Maggie pointed out reasonably.

"Not here. Someplace private. Without his lordship. How about meeting me for lunch at the Randolph?"

"All right. Let me know what day suits and I'll check my schedule."

"Good. And don't tell anyone. I have news." He glanced nervously over his shoulder again.

Maggie badly wanted to ask Stanley what this was all about but decided to be a good co-conspirator. Even though the last time she had met Stanley for lunch at the Randolph, the outcome had been quite dramatic. She hoped whatever it was Stanley wanted to discuss, it was something less disruptive.

Soon it was time to go in to dinner. Maggie sat between Sir John and Faisal, who was still avoiding eye contact. The two men continued a discussion they had begun over cocktails about the West's military presence in the Middle East. Apparently both men agreed about "bringing the boys home."

At the other end of the table the conversation was about publishing and the impact of eBooks and do-it-yourself authoring. Not surprisingly, Malcolm and Stanley took opposing sides.

After their guests had variously driven off or retired to their rooms, Thomas remarked, "So that was a pleasant evening."

"Yes. And I needn't have worried. After his untimely interruption, Faisal avoided making eye contact. He and Sir John found they had some grounds for agreement on world affairs and Thalia seemed to survive an event she considered to be overly multi-culti."

"And Constance was on her best behaviour," Thomas pointed out.

"Yes. She and Faisal have also found common ground for agreement. Both being in the pro-niqab camp."

"You being anti-niqab."

"Well, yes. At least in the West. What they do in Saudi…"

"What they do in Saudi Arabia is of absolutely no interest to me," Thomas interrupted.

"Oh?"

"No. None whatsoever."

They were in Thomas' room. As he loosened his tie and undid his cuff links, Maggie was suddenly reminded of

Deirdre. And realised she had not thought about Deirdre or Carrington the entire weekend. She felt stricken with remorse that she could have been so forgetful. And was suddenly tearful.

She remembered a verse from Omar Khayyám,

The Moving Finger writes; and, having writ,
Moves on: nor all thy Piety nor Wit
Shall lure it back to cancel half a Line,
Nor all thy Tears wash out a Word of it."

Then Thomas distracted her.

SUSAN ALEXANDER

Chapter 21

Back at Merrion on Monday night, Maggie was getting ready for bed. Thomas had remained at Beaumatin, so she was staying in her rooms at the college. She was about to draw the drapes in her bedroom when she heard voices and noticed a light flickering in the quad below. She opened the window, leaned on the windowsill and looked down.

A bonfire was burning. Half a dozen figures in black robes gyrated around it. They were ululating. The sound made her shiver.

It was the Niqabis. What were they up to now?

It was after midnight. The porter would have locked the entrance and gone home. She decided to investigate and slipped on a robe.

By the time she got downstairs, the fire was burning higher.

Maggie rushed out and yelled, "What are you doing?"

The figures began to scatter.

Maggie grabbed at a niqab. The figure turned and pushed her, hard. She landed on her back on the grass. By the time she managed to get up, everyone had disappeared.

Stephen came running up. The few students who were in residence between terms had come out and were gawking.

"Maggie! What's going on?" Stephen demanded.

"It was the Niqabis," she began, then looked more closely at the fire which was dying down.

Oh dear.

Among some lengths of wood, bits of branches and wadded-up newspapers were books. Her books. *Fitting In*. In which she presented her research that showed immigrants to the UK did better if they integrated. Learned to speak English. Sent their children to local schools. And left the niqabs behind. There must have been thirty or so of the volumes in various states of char.

Maggie was stunned.

"It's my book. They were burning my book."

"What?"

"Look."

Stephen peered.

"Good God."

Maggie pushed back her hair, which had completely escaped from her hair clip.

"What should I do? Call the police?" Stephen asked.

"I'm not sure I want another visit from Inspector Moss."

"Campus security, then."

"They should certainly be informed. And maybe they can check the security cameras. Although everyone I saw was robed. Veiled. But perhaps they can figure out where they came from. And went."

Stephen noticed Maggie had her arms folded across her chest. She looked cold and the night air was chilly.

"Maggie, I'll wait here for security. Go back to your rooms. I'll join you there. I think we could both use a drink."

"I won't argue with that," Maggie agreed.

Twenty minutes later, Stephen knocked on her door.

"Our security service is investigating. Although I'm not sure how much success they'll have. In terms of finding out who is behind this. The fire. And the stalking."

"I hate to mention this, but could there possibly be a connection to Faisal?"

Stephen grimaced.

"I really hope not. Can you imagine the conversation? 'So, Faisal, have you been sending niqab-clad book-burners to harass our new Weingarten fellow?' What do you suppose he'd say?"

"He'd deny it, of course."

"And it's quite possible he has nothing to do with it."

"Do you think so? The book came out months ago. And nothing happened except for the usual media frenzy. The, er, harassment is recent. Since Faisal's arrival. Do you think that's only a coincidence?"

Stephen looked unhappy.

"Of course I wouldn't want anyone to make an accusation without evidence. But perhaps, if you get the chance, you could mention what's been happening. Like it was just the usual Merrion gossip. See how he reacts."

"I could do that."

"And I'll also ask Chitta to see if she can find out anything."

"And maybe the security chaps will discover something."

Maggie gave Stephen a "Yeah, right" look.

Chapter 22

Maggie had gone up to Chitta's room to ask her friend about a journal article she was trying to locate when the women heard footsteps on the stairs. Several sets of footsteps. Not the usual trainer-wearing student's hurtling down late to a tutorial but heavy. Authoritative.

They looked at each other and Chitta crossed to her door and opened it. Maggie went and stood behind her.

Two police constables trod past.

Someone pounded on a door.

"Ross! Open up!"

They recognized that voice. It was Inspector Moss.

"We know you're in there. Open the door, Ross!"

More pounding.

Then a snarled, "What do you lot want?"

"Gordon Ross, you are under arrest for suspicion of the murders of Alastair Carrington and Deirdre Ross. You do not have to say anything but it may harm your defense if you do not mention when questioned something you later rely on in court. Anything you say may be given in evidence."

"What?"

"Constables." Moss again.

"No! No! You can't... I didn't..."

There were sounds of scuffling. Grunts. Muttered swearing.

"Take your hands off me!"

A thump as a body slammed into a wall. More thumps.

"Leggo!"

"It's no use, Ross. You're nicked."

Silence. Then footsteps descending.

Maggie and Chitta stood in the doorway, transfixed.

Ross reached the landing. He was in handcuffs, with the two police constables grasping his arms firmly. Moss and Bixby were close behind.

Gordon saw Maggie and stopped. Tried to jerk away from the PCs.

"Eliot! Eliot, you've got to help me. I didn't do it. I didn't kill Deirdre. I didn't kill Carrington. You've got to believe me. You've got to help me. You helped Draycott. He told me. Please…"

Ross was disheveled and blood trickled out of one nostril. His eyes were anguished. Pleading.

"Eliot, please. I'm begging you."

"That's enough, Ross. You're embarrassing yourself. Act like a man," said Moss contemptuously.

The constables hustled Ross down the remaining stairs.

"Inspector Moss?" Maggie put her hand on the detective's arm to detain him.

"What is it?" Moss was irritated.

"Are you sure…"

"We found a vial of cyanide in Ross' room. Hidden behind some books. And you yourself told me Ross pushed his wife."

"Yes, but…"

"I've no time for this."

Moss jerked away and continued down the stairs, followed by Bixby. Bixby's cheek was bruised and his lip was cut.

Maggie and Chitta went back inside and closed the door.

"Well." said Chitta.

Maggie looked troubled.

"You were sure Gordon pushed Deirdre. We both were. We heard it," Chitta reminded her friend.

"I know. And I still think he did. But…"

"But what?"

"It was what he said. The way he said it. It made me wonder…"

"You're just upset by that scene. It was pretty awful. Brutal. In fact, I could use some tea. Join me?"

"All right. Thank you," Maggie surprised herself by accepting

They had tea, largely in silence. What was there to say? Afterwards, Maggie thanked Chitta and returned to her rooms. She was thoughtful. There had been something about Gordon. His desperation.

Maggie had been suspected of murder before. On the basis of evidence that was just as convincing as Moss' against Gordon. And which had been wrong. Thomas had also been arrested. Twice. And if it had not been for what Thomas liked to call Maggie's pig-headedness, he might have stood trial. Even been convicted. It was not something Maggie liked to think about.

Maggie was an academic and committed to keeping an open mind. To not jumping to conclusions. She decided she would try to talk to Gordon and listen to what he had to say.

Chapter 23

Maggie had found out who Ross' solicitor was from Stephen—his name was Burgess—and the man had arranged for Maggie to visit his client.

Maggie had never been in a jail before and quickly decided she would never want to have that experience. Jail had also done nothing for Gordon. He had deep circles under his eyes and his face sagged. He looked older. Defeated.

When Maggie entered the small, bleak visitation room, he glared at her.

"You're the one who asked for my help, Gordon. I'll leave if you've changed your mind."

"No. No. Calm down. You women. Always the drama."

Maggie pressed her lips together and reminded herself that just because Gordon was a jerk did not mean he was a murderer.

"And it's your fault that I'm in here. You and Kazi. Telling that wanker Moss that I was the one who pushed Deirdre…"

Maggie decided arguing would be a waste of time.

"So if you didn't push Deirdre, who did? A poltergeist?"

"I don't know. I had gone back into my rooms. Closed the door. Came out again when I heard the racket."

"You didn't see anyone?"

"No."

He paused.

"Maybe she tripped."

Maggie shook her head.

"She didn't. She cried out 'No. Don't. No.' That eliminates an accident."

Ross scowled.

"And what about Alastair?"

"I dunno. I had nothing to do with that."

"Moss thinks you were trying to poison Deirdre and Alastair got the glass of sherry by mistake. Because Deirdre wasn't drinking. Because she was pregnant."

"Stupid cow. She knew I didn't want another brat. Another little pissant. She did it on purpose."

Maggie stood. "If you talk about Deirdre like that one more time I'll leave. And you can spend the rest of your life in prison."

"Take it easy."

"I mean it."

"Sorry," he finally said grudgingly.

"Moss says they found cyanide in your room."

"That was planted. Someone is trying to frame me."

"Who?"

"I don't know. Same person who pushed Deirdre."

"So someone wanted to kill Deirdre and figured you would make a convenient scapegoat?"

Ross shrugged.

"Who would want to kill Deirdre?"

"No idea. That's why I need your help."

Maggie had an unwelcome thought.

"Perhaps the cyanide wasn't meant for Alastair. Or Deirdre. But for you. You drink sherry. And pushing Deirdre down the stairs, after you'd had that fight, was a way to get at you."

Gordon thought. Nodded.

"So we need to consider that you as well as Deirdre might have been a target. Although we can't completely eliminate Alastair. Or that the person who put the poison in the sherry and the person who pushed Deirdre is the same."

"So Moss is taking the easy way out by pinning both deaths on me," Ross whinged.

Maggie shrugged.

"Who hates you enough to want to kill you, Gordon? Or see you convicted for murder?"

"I have some former colleagues in Glasgow. The University. Jealous sods. Hated my guts."

"All right."

"And then there are the vultures."

"Vultures?"

"My ex-wives."

"Mrs Ross Numbers One and Two?"

"Yes. Stupid cows."

Maggie refrained from pointing out that Ross had chosen to marry the 'stupid cows.'

"And your child? Do I remember your saying you had a child?"

"The little pissant? Haven't seen him since he was four. Since I left Fiona."

"Well, I'll need contact information for all of them. And the names of your former colleagues."

"I can give you the names of the tossers. But the vultures? No idea. I paid them off to make sure they'd get out of my life."

"And your son?"

Ross shrugged.

"Ask his mother."

Maggie tried not to show how she felt about Ross' attitude towards women and his callous indifference to his child.

"I'll at least need their names. And whatever addresses you remember. Oh and the names and whereabouts of Deirdre's family. And friends. Male and female."

"Deirdre didn't have any male friends."

"Are you sure?"

"I wouldn't allow it."

Maggie bit back a scathing comment.

"And I'll need Deirdre's email address. And password."

"Email? Why?"

"As I suggested, in case Deirdre was the intended victim. There may be some useful information in her emails."

"I doubt it. Her emails were pretty insipid."

"You read them?" Maggie was surprised.

Ross looked embarrassed.

"We shared a personal account. grdr@gmail.com. The password is… Wait. That means you'll see my emails."

"Do you have something to hide? And I'd assume the police have already read them all."

Ross muttered something.

"All right. The password is, er, Culloden1746."

"Culloden1746?"

"Yes. With an uppercase 'C.'"

Maggie thought Culloden sounded familiar. Wasn't it some battle? She briefly wished she knew more history. Thomas would certainly recognize the name.

"All right. If you could have your solicitor—Burgess isn't it?—get me that information as soon as possible, I'll see what I can do. Oh. And before I forget, I may need to enlist some outside help. Which will not come free. How do you want to handle any expenses?"

"Expenses?"

"Gordon, I'm not going to go to Glasgow myself to check out the whereabouts of your various ex-wives and former colleagues. To see if they had or needed alibis. So do you want my help or not?"

Gordon looked unhappy. Finally he said, "I had to give that blood-sucker Burgess a big retainer. I'll tell him to pay any invoices you submit. As long as they're reasonable ones, mind."

"Fine."

Maggie stood.

"I'll do my best, Gordon," she said. She didn't add that it would be for Deirdre, not for him.

Maggie still felt sick every time she thought about Deirdre. She blamed herself. She should have done something. She was sure she could have stopped it, him, whoever had pushed the woman down those stairs. Rather than just standing there…

But shoulda, woulda, coulda. It was too late. All she could do now was try to find out what had really happened. To Deirdre. And Alastair. If it had been Gordon. Or someone else. And why.

"You are not going to cry, Maggie Eliot," she told herself sternly. "Only a lesser woman would think tears are a substitute for action."

Chapter 24

Stanley had arranged to meet Maggie for lunch at the Randolph.

He had been mysterious about the reason for their appointment and Maggie was curious. And nervous. The last time she had lunched with Stanley at the Randolph, the meeting had resulted in her becoming the Weingarten fellow. But only after some serious turmoil. She hoped the current occasion would not have quite such a tumultuous aftermath.

Stanley entered the lobby and Maggie stared. Stanley was wearing a suit, dark grey, perfectly tailored, certainly not British. Possibly Italian. Maggie could not remember seeing Stanley in a suit before. He looked good. He was also carrying an elegant leather briefcase. Another Stanley first.

"Maggie!" he beamed and gave her a kiss.

"I'm hungry. It's been quite a morning. And I have to get back to my meeting as soon as lunch is over."

Stanley was greeted assiduously by the hotel's staff—he was apparently known at the Randolph—and they were taken to a private dining room.

Now Maggie's nervousness had grown into acute anxiety. What did Stanley have to say that required such privacy?

But Stanley was cheerful.

"Something to drink? I'll have a Glenfiddich," he told the waiter.

Maggie requested Chardonnay.

"We would never do this in Silicon Valley," Stanley commented.

"Hm?"

"Have a drink at lunch. Or even have lunch. Or at least have lunch away from our desks. England is much more civilised."

They ordered. Stanley had steak and Maggie a salad with smoked salmon, even though by then she was so nervous she was afraid she would not be able to swallow a bite.

Stanley chattered about Chitta's pregnancy and his excitement about becoming a father About the progress that had been made on his foundation's projects. When they had been served and were alone, he suddenly turned serious.

"Much as I enjoy your company—we should have lunch like this more often—I'm sure you're wondering why I need to see you."

Maggie put down her fork.

"You have made me curious," she admitted in what she hoped was a normal tone of voice.

Stanley hid a smile. He knew exactly how nervous he was making Maggie. He decided not to prolong the agony.

"I've received a very interesting offer for DigiData. As part of the deal I've had them agree to buy 3Dox as well."

The previous summer, Maggie had saved Stanley from being murdered. As a thank you, Stanley had "gifted" Maggie with shareholdings in two companies. She had worked with them on a project that converted more than a century of records of Beaumatin's gardens into a digital database as a birthday present for Thomas.

"Oh dear. I'm sorry, Stanley. I'm afraid I've been rather negligent…"

With the combined demands of her personal and professional lives, Maggie's involvement with the companies had been cursory at best.

"Not to worry. I've kept my eye on both. DigiData has outperformed even my most optimistic projections. 3Dox not so much. In fact, had this opportunity not come up, I would have had to consider pulling the plug."

Stanley was famous for cutting his losses on any investment he did not feel was performing up to his expectations.

"But the database project DigiData did for you turned out to be a goldmine. Besides selling it as a way to keep records of a garden, they made a bunch of different versions. For wine cellars. For art collections. For libraries. You can imagine the possibilities.

"So after some haggling I've agreed to sell. But I need your signature on some papers for the deal to go through. The deadline is at the close of business today. As I have another meeting this afternoon, I hope we can do this now."

Thomas had once told Stanley that he needed to give Maggie a firm deadline when he wanted her to make a decision and Stanley had subsequently found from experience that this was a good strategy.

"Of course."

Stanley looked surprised.

"Stanley, I feel quite guilty that I have not been more actively involved with the companies since the garden database project was completed. And I certainly never felt that I deserved... that I had done anything to merit such generosity on your part."

She did not add that when Stanley had given her the shares, Thomas had forbidden her to accept them and she was fairly sure he assumed she had refused the gift. So getting rid of her holdings would also be a relief. She hated deceiving Thomas, even if she could rationalise that his tendency to dictate her actions sometimes made it necessary.

"You're not going to study the paperwork? Or refer it to your London solicitor?"

"I trust you, Stanley. Is there some fine print I should know about? I assume you'd tell me if there were."

"You haven't asked what you will make from this transaction."

Maggie looked startled.

"I haven't because I don't expect to make much of anything."

Stanley shook his head.

"While it's true the amount is not considerable, or at least not in comparison to what I usually make on a deal, neither is it negligible. In fact, you will find it increases your net worth significantly."

"Stanley, what do you know about my net worth?" Maggie demanded.

"A great deal. Fond as I am of you, I was not going to offer a top position in my foundation or a generously funded fellowship to someone I hadn't checked out. You yourself convinced me of that," he pointed out.

"Oh."

"So unless you have some secret offshore accounts or some dummy corporation in the Caymans I don't know about..."

"Certainly not!"

"I didn't think so. In comparison, the Raynham holdings are not nearly so transparent. In fact, my people could hardly find out anything about them at all."

"And I can tell you even less. Except that whatever paperwork you may be carrying in your briefcase, it will be nothing compared to what I had to sign when I married Thomas."

"I can imagine."

Stanley took a bite of his steak. He noticed Maggie was not eating.

"I assume you think it bad manners to ask. So I guess I'll have to tell you. What you're going to make from all this."

He named a figure.

Maggie was glad she was not eating or she would have choked.

"What?"

He repeated it.

"Stanley, it's too much. I can't possibly..."

"Of course you can. I told you it wasn't a big deal. As it is, this is hardly worth my time, but since you were involved..."

"But..."

"Don't be boring, Maggie."

No one had ever told Maggie she was boring.

"Can't I just give you back my shares?"

"No. It would derail the deal. And it's a good deal. I negotiated it myself. Normally I'd have one of my junior associates do something this trivial."

Stanley ate his last bite of steak and pressed a button on a remote that was on the table. A waiter appeared.

"Coffee?" he asked Maggie.

She nodded.

"And some green tea, please."

The man looked askance at Maggie's largely untouched salad but he removed it without a word.

Stanley took out some documents from his briefcase and indicated where she should sign.

Maggie skimmed the pages and signed.

"I assume there's no clause about giving up my first born if I fail to comply with some condition," she joked.

"No. Even in my business that would be unusual. And probably unenforceable."

He handed her a card. "Have your solicitor call this man this afternoon. These deals settle very quickly. And you'll need some tax advice."

"I will."

"And don't spend it all in one place."

"Hm…"

"Do you know what you'll do with this?" Stanley asked.

"In fact, I do. Or I have an idea."

She took a sip of coffee.

"You've been to the house in Maine. Which is a family place, even if my name is on the deed. And I have a place in Boston. Where I also won't be spending much time, at least as things stand now. As long as I'm Lady Raynham. And I still own a flat in Oxford where I used to live. But when Thomas… When… Anyhow, now that there's Hereford Crescent, my flat is rented. And I've been feeling, well, a lack of my own space.

"So I may buy something. Not in Gloucestershire. Or Oxfordshire. Maybe in London. I love London. I was already thinking about looking for a pied à terre there. But with this, this bounty. Well, it certainly opens up the possibilities."

"Not a villa in Provence? Or a Tuscan farmhouse?"

"Too far away. And Beaumatin is rural enough. Mrs Cook is happy to let me feed the chickens if I need to feel bucolic. Although it does bring to mind Marie Antoinette playing shepherdess."

Stanley laughed.

"And of course you and Chitta and Baby Einhorn will always be welcome. Assuming I can find a place."

"With a budget like this, you should have quite a few options. Unless you're hankering for a mansion in Kensington."

"Good heavens, no."

Stanley was putting the paperwork back in his briefcase.

"Oh Stanley, really. I feel…."

But Stanley was standing. He gave her a quick peck on the cheek.

"Live long and prosper," he grinned and cut her off.

Chapter 25

Maggie was observing Thomas expertly carve a roast chicken Mrs Royce had prepared for their dinner. She admired his hands. They were long-fingered. Slender. Elegant. Strong.

She loved watching his hands as they deftly uncorked a bottle of wine. She loved watching them control Troubadour, the high-spirited, dappled grey stallion that he rode. She loved his hands when they…

"Maggie!"

Maggie became aware that it was not the first time Thomas had said her name.

Maggie blushed and Thomas decided that perhaps she had not been in "Eliotshire," which was what he called it when she became absorbed by some scholarly problem, but may have been thinking about something else. His mouth twitched.

"Breast or leg?" he asked again.

"Um, a bit of breast please." Maggie knew Thomas liked the leg and, as she had no preference, took the alternative.

After dinner, they retired to the library, Thomas with some whisky and Maggie with some white wine. She expected him to turn on the History channel but instead he sat quietly for a moment, then looked at her and said, "I was out doing an errand and ran into Stephen on the High Street this afternoon."

"Oh. Yes?"

"He told me Moss had arrested Gordon Ross."

"Yes. While Gordon was in his rooms. Chitta and I were there. Ross did not go quietly."

"I can't say I especially care for Ross. And men do kill their wives."

"And vice versa."

"And vice versa. But Carrington? Had Ross intended that sherry for Deirdre?"

"That's what Moss thinks. That Deirdre wasn't drinking alcohol because of the pregnancy, so poor Alastair got it by mistake."

"A bad business."

Maggie decided it was better that Thomas did not know that she was not as sure as Inspector Moss about Ross' guilt and was going to try to help the man.

"Yes," she agreed.

Thomas paused to take another sip of whisky.

"Stephen also told me about the stalking. The Niqabis, as you're calling them. And the book burning. And he was surprised you hadn't mentioned them to me already."

"Oh."

"Well?"

Maggie looked stricken.

"I was going to. It's just that... "

"Yes?" Thomas was becoming chilly.

"Well, I... We don't really know what this is about. Or who is behind it. Whether it's just some students cutting up about the book—you know I wasn't around during Hilary term when it came out—or whether it has something to do with... Faisal."

"Faisal?"

"The Niqabis started very soon after he came..."

"Faisal wouldn't..."

"I'm not suggesting that he did. But his presence could have inspired..."

"Humpf."

Silence.

"Well, Papillon, I know I agreed that you could stay at Merrion when I'm not in Oxford... and you're not at Beaumatin," he added pointedly.

"Yes?"

"But until this is straightened out, I want you to limit your time at Merrion and sleep at Hereford Crescent when you do have to be here."

Maggie wanted to say that this was exactly why she hadn't mentioned the Niqabis and the book burning to Thomas. Instead she said, "But I'm sure it's not, er, serious, Thomas. Just some undergraduates being... undergraduates. They'll get bored soon and move on to the next thing."

"Nevertheless."

Maggie recognised the implacable tone and realised arguing would be futile.

Thomas took her silence for acquiescence. He picked up the remote and turned to a programme on the role of the railways in World War I.

Maggie had no interest at all in railways and only slightly more in World War I. She tuned out.

After a few minutes, Thomas noticed. He paused the programme.

"We could watch something else if you prefer," he offered.

"Oh no. It's all right. I'm quite content just sitting here and... basking in your Thomas-ness."

Thomas looked at his wife. Who was brilliant. Elusive. Vulnerable. Innocent despite what Faisal had said. With her wonderful eyes. And impossible curls. Who had an extraordinary capacity for forgiveness. And pig-headedness. And who had apparently married him not for his title or his estate or his wealth but simply for himself. He felt a rush of strong emotion and decided he was not particularly interested in World War I railroads either. He clicked off the television.

Chapter 26

Maggie was nervous. She was about to meet the private detective recommended by Maddy Rana, a solicitor in the London law firm that handled the Raynham family affairs.

"And please keep this just between the two of us, Maddy. It's hard to explain but it has nothing to do with Thomas. It's for a friend... no, not a friend. A colleague here. At Merrion. He needs... Anyway just so there are no misunderstandings."

Maddy assured the wife of one of the firm's most important clients that she understood and could be relied upon to be discrete.

"Thank you. I expect to be in London sometime soon and I'll explain then."

The woman's name was Gina Burke. Beyond that Maggie knew nothing aside from Maddy's saying that the detective was professional and efficient. Miss Burke had done work for the firm for five years and they were very satisfied with her services.

There was a knock on her door. Burke was prompt. Maggie walked to the door and opened it.

Standing there was a woman of around thirty. Of medium height, she was stocky rather than fat, with blunt-cut dark hair and hazel eyes. She was wearing a conservatively-cut dark grey suit, a white, man-tailored blouse and low-heeled shoes. No jewellery except for small silver studs in each ear. Her posture proclaimed a no-nonsense attitude.

"Lady Raynham?" the woman asked politely.

Oh dear. Maggie had forgotten that Maddy would probably have used her title.

"Um, yes. Although in Oxford I normally use my professional name."

She indicated the plaque on her door. It read, "Professor Eliot."

"And you must be Ms Burke. Please come in. Would you like some coffee? Or tea?"

"Some tea would be nice."

"Earl Grey? Assam? Darjeeling? English Breakfast?"

"English Breakfast, please."

"Milk? Lemon?"

"Milk. No sugar."

"I'll just be a moment. Please sit down."

Gina pulled out one of the wooden chairs around the refectory table and sat.

Maggie made the tea and poured herself some coffee. She handed Gina a mug and a small pitcher of milk, then sat across from her at the table.

Gina took a sip of tea and then said, "So, er, Professor Eliot. Why do you need a private investigator? Maddy Rana was vague."

"Oh dear. That's because I didn't tell her. Well, it's complicated. I'll explain."

So Maggie told the detective about the deaths of Alastair Carrington and Deirdre Ross. And the arrest of Gordon Ross. And his insisting that he was innocent.

"And I've had some experience of innocent people being wrongfully arrested and... Well, I was there. I saw both Alastair and Deirdre die. And Deirdre had just found out she was pregnant. She was so happy. She had a picture..."

Maggie stopped. She was not going to start crying, she told herself.

"Anyway," she said after a moment. "I want to make sure whoever did commit these murders is punished. The police detective in charge—his name is Moss—does not inspire much confidence. He's convinced it's Ross. Because it's the easy solution. But I... I want to make sure that it really was him."

"You've decided to be an amateur sleuth? Lady Peter Wimsey?"

"No! But as I said, I've had experience of the police being wrong. And that's why I want you to... to undertake the investigation. Ross, who is a very unpleasant person, has agreed to pay for your services."

Maggie explained about Gordon and Mrs Ross Numbers One, Two and Three.

"I'd like you to help me eliminate his former colleagues and his ex-wives as suspects. As the police don't seem to consider that this is necessary. I can't think of anyone at Merrion who would want to kill Alastair. Or Deirdre. Or even Gordon for that matter, even if he is a jerk. Or to want to frame him. By pushing Deirdre down the stairs or by putting cyanide in his rooms. So it seems the place to start would be with people outside the college who might have reason to hate him."

Gina thought. Finally she said, "Murder. Murders. Not my usual territory. But all right. I am good at finding people. That I can do. And I suppose I can also discover where they were when the homicides occurred. Is that what you want?"

"Yes. And also your assessment of the people. If you think anyone seems a bit, well, in the US we'd call it squirrelly. Suspicious."

"All right."

Maggie handed her a list.

"These are the names Ross gave me. Of former colleagues who might bear a grudge, according to him. And Mrs Ross Numbers One and Two. Of whom he says he's lost track. And his son Hamish. How could someone loss track of his child?"

Maggie was indignant.

"You'd be surprised. A lot of my work involves tracking down spouses. And their children."

"Then this should be something you're used to."

"Yes. Although my searches usually involve divorces. And child support. Not homicides."

"I appreciate what you're going to do. I'm so far behind on my own work, there's no way I can go to Glasgow. I was on leave last term because… Anyway and then my arm was broken, which hasn't helped. And I'm starting a new position which has quite different responsibilities than my previous fellowship."

Maggie ran her fingers through her curls and her hair clip fell to the floor. She bent over and picked it up.

"Sorry. So we're all right? Oh, and what's your fee schedule? And I assume you'd like a retainer?"

Gina removed a sheet of paper from her purse and handed it to Maggie.

"Those are my fees. And of course I charge expenses. The trip to Glasgow, for instance."

"Of course."

Maggie put the fee schedule on her desk.

"When can you start?"

"Right away. As soon as I return to London. I'll do some research. Did you check to see if Ross' Glasgow colleagues are still at the university?"

"No. Sorry. I haven't had time," Maggie admitted.

"That's all right, Professor Eliot."

"Maggie, please."

"Then it's Gina."

The women smiled at each other.

"I'll be off then."

"And here's my card. It has all my contact information. And I'll look forward to hearing from you."

Chapter 27

Gina had not been gone ten minutes when there was another knock on Maggie's door.

"Come in."

It was Chitta. She looked serious.

"Maggie, are you busy?"

Maggie gestured to the piles of papers and journals and books piled on her desk.

"Yes, but nothing that can't wait. What's up?"

"There's someone I think you should talk to. She's in my rooms."

"Oh? Do I get a hint?"

"I think she should tell you herself. But… Well, it's about Gordon."

"Oh."

Maggie had told Chitta about her lack of certainty concerning Gordon's guilt and her decision to try to ascertain the truth. So she followed Chitta upstairs. Sitting in one of Chitta's retro butterfly chairs was a young woman. She was attractive and athletic-looking, with long, straight blonde hair and grey eyes. She stood when they entered and Maggie realised the woman was almost as tall as she was herself.

"Maggie, this is Megan Thompson. Megan, this is Professor Eliot."

The women shook hands.

"Megan is one of Gordon's doctoral students. Megan, would you please tell Professor Eliot what you told me?"

Maggie looked at Megan. Her eyes were red-rimmed, as though she had been crying.

"I came for my weekly meeting with Gord... with Professor Ross. He wasn't in his rooms, which was unusual for him. I asked Professor Kazi if she knew where Prof... where Gordon was."

She said his name defiantly. From her accent, Maggie concluded Megan was American.

"Why don't we all sit down while we talk," Chitta suggested.

Megan settled herself back in the butterfly chair, while Maggie and Chitta sat in some of Chitta's moulded plastic dining table chairs, one orange, the other olive green.

"Professor Kazi told me Gordon has been arrested and is in jail. For murdering his wife. And the Master. I freaked out because..."

Megan re-crossed her legs. She was wearing tight jeans and a baby pink sweater.

"I'm a doctoral student. Competent, according to Gordon. Not brilliant enough to be sure I'd get a research fellowship when I finished. But he told me he could fix it so I'd get one if I.... If I..."

Megan would not look at Maggie.

"If you had sex with him?"

Maggie was outraged.

Megan blushed and hung her head.

"You didn't report him?"

"No. I really want a fellowship to do a post-doc. And it wasn't such a big deal. I'm hardly a virgin. He didn't want anything kinky. It was more just 'close your eyes and think of England.' Or in my case, of the fellowship."

"How long…"

"Since last October. Michaelmas term."

"But that's not all," said Chitta.

"Oh?"

"I did some checking and, well, I wasn't the only one Gordon had done this with."

"You mean Deidre? She had been his student…"

"Oh, that's ancient history. No, I know seven other women he's made moves on. Promised them fellowships. Post-docs. Recommendations."

"And no one made a complaint?" Maggie asked incredulously.

"And risk not getting their doctorates? While Gordon never actually threatened me, I assumed… He kinda implied…"

Maggie felt disgust like a wave of nausea.

"You're not in love with Gordon?"

"Puh-leez," Megan rolled her eyes.

"What about the other women?"

Megan shrugged.

"Do you know how hard it is being a woman in the field of public policy? Political science? PPE? How many of your students are female?" she asked the women.

"A minority," Maggie admitted.

Chitta nodded in agreement.

"Anyhow, one day I was going into my tutorial and this other woman was just leaving. She looked a bit messy. And, well, like she had just had sex. But didn't seem very happy about it. No afterglow.

"The next day I saw her in a coffee shop. I sat down at her table. Started talking. And it all came out. And it seemed she knew another woman who was now doing her post-doc and...

"Anyhow there are eight women I know about. We even have a page on Facebook. Gordon's Girls. You have to be invited. It's a support group."

"But why haven't you reported him?"

"Because Gordon delivers. He gets us those fellowships and post-docs. He has a terrific reputation in his field. His recommendation means a lot. And he has a lot of contacts. Plus there's poor Laila."

Who?"

"Laila Khan. She's from Pakistan. She turned Gordon down and the next thing she knew she couldn't get her dissertation proposal approved and she lost her visa and had to go back home where her parents married her off to some army officer. She's living in Peshawar with two kids. And she was brilliant. She could have been Prime Minister. Or run the World Bank. Or the UN. Bastard."

Maggie felt sick to her stomach. She reminded herself that what she was doing was for Deirdre. And Alastair. And if Ross escaped being convicted, she would make sure he was booted out of Oxford. And find he was unable to get another academic position. She knew Stephen would be just as appalled as she and Chitta were by Ross' conduct.

On the other hand, this made all eight of these women potential suspects. They all had reason to hate Ross. And it could have carried over to the college and its master, whom they might have assumed had known what was going on. Although Maggie was sure that Alastair, like Stephen, would never have tolerated Gordon's conduct had he known about it.

"All right, Megan. Besides yourself, who are the other 'Gordon's Girls?'"

"Besides Sarah, the woman I told you about, who's also a DPhil candidate, and me, there are two who are doing post-docs here. Two are in London. One is in Washington. D.C. And one is in Cambridge. Our Cambridge. At Harvard."

"All right. Well I assume you and Sarah will be the most affected by... Gordon's current situation. So I promise that Chitta and the Master and I will make sure your work is not disrupted."

Maggie glanced at Chitta, who nodded.

"But in return..."

Megan made a face.

"I'm not Gordon, Megan. But I want to find out who murdered poor Deidre Ross. And Alastair Carrington. Every one of you has a motive. So in return I'd like to know where you all were when Deirdre was killed. Ross may be pond scum, but that doesn't necessarily mean he's a murderer and I want the person who is guilty to be punished."

"All right," said Megan grudgingly.

"Do you have contact information for the other women?"

"Yes."

"If you could give it to me, I'll have a woman I'm working with on this check them out Her name is Burke. Gina Burke."

Chitta handed Megan a piece of paper and a pen and Megan wrote out the list of names.

"Thank you, Megan. And don't worry. Professor Kazi and I will make sure you and—is it Sarah?—are not adversely affected by the situation with Ross. Well, not any more than you have been."

Chitta nodded.

Megan sniffed one last time and left.

Chapter 28

Maggie had gone into the town centre to do some errands. She was walking back to Merrion with her parcels when she saw a flutter of black out of the corner of her eye. She turned and froze.

It was the Niqabis. There were four of them. Shrouded in black. And this time they did not try to hide themselves but stood still. Waited.

This was ridiculous, she told herself. She was not going to be intimidated by some students—she assumed they were students—in Halloween costumes.

She continued on her way. Then she paused, turned and realised the Niqabis were still following her, keeping about twenty yards back.

Maggie began to walk again. After another block she again paused and turned. This time the pack was only about ten yards away.

Maggie began to feel slightly panicked.

Get a grip, Eliot. You're reacting exactly the way they want you to, she scolded herself.

She was about to set off again when she noticed a sign in a store across the street.

Stonor Antiques.

The name seemed familiar. Who was...

Then she remembered. Clive Stonor was Gweneth's uncle. Her father's brother. The disapproving Muriel's brother-in-law. Maggie had met Clive at Chloe Osborne's wedding the previous September and he had told her about his shop in Oxford. Invited her for tea. Until that moment, she had completely forgotten about it.

Now might be a good time to pay a visit, she decided.

She dashed across the street and went inside.

A bell gently tinkled.

She was in a large room filled with beautiful antique furniture—sofas and cabinets and bookcases and side tables and dining chairs and assorted bric-a-brac. Wood surfaces glowed, crystal sparkled, brass shone.

A man came through a door at the back of the room. He was about Maggie's height, slight, with thinning white hair, mild blue eyes and patrician features. He wore a beautifully tailored dark blue suit and a tie in a stripe that Thomas would have recognised.

The man frowned briefly, then smiled and said, "Lady Raynham. What a pleasant surprise."

"Hello, Clive. And it's Maggie, please. And my sincere apologies for not coming to see you months ago. Life has been… a bit hectic."

She gestured at her cast.

"And I missed seeing you at Constance's wedding. I developed a cough and, before you could say Jack Robinson, I had bronchitis."

"I'm so sorry. I trust you are better now."

"Fit as a fiddle," he beamed.

"So what brings you to my humble emporium? Surely there is nothing here you cannot find in that treasure trove of an attic you have at Beaumatin. Or is it that you need help disposing of some valuable trinket?"

When they had met, Clive had told her that one of the services he provided was the discrete sale of family treasures.

"Neither. This is strictly a social call. One I should have made months ago. And I distinctly recall an invitation to tea."

"Excellent. Although I believe you would rather have coffee."

"You remember."

"My Anthony taught me to take note of people's preferences. People feel special and it's good for business."

Anthony had been Clive's partner for thirty-seven years.

"But in your case, my dear, I do it because I like you," he added quickly.

"Oh. Well, thank you. But only if it's not a bother."

"No trouble at all. In fact, I was just about to make some tea for myself."

He led Maggie into a back room where there was a kitchen with a table and two chairs. A window with a view of a small garden was hung with curtains in a Jacobean pattern.

Clive busied himself. He turned on the water heater, brought out a lovely Spode tea pot, some matching cups and saucers and a cafetière. He spooned some loose tea into the pot.

"I love making tea. And coffee. The ritual is so comforting, don't you agree?"

Maggie nodded and realised with a pang that, with Mrs Cook at Beaumatin and Mrs Royce at Hereford Crescent, she rarely made either coffee or tea. She also realised that she missed it.

Eventually both coffee and tea were ready.

"Milk? Sugar?"

"Just some milk, please."

Clive handed her a cup.

"So how have you been? I followed the launch of both of your books. And watched some of your interviews. I thought you handled the media quite well."

Maggie laughed.

"It would be harder if some of the people interviewing me actually read what I'd written. And bothered to develop some informed opinions."

She sipped her coffee.

"And you?"

"You've come on an important day. I was just about to call an estate agent I know in London and put my house there on the market."

Maggie remembered that at Chloe's wedding, Clive had told her about the house that he and Anthony had shared and that he felt it was time to sell. To "downsize," as he had put it.

"Oh? Tell me about the house."

Maggie had the glimmerings of an idea.

"I can do better than that. I can show you."

Clive got up, opened a door in the hall that led between the shop and the kitchen and went up a flight of stars. In moments he was back down holding a photo album.

"Do you know London? It's in Belsize. South of Hampstead. Not far from the Swiss Cottage tube station. Not too far from Paddington by taxi. Lots of elegant Victorian houses with some nice shops and restaurants in the village."

Maggie had never been in that part of London but let Clive continue.

He opened the album to a picture of a nineteenth-century brick townhouse of three stories. Steps led up to a porch covered by a portico held up by Doric columns. A bow window overlooked the street.

"There is a lower, garden level with a large kitchen. There are six bedrooms on the top two floors and an attic under the roof. There is a sizeable garden in the back. A bit neglected now, I'm afraid."

He turned the pages and showed her pictures of comfortably proportioned rooms with high ceilings and hardly any furniture. Bare white walls. Parquet floors. No crystal chandeliers or ornate plastering, Maggie noted.

"You must have so many memories. Aren't you sad to give it up?" Maggie asked.

"Nostalgic, perhaps. But sad, no. I haven't been there in, it must be, eighteen months now. A woman comes in to clean once a month and a neighbour keeps an eye on things."

Maggie took a deep breath.

"Um, Clive? I have a proposal."

"Yes?"

"I'd like to see your house. And if it's as nice as it looks in your pictures, I'd like to buy it."

Clive's brows rose.

"You think Raynham would like to add this to his real estate portfolio?"

Much of the Raynham wealth was held in a substantial real estate trust.

"No. No. *I* would like to buy it."

Clive frowned.

"Maggie, London real estate…"

Maggie followed Clive's thought.

"I know what London real estate prices are, Clive. And no, I am not thinking of spending Thomas' money. Do people really believe Constance when she tells people I married Thomas for his fortune? I have my own resources beyond my academic's salary. And… Let's say an investment of mine paid off at the same time I feel the need to have my own space."

Maggie explained about her mixed feelings when she had rented out her small but comfortable Oxford flat and moved into the Hereford Crescent house. And her awareness that her rooms at Merrion were hers only as long as she had her fellowship.

"And I'm not sure I'll ever feel like Beaumatin is really home. But please, don't quote me."

Clive was still looking sceptical.

"And don't think I expect an 'insider' price. I want to pay the full market value. Plus there won't be an estate agent's fee."

While Clive still hesitated, Maggie had another idea.

"The building. It's not listed is it? The interior could be changed?"

"You can't make changes to the exterior, the façade, the windows, what have you, but inside you can pretty much do what you want."

"Could it be made into two flats?"

"There were four flats when Anthony bought it. He turned it back into a single family home but all the pipes and things you'd need are still there."

Maggie was remembering the frequent complaints of Victoria, the wife of Thomas' second son James, about how cramped their two-bedroom apartment was with two boys and how the prices of flats in London made finding a larger place almost impossible on James' military salary.

"Won't you at least let me look at it?" Maggie wheedled.

"Well, it would keep it in the family," Clive admitted grudgingly, then noticed Maggie's expression.

"My dear, your daughter-in-law is my niece. That makes us family."

"Oh."

Maggie smiled.

"When could I see it?"

"Um…"

"Sometime this week?"

"In a hurry?"

"Our first wedding anniversary is at the end of May. I'd like to surprise Thomas."

"I thought his lordship doesn't care for London," Clive pointed out.

"Well, he doesn't appreciate the Tate Modern. But there's more to London than that. And I do love London. There's so much to do. And, as I said, to have my own space, something that's mine…"

Clive considered.

"Thursday?"

"You would close your shop?"

"You might not have noticed, but business is hardly booming. And Friday is a day when people are more likely to come in."

"Thursday, then."

"And no promises. I don't want you to be disappointed," Clive warned.

"No promises. And please don't tell anyone. If this happens, I want it to be a complete surprise for Thomas."

Even though Thomas was not someone who liked surprises. But Maggie decided to ignore that fact.

When she emerged from the shop, the Niqabis had vanished.

Chapter 29

When Maggie got back to her rooms, without any further Niqabi sightings, she received a text message from Gina. She was in Oxford, she had information, if Maggie had the time, she would drop by.

Maggie texted back that she was in her rooms at Merrion and would be in all afternoon. Anytime was fine.

Just after four o'clock there was a knock on Maggie's door and Gina entered.

Maggie stared. The woman looked nothing like the person she had met just days before. She was wearing a yellow man's shirt over well-worn jeans, work boots and a black leather biker jacket. Her hair had been gelled into artful disarray and her eyes were ringed with black liner.

"I've been talking to your Gordon's Girls. I thought I'd get a better response with this than wearing a suit."

Maggie admitted Gina could pass for a graduate student.

"Anyhow, I talked to Megan. And Sarah. And Katy. And Chris. The ones who are in Oxford. And Chis knew of another girl. Martine. I talked to her as well."

Gina took a small notepad out of a pocket and consulted her notes.

"They all hated Ross. But they all knew what had happened to Laila. So they put up with it. Because he delivered. And apparently he wasn't much in the shagging department, which helped. Katy said it was like going to the gynaecologist. It was just something you endured. And they were all someplace else when Deirdre died.

"Chris was on a train back from London. She couldn't produce a ticket but if it came down to it I assume there would be CCTV footage. Sarah was in the Bodleian. She says a librarian friend would remember the visit. Katy was with friends. She gave me their names. Megan was in Amsterdam. She had the stamps in her passport. Chris wasn't sure but thought she had gone shopping and could probably find the receipts if she looked hard enough and Martine has a part-time job in a bookshop and was working.

"The other four who are no longer in Oxford were also apparently where they were supposed to be. At least they were there when I contacted them. They also had some very unkind things to say about Ross."

Gina paused.

"Are you going to do something about this guy? If it turns out he's not a murderer? You're not going to let him come back and keep on doing this, are you?" Gina demanded.

"No. The Master of Merrion is a friend and I'm sure he'll feel the same way about this that I do."

"So you'll fob this pig off on some other unsuspecting university, like the Catholic Church moved on their pederast priests," said Gina cynically.

"No. Ross will have to find another line of work."

"Is it because he's working class and not some old Etonian that you're not going to protect him?"

"No, Gina. But neither do I want to see Merrion make the headlines of the *Daily Post*. Nor do I want to hurt any of Gordon's Girls who also have to consider their reputations."

"The double standard?"

"Alive and well unless I missed that press release."

Gina snorted.

"All right. Also, I checked out those old colleagues in Glasgow whose names Ross gave you. And they were also all where you'd expect them to be. At their universities. And were surprised to hear Ross' name. And had some very harsh things to say about their former associate. I would repeat them but I'm afraid the language would make your ladyship blush.

"Finally, I've tracked down Mrs Ross Number Two."

"Oh. Where is she?"

"Chipping Norton."

"Did you speak with her?"

"No. I thought you might want to do that. She's an estate agent. Uses her maiden name. Helen Armitage. I thought she might be more forthcoming if we visited her together."

Maggie gave Gina a look.

"And don't worry. I'll wear my good suit. And you can use your title."

"I take it you don't mean Professor Eliot."

"No, your ladyship."

"You're probably right. Tomorrow? I need to go to London on Thursday."

"Tomorrow it is. Can you be ready by nine o'clock?"

"Nine is fine."

"I'll pick you up at the gate then."

After Gina left, Maggie made some fresh coffee, then started calling people.

Her first call was to Malcolm.

"Malcolm? I'm going to be in London Thursday and wondered whether it would be possible to meet with your graphics person who's designing the covers for the Developing World series."

"Of course. Morning?"

"Morning is good. Say ten, ten thirty?"

"I'll set it up. May I take you to lunch?"

"Um, thank you, Malcolm, but I have another appointment."

"Too bad. Next time, then."

Maggie's second call was to Simon Peevey, a solicitor who served both the Raynhams and the Ainswicks. He specialised in estates and trusts and handled the legal complexities of the Raynham real estate portfolio. Maggie figured if anyone would have an idea about how to do what she wanted to do, Simon would. And also know about its tax implications.

"Simon? Maggie Eliot. Er, Raynham. I'm going to be in London Thursday looking at a house I'm interested in buying. It will be my house—I'll be paying for it out of my own funds. I want it to be a surprise for Thomas for our anniversary, so please, this is confidential. The owner is Clive Stonor. Gweneth's uncle. Yes, Clive. It's in Belsize. I wondered, if I gave you the address, if you could meet us there. Around two, two-thirty.

"You can? That's wonderful. I'll email you the address."

Maggie's final call was to Victoria.

"Victoria? It's Maggie."

There was a pause and Maggie frantically wondered how to identify herself. Your step-mother-in-law? Your father-in-law's wife? Lady Raynham Number Two?

The coin dropped for Victoria.

"Oh. Er, hi, Maggie. Sorry. You surprised me."

"I'm calling because I'm going to be in London Thursday and wondered if you'd be free to meet for lunch. I know it's a bit short notice…"

Another pause.

"All right. I'll see if I can get someone to stay with the boys."

"Great. I'd say bring them but it's probably better if… Anyhow it will be near Swiss Cottage. I'll text you with the place. Is noon all right?"

"Yes."

"I know this is unexpected. I'd tell you, but I want it to be a bit of a surprise."

"All right."

Victoria was hiding her enthusiasm about having lunch with her "step-mother-in-law." Which was not so amazing, given the tenuous nature of their relationship. Well, what she planned should change that.

Susan Alexander

Chapter 30

Gina was on time. She met Maggie in a smart silver Golf GTI and they set off for Chipping Norton. Gina was an expert driver, traffic flowed on the A44 and by ten o'clock they were at Armitage Estate Agents, the ground floor of a townhouse on the high street.

Pictures of two country houses mounted in ornate picture frames were displayed on easels in the front windows. Maggie looked at the prices and realised why the houses had been given the same treatment a Gainsborough would be given in a window of a top London gallery.

The women glanced at each other. Gina looked smart in a man-tailored grey suit. Maggie had dressed carefully in a little navy blue suit that had a narrow pleated edging around the cuffs and down the front. She had just managed to slip the sleeve over her cast. She had worn the emeralds Thomas had given her at their wedding and her hair was almost under control. She had even put on makeup for the occasion.

"I made an appointment for 'Lady Raynham,'" Gina murmured.

They entered and found themselves in an elegant room. Two comfortable armchairs were placed in front of a mahogany Georgian desk. In another corner, two chairs upholstered in a navy and taupe check were separated by a coffee table that held issues of *Tatler*, *Country Life* and *Cotswolds* magazine. Oils of a horse and a Victorian woman holding a King Charles spaniel hung on wallpaper subtly striped in taupe and cranberry and a good Oriental carpet covered the floor.

A door in the back wall opened and a woman entered. In her early forties and handsome, with chin-length blonde hair and grey eyes, she wore a deep red suit with a cream silk blouse. A Rolex adorned a wrist and an impressive diamond engagement ring graced a finger.

"Lady Raynham?" asked Helen Armitage.

Maggie produced a smile.

"Yes. And this is my associate, Gina Burke."

"And how may I help you? Your Miss Burke was not very forthcoming. I assume you're not here to tell me you're putting Beaumatin on the market and you want Armitage to handle the sale," the woman said with a brittle smile.

"No. I'm afraid not. In fact, our visit is not about real estate but something else entirely."

Helen Armitage hesitated, then finally said, "Well, please, sit down anyway. Would you like some tea?"

"No, thank you."

The women sat.

"So, Lady Raynham…"

Maggie figured it was better not to invite this woman to call her Maggie.

"It's about your former husband. Gordon Ross."

Helen Armitage stiffened and pressed her lips together.

"You know he's been arrested for murder. Two murders."

"Yes. I read the papers. But what does this have to do with you? You're not the press, are you?" she asked suspiciously.

"No, I'm not, I assure you. I'm a professor at Merrion College. Gordon is a colleague."

Maggie handed over one of her cards.

"Eliot?"

"My professional name."

"Humpf."

"I was there when Alastair Carrington died. And when Deirdre was pushed down the stairs."

"Yes?" Indifferent.

"And I was there when Gordon was arrested and... He swore he was innocent and asked me to look into it. The murders. And while I have no reason to want to get Gordon off if he's guilty, I do want whoever did kill Alastair Carrington and Deirdre to be, um, brought to justice."

"How quixotic. But what does this have to do with me?"

"We're talking to people who know, or knew, Gordon. To see if they might be able to suggest who might hold a grudge. Might want to frame him."

Helen snorted.

"Who dislikes Gordon? Who doesn't dislike him? Do you want a list? I hope you have some time.

"And I suppose you'd like me to tell you where I was at the time of those deaths. The ex-wife. Always at the top of the suspect list."

She paused.

"But why are you here? And not the police?"

"Because the police are convinced Gordon is guilty. Based on circumstantial evidence."

"So you've decided to play Miss Marple?"

"You could put it that way. But Miss Burke is a private investigator. She works for the London solicitors used by the Raynhams for legal matters."

Maggie could tell Helen was considering how useful Maggie might be to her in the future.

"And talking to us instead of the police... Well, there is always the possibility that whatever the police do would get into the press. And I assume you would rather avoid that kind of publicity."

The estate agent grimaced at the thought of being connected with Ross and the murders in the media.

"Very well. What do you want to know?" she asked finally.

"What you can tell us about Gordon?"

"That bastard? He'd already dumped poor Fiona and the kid a few years before we met. I was working as an estate agent in Oxford and Gordon came in looking for a flat to rent. I showed him a few within his price range—you professors really work for a pittance, don't you?

"He eventually took one. The least expensive. But he was amusing. He had a certain charm if you could get past the chip on his shoulder about being from the wrong side of the tracks. I'd never met anyone like him. He asked me out."

Helen sighed.

"I was thirty and terrified that I was going to end up an old maid who'd die alone and be eaten by her cats. I was impressed by Gordon's being an Oxford professor. And I thought I could civilize him. In the meantime, there was a certain attraction in having a bit of rough. My mother would have called him NOCD."

"NOCD?" Maggie was puzzled.

"Not our class, dear," said Gina, with a slight edge to her voice.

"And Gordon? He was not immune to the fact that I had some family money. He liked my Mercedes. And my house. And he was tired of doing his own laundry. Not that I would have done it for him. I had help for that.

"So we got married. But after a year or so… Gordon likes them young. Not undergrads. He was too smart for that. But his graduate students. He always wanted the girls. I could tolerate the casual shagging. As long as it was discrete. I had already realised Gordon was not going to change. He would always be a social liability, at least as far as my circle was concerned. In fact, after a few dinner parties when he attacked my friends for being bourgeois and generally tried to carry on the class struggle, we were no longer invited out, except for Merrion events.

"But then he met Deirdre. She was infatuated. He was obsessed. They started going out in public together. You can imagine the gossip. The humiliation. And that was it as far as I was concerned.

"We got divorced. He complained about the settlement but mostly it involved his having to move out of the house—the house that I owned. And having to pay his own way again. I guess I was lucky I didn't have to pay him alimony.

"I left Oxford and set up here. I had connections. Business has been good. And I've met someone. A solicitor whose speciality is real estate. Also divorced. We're going to be married in June."

Helen looked down at her engagement ring.

"That's really all I can tell you."

"Did you know Deirdre was pregnant when she died?"

Helen looked startled.

"Pregnant? Gordon would have hated that. He was adamant about not wanting children. One was more than enough, he always said. Although I don't think he would have killed the poor girl. Just dumped her and moved on. He always had his groupies."

"We've been trying to locate his first wife. You wouldn't know anything about her, would you? Where she is? What name she's using?"

"No. I only know her name was Fiona. Gordon always called her 'that fat cow Fiona.' I know they had a child. A boy, I think. Whom he called 'the little pissant' in that charming way he has. But that's all."

"And you can't think of anyone who might..."

"No. Gordon may have been disliked, but that much? And poor Alastair. I always liked Alastair. Why would Gordon kill him?"

"The police think the poison was meant for Deirdre. Who wasn't drinking because of the pregnancy."

"Perhaps you should be looking more closely at her."

"We are," Maggie assured her.

Helen took an agenda out of a desk drawer.

"Now. What were the dates and times of those murders again?"

Gina told her.

Helen checked.

"At the time of Alastair's murder, Roger and I were at a dinner party with a dozen other people. Roger's my fiancé. And when Deirdre…"

She flipped some pages.

"I was showing Dmitri Dunayevsky, the Russia oligarch, some properties most of the day. If you need confirmation of that I am sure there are people who can provide it."

"I don't think that will be necessary. And thank you," Maggie said.

"Since I've answered your questions, I hope I can trust you not to mention my name in connection with the case. Reputations matter in my business."

"I understand."

Helen handed Maggie a beautifully engraved business card.

"And if you ever want to downsize or are looking for something slightly more rustic than your current residence, I would be happy to assist you," she gave a genuine smile.

"I'll remember," Maggie promised.

In the car on their way back to Oxford, Gina said, "So we seem to have eliminated all of the people on your list except for Fiona."

"Yes. I can't believe Gordon has no idea where she is or what happened to his son."

"Unfortunately, that's not as uncommon as you'd think."

"Really?"

"And perhaps Fiona did not want to stay in contact. Ross is a real asshole."

"Pond scum," Maggie agreed.

"But you're still going to try to prove he's innocent?"

"No. I want to find out if he did kill Alastair and Deirdre. And if he didn't, who did. It's not quite the same thing."

Gina shook her head.

"Anyhow I'll talk to Gordon again and see if he has been able to remember anything that could help locate Fiona."

"Better you than me."

Back in her rooms, Maggie frowned. She had her own work to do. And the trip to London tomorrow.

She called Thomas.

"Hello. I thought you should know. I have a meeting with Malcolm at the Global Press tomorrow morning. And after that, I'm meeting Victoria for lunch."

"You're meeting Victoria?" Thomas was surprised.

"Um, yes."

"Oh. Well, that's nice. Give her my love."

"I will. And I won't be back in Oxford until evening and Friday there's work I still need to do so, if it's all right, I'll be back at Beaumatin in time for dinner on Friday."

There was silence.

"You're staying at Hereford Crescent?" Pointedly.

"Yes. Of course."

"All right, Papillon. I'll see you Friday."

"Friday. And I'll call when I'm back from London tomorrow."

"Very well."

The call ended. Neither Maggie nor Thomas were big on endearments. Maggie's attitude was that some things were so obvious that they didn't need to be said. She also knew Thomas was unhappy with her being away. Well, it was not so long until Friday.

Susan Alexander

Chapter 31

Maggie was proof-reading the book she and Chitta had written for Stanley's Developing World series. It reviewed the evidence on the impact of female education on reducing poverty. It was finicky work and, before she knew it, she had nodded off.

An hour later she started awake. Something had woken her. Then she realised it was noise coming from outside. Chanting. And again there was the strange light coming from the quad.

It was another bonfire. Eight black-clad figures gyrated around it. They were burning her books again.

Oh dear. What should she do?

She called Stephen. It seemed he was also at work in his office.

"Stephen, it's happening again. The Niqabis have lit a bonfire in the quad. I wasn't sure whom to call..."

"I'll call security. Stay in your rooms."

Stay in her rooms? Not likely.

Maggie rushed down.

"What are you doing? Stop it!"

She waved her arms.

Instead of running off, as she had expected, the Niqabis advanced on her.

Maggie stood her ground. She wasn't going to be intimidated by some silly undergrads.

"The police have been called!"

Two of the figures ran up to her. One pushed her back into the other's arms, then grabbed her feet. She kicked but she was firmly held.

"Let go!" She struggled.

"Throw the infidel on the fire!" a male voice called out.

"Throw her on the fire! Throw her on the fire!"

The two holding her hesitated, then started to carry her towards the blaze.

"No!"

Maggie tried to kick but her ankles were grasped too tightly.

At that moment, Stephen rushed up.

"Hey!" he yelled.

The two holding her—she was sure they were men—abruptly dropped her on the ground and took off. The others also scattered.

Stephen was torn between chasing after the Niqabis and making sure Maggie was all right. He decided on Maggie.

"I thought I told you to stay in your room! You could have been hurt!"

He was furious.

Maggie had had the breath knocked out of her and could only gasp. She flapped her hands. When she could finally breathe, she burst into tears.

"Maggie!"

He pulled her up and hugged her.

"It's all right. Don't cry."

"I'm sorry. Sorry. It was just..." she sniffed.

Campus security arrived. Four men in a security firm's uniform. Two searched the perimeter of the quadrangle, one toed the fire which was beginning to die down and the fourth asked Stephen, "Was it those kids again? Playing dress up?"

The man shook his head.

"Well, we can check CCTV. Maybe find out which staircases they came out of. And see where they went."

"Please. Make it a priority. Professor Eliot came close to being seriously injured."

The man looked uncomfortable.

Stephen turned to Maggie.

"You should go to Hereford Crescent."

Maggie nodded.

Stephen turned to one of the security officers.

"Do you have a car here?"

"Yes."

"Then you can drive Professor Eliot home. I'll go with you."

He turned to Maggie.

"Is there something you need from your rooms?"

"Yes. I'll be right back."

"We'll wait."

Maggie went up and hurriedly gathered her laptop and her purse.

The ride to Hereford Crescent was silent. When they arrived, Stephen got out with Maggie and sent the car away.

"Drink?"

"Yes, please."

"If you'll wait in the library, I'll…"

Maggie returned with whisky, white wine and glasses.

She poured.

Stephen was still fuming. Maggie had known Stephen for more than eight years and had never seen him really angry before.

She took a sip of wine and sighed.

"Are you all right?"

"Yes. I'm all right. I'm fine."

"Right."

Silence.

"I'm just not sure what you can do."

"I'm going to speak to the Vice Chancellor, for one thing."

"Do you really think…"

"Maggie, do you know what could have happened if I'd gotten there just a few seconds later?"

"Yes, I..."

"Do know what burns are like? And how I could have faced Thomas..."

Thomas.

"Stephen, please don't tell Thomas."

Stephen glared.

"He's already made me promise not to stay in my rooms. I wouldn't have been there tonight except I was working and I dozed off. If Thomas knew, he'd lock me in the dungeon he claims he has at Beaumatin. And Stanley would need to find a new Weingarten fellow."

Stephen scowled.

"Tomorrow I'll be in London all day. And Friday I have one appointment in the morning and then I'm leaving for Beaumatin. And perhaps the CCTV will give a better indication of who's involved in this. Or security will think of some way..."

"The Niqabis. Have you seen them lately? Besides tonight?"

Maggie hesitated.

"Well?"

"Yesterday. Tuesday. I was doing some errands. And suddenly there were four of them. Following me. They didn't run off when I turned to confront them. It happened that I was in front of a shop owed by... well a member of the extended

Raynham family. I went in and when I came out, they'd gone."

Stephen frowned.

"The problem is, if I got the Thames Valley police involved, and they stopped someone wearing a niqab and it turned out to be an innocent woman… Well, you can imagine the uproar."

"I certainly can."

Stephen paused while he finished his whisky and refilled his glass.

"You haven't discussed this with Faisal, have you?"

"No."

"Now might be a good time. See what he suggests. Assuming he's not behind it. Although I still have the impression he would have preferred you had arrived a bit later."

"Thomas and Faisal have become close. Do you think Thomas could approach…"

"No! I told you what Thomas would do if he found out."

"All right."

"I don't think you can delegate this, Stephen."

"Quite."

He drained his whisky.

"You're sure you'll be all right?"

"Yes. And the Royces are here."

"And you're in London tomorrow?"

"Yes. I have a meeting with a graphics guy about the design for the Developing World series."

"Well, that should be Niqabi-free."

"Or as free as it gets in London. But yes, I should be safe enough."

"Then I'd better get back to Merrion."

"Thank you, Stephen."

"And I have your promise? No more risk-taking."

"Yes, Stephen."

Maggie walked Stephen to the door. He opened it.

"Good God."

On the top step was a pig's head. Flies crawled over its snout and around its clouded eyes.

"What the..."

Maggie saw. It was too much.

"Stephen, does your phone have a camera? Then take some pictures. I'm going to call the Royces. If you want, you can call the police. Or Thomas. Do whatever you think is appropriate."

Maggie walked over to an intercom on the wall and pushed a button.

"I'm sorry to bother you at this hour, Mrs Royce, but there's a problem. Could you and Mr Royce please come up to the front hall?"

In a minute the Royces were there, in their bathrobes. They gaped at the sight of the pig's head.

It had been a Gloucester Old Spot, with distinctive black markings on one ear and on the back of its head. Blood was caked around the edges of the neck where the head had been cut off and was smeared on the step.

"So, Stephen?" Maggie felt like she was fraying at the edges. Stephen noticed.

"Go to bed. The Royces and I will handle this."

He glanced at the couple, who nodded mutely.

"I'm sorry, Stephen. Thank you."

Maggie fled.

Chapter 32

The next morning, Maggie took a taxi to the train station. She had an important day ahead of her and her problems with the Niqabis could wait. She would compartmentalise.

She had a productive meeting with the Global Press' graphic artist and settled on two designs to show to Stanley for his feedback. Of course, the meeting was really only an excuse for the trip.

Maggie met Victoria at Bradley's, an elegant restaurant near the Swiss Cottage underground station that Simon Peevey had recommended.

Maggie had barely been seated when Victoria arrived. The woman looked cool and elegant in a silver grey dress and matching jacket. Pale blonde hair curled under in a prefect bob. Maggie was glad she had worn her good navy suit even though her hair was escaping from its hairclip as usual.

"Victoria!" The women air kissed and sat.

Maggie inquired after James and how his work was going. Victoria said that James was well but was vague about his work. She was more forthcoming about sons Thomas and John and described their latest exploits in great detail.

Maggie saw that there were oysters on the menu and ordered half a dozen as a starter and another half dozen as a main course. Victoria had asparagus and then turbot and they shared a half bottle of Pouilly fumé.

As Maggie started her second plate of oysters, she said, "Victoria. I remember you saying you were frustrated by not having more space in your flat. And I am well aware of the cost of London real estate. And I had an idea. But whether it appeals you or not, I need you to keep it a secret. Because I want it to be a surprise for Thomas."

Victoria's expression indicated nothing more than polite interest.

"I'm considering buying a London property. In fact, after lunch I'm going to look at a house that's near here. It belongs to Gweneth's uncle, Clive Stonor. Muriel's brother-in-law. I assume you know him."

Victoria nodded.

"It's a town house. Victorian. It has a garden level and then three floors. Clive says there are six bedrooms on the top two floors plus an attic. It's now a single home but it used to be broken into apartments and the infrastructure, the pipes and wiring, are still there. And while the place appears to be exactly what I'm looking for—I've only seen pictures so far—it is far too big for just Thomas and me. So I had an idea.

"If it turns out to be as nice as Clive's pictures indicate, I thought about keeping the bottom two floors and turning the top floors into a separate flat. And wondered if you and James might be interested in living there. And either buying it outright or working out a scheme so that any rent you paid would go towards your eventually owning the flat.

"And I know you can't give me an answer until you've spoken with James and seen the place. And considered all the issues. But, well, I'm going to meet Clive there after we finish lunch. And Simon Peevey, our solicitor, will be there as well. And I wondered whether you would like to come and take a look."

"Really?" Victoria was surprised.

"Oh. Um, all right. I'll come and take a look. Although I can't make any sort of commitment."

"Of course not. Just, whatever you decide, please don't mention this to Thomas."

"My lips are sealed. And I'll make sure James also knows not to say anything."

"Thank you."

"And... Well... I just found out I'm pregnant, so finding a larger flat has become critical. I'd hate to have to move to some dreary suburban town and have James spend hours every day commuting."

Maggie offered her congratulations. Again.

SUSAN ALEXANDER

Chapter 33

Maggie was excited on the train back to Oxford. Clive's house had exceeded her expectations. The interiors were light, airy and immaculate. The bottom two floors would provide more than enough space for her and Thomas, while the top two floors and attic would give the James Conyers family a generous living space and four bedrooms, while the garden would provide a perfect place for the children to play. Victoria left determined to convince James that the house was a perfect solution to their problems. Clive was delighted at the price Maggie proposed and Simon said he would start the paperwork as soon as he returned to his office. Maggie pledged everyone to secrecy.

When Maggie got out of the taxi at Hereford Crescent, she saw a car she recognised. It was Thomas' ancient Land Rover. In addition, there was a Bentley with its driver leaning against the car having a smoke and another large, dark-coloured sedan double-parked with its driver also waiting beside it. This man was in police uniform.

Oh dear. This wasn't good.

Maggie let herself into the house, while noting that the pig's head was gone and the front steps had been cleaned. She heard low voices coming from the drawing room. She took a deep breath and opened the door.

Four men were in the room. Thomas. And Stephen. The University Vice Chancellor. And a fourth man she did not recognize but from the quality of his tailoring and general demeanour assumed was also someone important.

She briefly reflected that had she arrived after dinner, the room would have smelled of cigars and cognac. As it was, the men were enjoying some of Thomas' whisky. She was also glad she was appropriately dressed, although she could not vouch for her hair. She wondered if the men had been comparing their tailors. But probably not.

She looked at Thomas and saw that he was in full twenty-eighth baron mode. Or perhaps he was more Genghis Khan.

Everyone stood.

"My dear, I assume you know everyone except for Horace Allenby, who is the Chief Constable of the Thames Valley Police."

Maggie shook hands.

Thomas indicated she should take a seat beside him on a sofa. She did and the others sat back down.

"We have been discussing the various incidents that have been occurring at Merrion. And last night, the pig's head..."

"How..."

"Mrs Royce informed me. Then Stephen called and told me about what had happened at the college last night."

So Mrs Royce was a snitch as well as a gossip, Maggie thought. And Stephen was avoiding eye contact.

The Vice Chancellor took on the role of group spokesman.

"Given that these Niqabis as you call them—a good term by the way—have begun to act outside of the University grounds and have gone beyond stalking to threatening serious physical harm, we have decided to turn the matter over to the police. Who are better equipped to review CCTV footage and

234

analyse any extant forensic evidence. And may already be aware of the identities of some of these troublemakers.

"And the University will also make some discrete inquiries about the possible identities of these women..."

"The Niqabis are not all women," Maggie interrupted.

The men looked at her.

"Some are men. I know because..."

Maggie did not want to say she knew because she had felt the bodies underneath the niqabs when the two had picked her up and were trying to toss her onto the fire.

"I could tell by their voices. At least two were definitely male."

The Vice Chancellor looked pained.

"I suppose it was inevitable that a few of our students would become radicalised," Stephen said regretfully.

The Vice Chancellor continued.

"In the meantime, especially since it is between terms, we believe it would be better if you stayed away from Oxford..."

"But that's what they want, isn't it? I thought we weren't supposed to give in to... terrorists."

Maggie hated using the "t" word but went for the effect.

"Hm. I can see... Very well. Can you minimize the time you spend at Merrion and be sure you leave before dark? Just until this is sorted, of course."

The Vice Chancellor prided himself on being the voice of reason and the effector of the artful compromise. And whatever occurred outside the University grounds was not his problem.

Thomas' hand closed tightly around Maggie's wrist.

"Well, my dear?"

His tone was mild but his grip was like a vice.

"That seems like a more viable arrangement," she finally said.

"And I will alert my men and provide a number you can call directly if you experience any further harassment or vandalism," said the Chief Constable.

"Yes. This is a bad business. To have such unpleasantness at Oxford. It must be stopped and the perpetrators dealt with," stated the Vice Chancellor.

The other men muttered in agreement.

"Well then." The Vice Chancellor stood, followed by the others.

"I trust you will keep us informed about your progress, Chief Constable," Thomas said.

"You can be sure, Lord Raynham. I will have my best men on this."

Maggie hoped it would not be Inspector Moss.

"Do you think this could have any relation to the homicides?" Maggie wondered aloud.

The men stared at her. Thomas stiffened.

"Alastair Carrington. And Deirdre Ross," Maggie added for clarification.

"I will put that question to Detective Inspector Moss. Although I understand we have a suspect in custody," said the police chief smoothly.

Thomas showed the men to the door. Maggie waited in the drawing room for the inevitable.

He returned. Maggie could tell he was furious.

"I thought we agreed you were not going to stay at Merrion."

"I wasn't. I got engrossed in my work and forgot about the time. I was leaving to come back here when..."

"And then you don't tell me the house has been vandalised and I have to hear about it from a servant? And have to wheedle information out of Draycott? Again?"

Maggie vowed she was not going to hang her head like a guilty child.

"It had been a bit of a day," she began when the ornate antique clock on the mantle chimed.

Thomas noticed the hour.

"I have an engagement. We'll discuss this further when I return."

He left. Maggie heard the front door open and close.

Rats. Rats and phooey.

Maggie knew any discussion would be completely one-sided. And that she had been put in a position of "You just wait until your father gets home!"

Well, she was not going to sit around and cower until Thomas got back. She declined Mrs Royce's offer of dinner and took a glass and bottle of Viognier to her study. She set up her laptop and opened the wine. She reminded herself how excited she was about the Belsize house. And that, even with Victoria's help, it was going to be an epic task to have the house even minimally ready for their anniversary.

Always assuming…

Thomas was as angry as she had ever seen him. Perhaps it really was good that she was going to get her own space. She wondered what his engagement was. Faisal, most likely. Didn't Thomas even consider that Faisal might have some connection to the Niqabis?

Probably not. She could imagine the men commiserating over their whiskies about the perversities of women and the proper treatment of wives.

Maggie decided to compartmentalise and spent the next two hours looking at furniture and fabrics on the Internet.

Maggie thought about the Belsize house. It was perfect, with lots of space and light. Victoria had been ecstatic and she saw no reason James would not be pleased as well with the large garden for the children to play in and a Waitrose not too far away and the Jubilee line at Swiss Cottage that went straight to Westminster. Maggie assumed that would be close to where James worked.

Maggie was on her third glass of wine and suddenly felt exhausted.

She decided to go to bed. Her bed. She was not going to wait up for Thomas to return and continue his harangue. And if he were in the same state as the last time he had had dinner with Faisal… Assuming he was having dinner with Faisal.

Maggie shut down her computer, went into her bedroom, skipped her nightly beauty rituals, pulled on a long slip of a nightgown in peach satin and went to sleep.

Chapter 34

Thomas had indeed been having dinner with Faisal. He had enjoyed a savoury lamb stew and some red wine that stood up to the spices. And some whisky. Quite a bit if he had been keeping count. Which he hadn't.

He told Faisal about the stalking. And the book burnings. And the pig's head. Faisal's response had been that it was not so surprising given the current polarized political climate. As well as Maggie's being seen as being anti-Muslim. He did not add that he was one of the reasons that she was perceived this way.

Thomas went on to talk about Harriet. Who had been so lovely. So gentle. So content with her role as wife and mother. About how devastated he had been by her death. And then meeting Maggie. Who was so different than his first wife. Accomplished. Independent. And not at all inclined to listen to her husband or take his good advice.

Faisal was a sympathetic listener and refilled his guest's glass with some more fine whisky.

Thomas floated back to his house and up the stairs. He looked in his bedroom. It was empty. As he opened the door to Maggie's room he was afraid for a brief instant that he would find that empty as well. But Maggie was peacefully asleep.

He looked down at his wife and considered waking her and continuing his tirade. But that would have been brutish and he was not a brute.

He went back to his bedroom and began to undress. As he unfastened his cufflinks he thought perhaps that his rage at Maggie's putting herself in danger was to cover his terror that he might lose her. Like he had lost Harriet. He knew he would not survive that kind of grief a second time.

He put on his bathrobe and went back across the hall. Maggie was still asleep. Her curls lay in turmoil on her pillow and he caught a faint whiff of the scent she always wore. It was warm and flowery, like a garden on a June day. Anger fought with desire. Desire won.

He picked her up.

"Thomas?"

"Shh."

And he carried her back to his bedroom.

Chapter 35

At breakfast the next morning, while he had a soft boiled egg and Maggie sipped some coffee, Thomas announced, "We can leave for Beaumatin as soon as you're ready."

Then he noticed that his wife was dressed in an elegant deep grey suit and a creamy silk blouse.

"You're looking very business-like," he remarked.

"Um. I have an appointment. Not at the University. Out of town. Concerning a research project. It should only take a couple of hours. Then we can have lunch and leave. Or we can leave as soon as I get back and have a late lunch at Beaumatin. Whichever you prefer."

Maggie waited apprehensively for Thomas' reaction.

"You're not going near the University?"

"No."

"Very well. I'll wait."

"Thank you. I'll be back as soon as possible."

Maggie had arranged with Burgess, Ross' solicitor, to meet the man again. She was taking Gina with her. She wanted to tell Gordon what they had learned from the information he had provided. As well as having some additional questions, she wanted to get Gina's opinion of the man. Not that he wasn't pond scum. But was he murderous pond scum? She still was not sure.

Maggie picked Gina up in Summertown where she was staying "at a friend's." Traffic was light and they were at the prison in good time.

Gordon was his usual charming self.

"So there's two of you now. Who's she?"

He jerked his head at Gina, who was also looking business-like in a black pantsuit and a grey blouse.

"This is Gina Burke, the private investigator who's helping us."

"I hope you're worth it," was his comment.

Maggie ignored it.

"Gina checked out your former colleagues whose names you gave us. None of them had anything nice to say about you, but all were at their respective universities at the times of the murders and seemed surprised they were asked to provide alibis.

"We also found Helen Armitage, your second wife. While she also is not a member of the Gordon Ross fan club, she also had alibis for the times of both killings.

"And we found some of your students. Or they found us. Megan. Martine. Chris. Katy. Some others. They'd formed a club. They call it 'Gordon's Girls.' They even have a page on Facebook. And they told us about your behaviour."

"So? What's it to you what I do in private?"

Gina looked disgusted.

"The reputation of Merrion matters to me. And to Chitta and Laurence and Andrew and Stephen and our other faculty. All of these women have grounds for legal action

244

against you and the college. And if you are ever cleared of these murder charges, you can be sure that Stephen will address your misconduct."

Gordon shrugged.

"That's the least of my worries."

"However, having found out about the Gordon's Girls, they also had to be eliminated as possible suspects. Fortunately for them, but unfortunately for you, none of them could have committed the murders.

"So that leaves one person we have been unable to find. Or two. Your first wife, Fiona, and your son, Hamish. There's absolutely no trace of either."

"Well, I told you her maiden name was MacNelly. Did you look for her parents?"

"Do you know how many MacNellys there are in Scotland?" Gina demanded.

"That's your problem."

"No, it's yours. As long as we haven't found anyone else who could have murdered Alastair. And Deirdre. So can you think of anything that could help us find Fiona? Did Fiona have any siblings?" Maggie persisted.

Gordon frowned.

"She did have a sister. Her name was... Susan. Or Susie. Or Sue. And I think I remember that we went to her wedding. I didn't want to go but Fiona insisted. Stupid cow. She married some guy. What was his name? Something common. Not Jones. Not Smith. Something Scottish. What was it?"

Gordon frowned.

"I don't know. Maybe it was Brown. Yes. It could have been Brown."

"So Fiona has or had a sister whose name was Susan MacNelly who may have married a man named Brown. Do you remember the date of the wedding?"

Ross frowned.

"The little pissant was two. Or maybe three. So 1995 or '96? And I think it was summer."

"That's not much to go on," said Gina.

"Well, it's more than we had," said Maggie.

"But it will take time. There are even more Browns in Scotland than MacNellys."

"Going to drag your feet so you can submit a bigger bill? I know how you people work," Gordon sneered.

Gina stood, put both hands on the table and leaned over.

"Look, Ross. There are lots of things I'd rather be doing than trying to get your ass out of nick. As far as I'm concerned, you're pond scum. Lower than pond scum. But Lady Raynham wants justice for Carrington and poor Deirdre. Which means making sure the right person gets sent to prison. As far as I'm concerned, you can rot in here until hell freezes over."

Gina turned and walked towards the door.

"I couldn't have said it better myself," agreed Maggie as she followed the detective.

Chapter 36

Maggie was back at Hereford Crescent before noon. Gina had promised she would report back on her search for Fiona as soon as she learned anything.

Thomas decided he wanted to leave straight away for Beaumatin. They took the new green Land Rover Thomas had given Maggie for her birthday the previous June and were back in time for a late lunch.

After lunch, Thomas rode off with Ned to do his usual tour of the estate and Maggie went to her study and called Anne.

"Hey, Anne."

"Hey, Maggie. What's up?"

"A lot. Are you around?"

"Yes. If you're free, come by tomorrow and provide moral support while I do my annual kitchen clean."

"Hm. Moral support I can certainly provide."

"And you'll also be useful for getting things down from the top shelves."

At 5'11", Maggie had half a foot on Anne's 5'5".

"At least I've been warned. What time?"

"Ten-ish? I'll have fresh coffee."

Anne approached Maggie's levels of caffeine addiction.

At dinner, which was a roast loin of pork, Maggie ventured, "If it's all right I'm going to go see Anne tomorrow morning. She needs support for her spring kitchen cleaning."

"In Broadway?"

"Yes. And to the best of my knowledge, a niqab has yet to be seen in the village."

Thomas considered.

"I'll be back well before dinner."

"Yes. Of course. I'm sorry, Papillon. I'm a bit sensitive about your well-being these days."

"And is the Triumph still running? It's supposed to be a nice day. I can take that and leave you the Land Rover. Just in case."

The Triumph, vintage 1954, had belonged to Thomas' father and still had a place in the Beaumatin garage.

"I'll make sure Ned has it ready."

He stood and pulled out Maggie's chair.

"Come. There's a nature show on about Madagascar. A place I've always wanted to visit. Did you know eighty percent of their species are unique? Lemurs. I'd love to see a lemur in the wild."

Maggie wondered if she should have gotten Thomas a trip to Madagascar rather than a house for their anniversary. Well, there was still his birthday.

"Sounds fascinating," she smiled.

Chapter 37

Anne lived in a beautifully restored Georgian house in Broadway, which was in Warwickshire. Or perhaps Oxfordshire. Or possibly Worcestershire. Maggie could never keep her shires straight. It was definitely in the Cotswolds. One view of the luminous, golden-hued stone used in the buildings on the high street made that obvious.

Laurence greeted Maggie at the door.

"You're warned. It's worth your life to go into the kitchen right now. I'm hiding in my study. My excuse is that I have a journal article to finish," Laurence winked.

Maggie found Anne standing on a stepstool and removing items from a shelf. Every available inch of counter space was crammed with cans and jars and bottles and boxes.

"My goodness."

Anne turned.

"Oh wonderful. You've come. I can put you to work immediately. You can start by checking the sell-by dates on all of these," she pointed to the collection on the countertops.

"And maybe after you check, put them into groups of 'likes,' like all the preserves together and all the spices together and all the carbs, the pastas and rice and couscous, together and…"

"Anne…"

"Oh wait. A better idea. Can you reach these? I can't. You can hand them down to me and then you can do those other things."

"Anne!"

"Yes?"

"How about some coffee first?"

"Coffee? Oh. Of course. I promised you coffee, didn't I? All right."

Anne clambered down from the stepstool.

"I'll make some fresh. But while we're waiting, you might start on those sell-by dates."

Maggie dutifully picked up a jar. Tandoori paste. She turned it this way and that. Frowned.

"Do you have a magnifying glass?"

"Believe it or not, yes."

Anne rummaged in a drawer and handed a magnifier to Maggie.

Maggie squinted through the glass.

"2011. Definitely beyond."

"Oh dear."

Anne dragged out a plastic garbage bin from under a counter.

"Just put it in here for now."

Anne made coffee while Maggie checked dates. Three more items went in the bin.

Anne handed Maggie a mug of coffee.

"So what's going on?" Anne asked.

"Quite a bit, actually. I guess the most, um, interesting thing is that I'm buying a house. In London."

"You're buying a house? In London? But why? You've already got Beaumatin. And Hereford Crescent. And I thought the Raynhams owned real estate in London."

"Yes, they do. But, like Hereford Crescent and Beaumatin, they belong to the Raynhams. The barony. And I've been feeling a bit like a tenant. I'm only in residence as long as Thomas and I are together. I've been feeling... Well, like I needed someplace that was mine. That was not provisional."

Maggie told Anne about Constance and what had happened at dinner.

"That girl. She really needs someone to beat some manners into her. And she's pregnant? And left Nils?"

"Yes. Thankfully she's staying with William and Gweneth and not at Beaumatin."

"Humpf."

"And then I got this windfall..."

Maggie told Anne about the shares Stanley had given her and the sale of the companies.

"Goodness gracious."

"And at the same time... Did you meet Clive Stonor, Gweneth's uncle, her father's brother, at Chloe's wedding?"

Anne tried to remember.

"I'm sure we were introduced but I'm not certain..."

"He has an antique shop in Oxford. And I dropped in and he told me he was about to put a house he has in London on the market and... Well, I told him I might be interested in buying it. It's a wonderful house. In Belsize. Convenient to Paddington. And the underground. And there are shops. A Waitrose. And then there's James and Victoria and the boys."

Maggie told Anne her inspiration about having them take the top two floors.

"Victoria's been complaining ever since I met her about how cramped they are in their flat. And how unaffordable London is. And certainly we will never use all the space. The house has six bedrooms. And a large garden. Well, large for London. And she's pregnant so they really are desperate for more room."

Maggie showed Anne some pictures she had taken on her smart phone.

"I really want it more as a pied à terre. Someplace to stay in town."

"What does Thomas say?"

"Nothing yet. I want to surprise him. For our anniversary. I've left Victoria in charge of overseeing the work that needs to be done. Apparently she worked as a decorator before she married James. And Simon Peevey is taking care of all the paperwork. I have no idea of the tax implications of all this, so I'm leaving that in his hands too."

"My goodness."

"There'll be a guest room. So if you and Laurence ever need a place to stay in London..."

"Thank you. We'll certainly take you up on that. Given what hotels cost."

Maggie put another expired can in the bin.

"And then there's Merrion..."

"I know."

"You know?"

"Well, you know how things spread. Stephen told Laurence who of course told me."

Maggie sighed.

"About Gordon? Or the Niqabis?"

"Um... Both."

"Both."

Maggie picked up a jar of cherry preserves. Squinted at the date. Reached for the magnifier.

"Well, there's one thing you don't know. Because Stephen doesn't."

"Oh?"

"But you have to promise not to say a word. Not even to Laurence."

"Cross my heart and kiss my elbow."

Maggie put the jar of preserves with the other jams. Then she told Anne about "Gordon's Girls."

"Maggie, that's horrible. Disgusting. And why haven't you told Stephen?"

"Because if Gordon's convicted for murder, it won't matter. If he's not, then I'll tell Stephen. Poor Stephen has enough problems without adding this to them."

"At least Deirdre didn't know."

"Yes."

Maggie thought about Deirdre's last moments and felt like crying. Again. Anne noticed.

"Maggie?"

"I blame myself. About Deirdre. I should have done something. I should have intervened when I heard Gordon yelling at her."

"Maggie..."

"I just stood there and listened. Like some old village snoop peeking out from behind a curtain."

"Maggie, it wasn't your fault. It's the fault of whoever pushed her."

"I know. That's what I tell myself. But it doesn't seem to help."

Maggie sighed.

Anne changed the subject.

"What's happening with your stalking problem?"

"The Niqabis? Well, on Wednesday night, things got a little out of hand."

"A little? Stephen told Laurence they were trying to throw you onto their bonfire."

"Um, yes. That was a new development. Normally they just follow me."

Maggie tossed a half-used box of bulgur with a sell by date of 2010 in the bin.

"When I got back from London Thursday I found the Vice Chancellor, the Thames Valley Chief Constable, Thomas and Stephen in the drawing room. I felt like I had accidentally walked into Brooks. Or Boodles. Did you know Thomas and the Vice-Chancellor were at Balliol together?

"Anyway, I hadn't told Thomas about the incident on Wednesday. But then there was the pig's head on the doorstep. Did Stephen tell Laurence about that? The Royces called Thomas and he immediately drove up from Beaumatin. And called Stephen, who told him about the bonfire near-miss. Thomas was furious. And is being over-protective. I had to beg for permission to come and see you today. And it's been decided to turn the matter over to the police and not rely on campus security."

"Good decision." Anne decided not to comment about Thomas.

"Yes. Except I'm not sure how they'll find out who're under the niqabs. Can you imagine what would happen if the police stopped someone in the street and demanded she take off her veil and it turned out it was just some poor innocent immigrant? You can imagine the headlines."

"Oh dear. Yes, I can."

"But the Niqabis? They're not just women. There are men under those niqabs as well. Poor Stephen is loath to speak to Faisal. But my gut says he's somehow involved. As it only started after he arrived and it's not as though my opinions hadn't been known before he came."

The women worked contentedly until lunchtime. Anne fixed chicken salad to go with her homemade bread and Laurence ventured out of his study to join them.

After lunch, Anne cleaned the empty cupboards while Maggie sorted the jars and boxes and bottles into "likes."

Suddenly Maggie said, "About Deirdre. It wasn't just the terrible things Ross said. Or standing right there when she fell. But she'd been to the obstetrician that morning. Her doctor had done a sonogram. Deirdre showed the picture to Chitta and me. The head. The heart. She was so happy. And she died with the picture clutched in her hand. The little baby. I keep seeing it..."

Maggie began to cry.

"Maggie!" Anne climbed down and hugged her friend.

"I don't know what's wrong with me. I just can't stop remembering. Do you think it's because I never had a child? That it's caught up with me? Or do I just need to adjust my HRT?"

"I think Deirdre's death was very traumatic for you. And the sonogram picture. I hadn't known. It wasn't mentioned. How terrible."

Maggie wiped her eyes and sniffed.

"Come sit down. The kitchen can wait."

Anne pushed Maggie into a chair. She went to the refrigerator, got out a bottle of Pouilly fuissé and took two glasses from a cupboard. She came back to the table and poured them each a drink.

"And it seems everyone I know is pregnant. Well, not you of course. But Chitta. And Gweneth and Chloe and Constance. And now Victoria. Constance called me 'a barren bitch.' Is that what I am?"

"No. Of course not. We've talked about this."

Maggie thought.

"You're probably right. About it being traumatic for me when Deirdre... And I've been under-estimating the impact."

"Yes. And if it's babies you want, enjoy the grandchildren. All of the pleasure and none of the bother."

"But I'm not really their grandmother..."

"Of course you are! Harry and Elizabeth and—is it John and Thomas? —don't care about genetics. If Thomas is their grandfather, then you are certainly their grandmother. And fulfil this role for them in their lives. It will be a loss for both sides if you don't, er, step up to the plate."

Maggie considered this.

"I quite envy you. I wish my sprogs would settle down and reproduce. Although perhaps not Edward and his current girlfriend. Caitlin, the Pilates instructor."

Maggie laughed.

"You are absolutely right as always, Anne. Now may I put things back on those top shelves for you?"

Susan Alexander

Chapter 38

Maggie had had a productive day in her rooms at Merrion and was preparing to leave. Thomas was driving up from Beaumatin and said he would pick her up.

Her mobile sounded. It was Thomas. He sounded grumpy.

"I'm stuck in traffic. I'm not sure when I'll get to Oxford."

"I'm sorry, Thomas. But don't worry. I can walk to Hereford Crescent. It's still quite light and if I see any Niqabis, I'll call the police."

The morning after the meeting at Hereford Crescent, the Chief Constable had given Maggie and Thomas a direct line to call if she were being stalked.

She could sense Thomas fuming.

Finally he said, "All right. But stay alert. And be careful."

"I will, Thomas."

Maggie sighed.

On her way out, she saw Faisal bin Abdulaziz, who was also leaving for the day.

"Hello, Faisal. Are you on your way back to Hereford Crescent?" she asked pleasantly.

"Yes," he admitted.

"May I accompany you? Thomas was supposed to meet me but he is tied up in traffic and is worried about my walking alone. Given what's been happening."

Faisal hesitated.

"I assume Thomas told you about what's been happening?"

Maggie was feeling mischievous and enjoyed putting Faisal in a bind.

"Yes. Unfortunate," he finally conceded.

"Thank you," she said as though he had agreed to escort her and smiled warmly.

They went past the Porter's Lodge, through the gate and turned in the direction of Hereford Crescent.

"How are you finding Oxford?" Maggie asked politely.

Faisal glanced at her and decided the question was sincere.

They discussed the University, how much it differed from the US and how much it was the same. As they were nearing Hereford Crescent, Maggie said, "I would like to invite your wives to tea some afternoon. With some of the other Merrion women. Chitta. Eunice. Anne Brooks and Claire Kittredge. There would only be women present. It must be difficult to be in a foreign country and not know anyone. And it is a fairly normal thing to do for newcomers to the Merrion community. Anne Brooks organised a tea for me when I first arrived."

Faisal's lack of enthusiasm was obvious.

"They only speak Arabic."

"I would ask some female students to act as translators."

"Let me see. Aliyah in particular is… shy."

"Of course."

They had reached Hereford Crescent. Suddenly Faisal stopped short. Stiffened. Maggie followed his stare.

Oh dear.

There were graffiti in bright red paint scrawled across the deep blue front door and on the stonework around the entrance. And on the steps. Maggie thought it looked like Arabic.

"Oh no. Thomas is not going to be happy. Can you tell what it says?" she asked.

"Yes. But they are not words I can say to a woman."

"Oh."

Maggie's mobile sounded. It was Thomas.

"Thomas?"

He had reached Oxford. Where was she?

"I'm with Faisal. At Hereford Crescent. And… There's…. I'm afraid someone's sprayed graffiti on the front of the house. In Arabic."

Silence.

"I could ask Faisal if he would wait."

"Do that."

Thomas ended the call.

"That was Thomas. He will be here shortly and he asked if you wouldn't mind waiting until he arrives."

Faisal frowned.

Finally he said, "Of course. I will need to call…"

"Of course. Please come in."

Maggie got out her key. Fortunately the paint had missed the lock.

Inside, she led Faisal to the library.

"Would you like some coffee? Tea? Whisky?"

Faisal hesitated.

"I'm sure Thomas will have some Laphroaig as soon as he arrives and sees…"

Faisal nodded.

"Please make your call. I'll be right back."

Maggie was returning with a bottle of whisky when Thomas came in. He made an angry gesture when he saw her.

"Faisal is here. He's in the library," she said quickly.

"Faisal's here?"

"Yes. I told you we were walking back from Merrion together and discovered the graffiti. It's Arabic. Faisal says he knows what it means."

"Humpf."

Maggie thrust the bottle at him.

"Take this in. You know where the glasses are."

"Have you called anyone?"

"No. I thought I'd leave that to you."

Maggie picked up her briefcase and went upstairs to her study. She unpacked her laptop. Plugged it in. Sighed.

The murders. The harassment. And now the vandalism. Thomas understandably upset.

Her mobile made the sound it did when she had received a text message.

She checked.

It was from Gina. The message was succinct.

"I have found Fiona."

Susan Alexander

Chapter 39

Maggie woke up. Something was making a noise. On the table beside her. Her mobile was sounding an alarm.

It was way too early. She really needed more sleep. But she switched off the alarm and resigned herself to getting up. To become fully functional, she would need a massive infusion of caffeine.

Thomas, who needed less sleep than she did, was already awake. When she began to disentangle herself from his arms, and legs, he tightened his hold.

"Don't go."

"Thomas, I have an appointment. If I don't get up right away, I'll be late."

He pulled her to him.

"I am the Right Honourable Thomas Hugh Alardyce Baron Raynham and I say, let them wait," he said and punctuated his words with kisses.

"Thomas!"

"Shh."

Maggie decided it was futile trying to argue with eight hundred years of baronial prerogative.

Later, after a frantic shower, Maggie scrambled into a white blouse and a navy pants suit. She was hurtling down Beaumatin's grand staircase while she pulled on her jacket.

Thomas, who was himself only half dressed in a white shirt, tweed pants and braces, was in pursuit.

"Maggie, slow down. You'll fall and kill yourself."

Thomas' older brother Charles had fallen down the same staircase one night when he was drunk and broken his neck. It was how Thomas had inherited the title.

"I'm late!" she called and gave an undignified whoop as she skidded around the corner of the landing and continued her hurried descent.

Thomas caught up with his wife by expertly sliding down the bannister. They reached the bottom together.

"I haven't done that since I was a boy," Thomas admitted.

"You forgot your hairclip," he added and handed it to her.

Mrs Cook and another woman were standing in the hall, open-mouthed.

"Oh. Gina. I'm so sorry. I'm running late, I'm afraid."

Maggie became aware that Thomas was waiting expectantly and realised that he had never met Gina. And had no knowledge of their efforts on Ross' behalf. And that, if he knew, he would certainly order her to stop. Which, of course, she wouldn't.

Oh dear.

"Hi. Gina. This is, er, my husband, Lord Raynham. Um, Thomas. Thomas, this is Gina Burke. She's a... research assistant."

Gina looked professional in a burgundy pantsuit and man-tailored blouse. She gave Maggie a quizzical look, but did not contradict her.

Hands were shaken.

"Before we go, I need some coffee. Gina, have you had breakfast?" Maggie asked.

"Yes, but some tea..."

"Of course."

"And I must finish dressing," said Thomas. He went back upstairs.

Maggie and Gina followed Mrs Cook back to the kitchen. Maggie noticed Gina was looking at the great hall and its ancestral portrait gallery with a strange expression on her face.

Gina had tea, Maggie consumed two mugs of coffee and both women succumbed to Mrs Cook's freshly-baked scones.

"I'm sorry, Gina. I'm afraid we're going to be very late."

"That's all right. I left the time a bit vague."

Maggie was relieved.

Back in the hall, they met Thomas. He had finished dressing and had on a waxed Barbour jacket and green Wellies over his tweeds. He held a cap in one hand.

Maggie watched Gina look at Thomas and tried to see him through her eyes. She knew her view of Thomas was coloured by how besotted she was about the man. She was also aware that, as an American, she had little of the baggage about social class that so many British people seemed to have.

"So you're off?" Thomas asked.

"Yes. To Birmingham."

"Birmingham?"

Thomas was surprised. It was clearly not the answer he had been expecting.

"Yes. Um…" Maggie glanced at Gina nervously, in the knowledge that she was about to tell Thomas what she had heard called a major "porky." She hoped the woman would not give her away.

"It's for a research project. We need to meet with some social service agencies about having some of their clients complete a questionnaire we developed. I expect it to be a completely Niqabi-free expedition. And to be back here late in the afternoon."

Thomas nodded. He walked them out to Gina's car. Gina had said she knew the route and had volunteered to drive.

Maggie again noticed Gina stare at Thomas, who was standing on the front steps of the great house beneath the Raynham coat of arms and its motto. Numquam cede. Never yield. She thought that Thomas was looking very twenty-eighth baron, which made her stomach flutter the way it often did when she looked at Thomas. But she also was aware that he might have quite a different effect on Gina.

As Gina drove down the drive and out onto the single track lane that went past Beaumatin, Maggie noted that her companion seemed to be in a bad mood.

"Gina?"

Stony-faced, Gina remained silent.

"Gina, is something wrong?"

Gina stopped at a pullover on the side of the road that allowed cars to pass.

"I can't figure you out."

"What do you mean?"

"I thought I had you pegged. And I'm good at pegging people. It's a skill you need to have in my business. And I had you down as a more or less regular person, not some posho. But that monument to privilege you call home? And your husband who, if you'll excuse me, is such a complete toff. He made me feel like I was something that had gotten stuck in the cleats of his Wellies."

"Gina, I was there and that's simply not true. If you're supposed to be so good at pegging people, oughtn't you to consider that Thomas is simply reserved? And tends to be reticent with people he does not know? He was the same with you as when he met the former Master of my college. And his wife, who is the daughter of an earl."

"He didn't seem to be so reserved when he was chasing you down the stairs," Gina pointed out.

"Oh. That. Well…"

Maggie flushed.

"Neither of us realised that anyone was there," she said finally.

"And as for being a regular person, whatever you mean by that, I am. Just a person. And I hope I treat everyone with equal respect whether he's a duke or a ditch digger. Not that I've ever met a duke. No, I guess I did meet one. Once. But it was only very briefly. And I was terrified that I'd fall over and make a spectacle of myself when I tried to curtsey."

Gina thought about this.

"So you already had a successful career. Why'd you marry the baron? You wanted another title? A better address?"

"No!"

Maggie briefly wondered why she felt she needed to explain herself to this woman. But continued anyway.

"I won't deny I knew who Thomas was when we met. He was standing on the front steps of Beaumatin. Looking very... Well, I call it very twenty-eighth baron. And I won't deny the title and the estate are an integral part of his identity. It was not as though we bumped into each other at the sock counter at Selfridge's and I had no idea who he was until after we had developed a relationship.

"But I married him... well, for the reasons most people get married, I suppose. And I try to avoid using my title, the Lady Raynham one, as much as possible except when it's necessary. As for the estate... Well, you saw the place. It's like living in a museum. We've been married almost a year and I'm not sure I'll ever feel really comfortable at Beaumatin or think of it as home. But it is Thomas' home and it's not like he can move someplace that would feel cosier.

"Anyway, I'm sorry I had to, um, dissemble about who you are and what we're doing and I appreciate your not contradicting me. Thomas... Well he can be very, um, Victorian and try to dictate...

"But if the prevaricating and Thomas and the whole aristo thing has put you off. If you feel you don't want to continue. Well, I'll understand. Although I would appreciate it if you could at least stick it out until we've seen Fiona."

Gina scowled. Reached a decision.

"Right. We'll go see Fiona. Then I'll see."

"Thank you, Gina."

Gina drove rapidly and expertly towards their destination. However, as they reached the outskirts of the city, she slowed to just above the speed limit. Maggie noticed.

"Do you need help with directions? Is there anything I should look for?" she asked.

"No."

Gina was abrupt.

Finally she said, "Since we're being all self-revelatory... I'm from Birmingham. My family still lives here. But we haven't spoken for more than a decade."

"I'm sorry. That must be hard."

Maggie wanted to ask why but did not want to be intrusive.

"You toffs. You want to know why, but are too polite to ask," Gina said perceptively.

"OK. So I had done some O levels. I just scraped by. I was the middle child. I had an older sister and a younger brother. In my family, no one went to university. Everyone worked. It didn't matter much at what. If you were a girl you worked until you got married and had kids. My dad worked as a delivery man for an express mail company and my mother helped out part time at a local news agent. My sister worked as a manicurist and was dating some bloke. My brother was still at school. I don't know what's become of him.

"I got a job at the local pub. I already suspected…"

She glanced at Maggie.

"That I was a lesbian," she continued defiantly and waited for Maggie's reaction.

When none came she continued.

"Although back then I really didn't know that I was… gay. I only knew that I didn't much like guys and I had these feelings for one of the girls in my class. Her name was Lizzie. We weren't exactly friends. She was someone I knew casually. Anyhow, one night Lizzie and some of her friends were at the pub. I went out to have a smoke and she followed me and before I knew what was happening, she kissed me. Full on the lips. Real passionate. And I… Like an idiot I responded. I thought she meant it. Wishful thinking. Her friends had snuck out and were watching and it turned out they'd made a bet that if Lizzie kissed me, I would kiss her back.

"The next morning my mum heard about it at the news agent's. My dad came home from work early. Both of them were yelling. They called me names. Told me to get out. So I did."

"I'm so sorry, Gina. I can't imagine…"

"Yeah. Well…" Gina cut Maggie off. She exited the motorway and began to navigate through a commercial area of the city.

"Anyhow, I emptied my bank account and caught the next train to London. I'd never been to London. I slept rough a few nights but then I got lucky and met a woman, Barbara, who took me in, introduced me around. She helped me find a job as a dogsbody for a detective who had an office in Soho.

His name was Joe. Joe Bishop. He took a liking to me and taught me the trade. You don't need a license although I've heard they may begin requiring one in a couple of years.

"When he retired, he left me the business. His wife had died, he had no children, and he said he had more money than he needed. He died last year."

Gina paused to enter some coordinates into her GPS.

"So in the end, Lizzie did me a favour. I have a career, a partner I love, a life I enjoy. While Lizzie has probably gained five stone, has four screaming, squabbling kids and a husband who spends his evenings at the pub."

"And your family?"

"Someday I may try to contact my sister. Find out if she thinks my parents would like to see me. If not..." Gina shrugged.

Susan Alexander

Chapter 40

City Taxi was a large garage in an unprepossessing neighbourhood of warehouses and auto repair shops and a storage locker facility.

"This is the address she gave," Gina said.

"Is she still Fiona Ross?" Maggie asked.

"No. She's now Fiona Banks. I assume she remarried."

They entered the garage and stood looking around in the gloom. At least a dozen taxis were parked inside and a couple of men were working on one of the cabs, vacuuming out the interior and washing the windows. A radio blared Kylie Minogue.

One of the men turned and saw the women.

"Help you, love?" he asked.

"We're looking for Fiona Banks."

"In the office in the back." He jerked his head to the rear, then continued to vacuum.

The women headed towards a glass-enclosed office. It was divided into two rooms. The first one was the dispatcher's and had a telephone switchboard and a computer. A young Asian man sat at the desk and took calls. The inner room was an office with a metal desk cluttered with papers and filing cabinets and a large white board that had a grid with names and shifts noted in thick black marker.

Behind the desk sat a woman in her forties. Fiona Banks was plump and wore a light blue knit pants suit that emphasized heavy breasts and a thick waist. She was a bleached blonde with a hard, lined face. Maggie thought that the ashtray overflowing with cigarette butts might explain the wrinkles.

"Mrs Banks?" Gina asked.

The woman stubbed out one cigarette and lit another.

"Yes. You're that woman who called?"

"Yes. I'm Gina Burke. And this is…"

"Maggie Eliot," Maggie cut her off before Gina could use her title.

"We're here about your ex-husband. Gordon Ross. And the murders. Do you know about the murders at Oxford? And Ross' arrest?"

Fiona nodded as she stubbed out a cigarette and lit another.

"So why does this have anything to do with me? I haven't had any contact with that rat bastard in fifteen, sixteen years."

"I understand. But we're speaking with everyone who knew him. Who might be able to provide some… insight. Gordon claims he's innocent, you see."

"Of course he would. He may be a wanker, but he's not an idiot," Fiona snorted.

"Yes, but if he is innocent of the murders, we don't want the person who really is guilty to avoid justice," Maggie explained.

"All right. So what can I tell you?" Fiona asked grudgingly.

"How did you meet Gordon?"

"I was working as a waitress at a tea shop near the university. In Glasgow. Gordon used to come in between classes. He was old for a student. In his mid-twenties. He'd had to work and save. He was the first person in his family to go to university, he told me.

"He'd come in and order a cup of tea and then had me refill the cup with hot water two or three times using the same teabag. It was obvious he didn't have a bean. But we got friendly. I was still pretty back then. He said he'd like to ask me out but he couldn't afford it. So one day I invited him for a pint. I should have known. But I didn't. I was young. Naive.

"I got a better job as a waitress at a pub. I would take leftovers for Gordon. After a couple of months, we moved into a bedsit together. I was supporting us both by then. Gordon proposed.

"We got married. Gordon had started his doctorate. I was still working, sometimes double shifts. Then I got pregnant. Gordon was furious but I insisted. I wanted a baby. And Gordon needed the money I was earning.

"I had hoped that once the baby was born, Gordon would change his mind. How can someone not love his own child? But Gordon..." Fiona shook her head.

"The baby was a boy and we named him Hamish. With three of us to support I had to work even harder. I would come home and find the baby crying. He hadn't been fed or had his diaper changed. Gordon called Hamish 'the little pissant' and complained he was interfering with his work. I started leaving Hamish with my mother."

Fiona lit another cigarette.

"The day Gordon got his doctorate, he told me he wanted a divorce. He packed up his stuff and left. Hamish was nearly four. I thought about moving back home, but my mother had never liked Gordon. She kept on saying 'I told you so' and I didn't need the aggro.

"My sister Susan had married a copper and they were living in Birmingham. She'd had a kid of her own by then and she suggested I come live with them. She could take care of Hamish while I looked for work.

"It took me six weeks. I didn't want a job in another pub. I didn't see any future in that. I applied to be a shop assistant and a grocery checkout lady, but they only wanted people with experience. Then I saw an ad for a taxi dispatcher. I figured, 'What the hell.' And asked for an interview.

"I guess George must have seen something in me. Anyhow, even though I knew damn all about dispatching, he said he'd give me a chance. I had a week to show him I could do the job.

"I'm not sure why I decided I wanted that job. The pay wasn't that great and you spend all day sitting on your ass at a desk and answering the phone. But I worked my butt off and, at the end of the week, George decided I could stay. He found out about Hamish and tried to..."

The phone on her desk buzzed.

"Excuse me."

"Sadiq? Let me check."

Fiona consulted the white board.

"Four to midnight. That's right. OK. Sure. Ta."

Fiona continued.

278

"I don't know why I'm boring you with all this. Anyhow, to make a long story short, George and I, we found out we made a good team. After six months, he proposed. He was also divorced. His wife had run off with one of his drivers. I accepted. Not because I was head-over-heels. I don't think George was either. It was more of a partnership. But I knew what I was getting. George was a hard man. But fair. And honest. He wasn't a user, like Ross. And he adopted Hamish. He had no kids of his own."

Fiona lit another cigarette and inhaled deeply.

"He died two years ago. Heart attack."

Fiona glanced at her cigarette.

"Chain smoker. I know I should quit, but…"

She shrugged.

"And what about Hamish?" Maggie asked.

"My boy? He inherited his father's brains. But fortunately not his character. He's at university. Got a scholarship. George encouraged him to study."

"Oh. You must be very proud. Where is he?"

"At Oxford."

"Oxford?"

Maggie and Gina exchanged glances.

"Um, Mrs Banks? Which college is he attending?"

"College? Uh. It's an unusual name. It reminds me of Robin Hood. Is it Tuck, like Friar Tuck? Or maybe Nottingham, like the Sheriff? Or…"

Maggie had an intuitive flash.

"Maid Marion?" she asked.

"Yes. That's it. Marion."

"Are you sure you don't mean Merrion?"

"Yeah. Like I said. Marion."

Before Maggie could say more, the phone buzzed again.

"'Lo? Who? Oh yeah? Bloody hell. Where? You're kidding. Hang on."

She waved a cigarette at the women.

"Sorry. Cab had an accident. This is going to take a while. Is there anything else?"

"If we have any questions, we'll be in touch."

"Right. Too bad they don't hang people anymore. That rat bastard... Yeah? Go on."

Maggie and Gina left.

Chapter 41

Maggie returned to Beaumatin in time to join Thomas for a cocktail before dinner. On the way, Maggie told Gina she had decided it was time to meet with Stephen Draycott and inform him about the results of their investigation.

"I don't feel like I should talk to Hamish on my own. Without, um, authorization. And I'll probably need to have Stephen present. He's the Master, the head of the college," Maggie added for clarification.

"I know what a master is," replied Gina shortly.

"Oh. Sorry. Anyway, would you like to come?"

Gina thought.

"You'll tell him about Gordon's Girls?"

"Yes."

"All right. I want to see this through. Even though…"

"I understand. And thank you."

"How was Birmingham?" Thomas asked.

"A bit grim. The parts we were in. They were not especially pleasant. Or attractive. Garages and metalwork shops. Housing estates. I assume there are nicer areas. Are there?"

"I've never been," Thomas admitted.

"Never been to Birmingham? But it's so close."

Thomas shrugged.

"I've been to Carlisle. Hadrian's Wall. And Portsmouth, On my way to the Isle of Wight. Some college chums were sailing at Cowes."

"Manchester?"

"No. But Cambridge. To visit some friends from Eton."

Maggie waited while Thomas tried to remember other places he'd been.

"Scotland. The highlands. With my father and Charles. For the shooting. And fishing."

Maggie shook her head.

Mrs Cook had gone to visit a cousin who lived in Cheltenham but had left dinner. A lamb stew with carrots, peas and potatoes. And Maggie saw a crumble of some sort on the sideboard. With a bowl of custard sauce.

As Thomas pulled out her chair for her, he remarked, "When my grandfather was young, a footman would have performed this courtesy for you. And served you dinner, which would have been four or five courses."

"And you would have dressed for dinner. And the ladies would have retired to leave the gentlemen to their port," Maggie added.

"Yes. My grandfather said there were three footmen. And four housemaids. He had a valet and my grandmother had a ladies' maid. Plus a cook, a kitchen maid, a housekeeper and a butler."

Of course a butler, Maggie thought.

"My grandfather's butler was a Mr Butterworth. Which you'd think would be someone who was plump and jolly. But he was tall and thin. Dark. Dour. Never smiled."

"You mentioned your father also had a butler."

"Yes. Old Oakes. He had started out as a footman with my grandfather. Worked his way up. Of course by my father's time, the footmen had gone. And most of the rest of the domestic staff."

"And people had stopped dressing for dinner."

"Yes. Except for special occasions. And, of course, at Oxford."

Maggie admired Thomas' perfectly tailored tweed suit, his pristine white shirt, his cuffs with gold cufflinks engraved with the Raynham coat of arms and the white handkerchief in his breast pocket.

"Well, much as I admire you in a tuxedo, I think you look perfectly splendid just as you are. That's the Raynham tweed, isn't it?" Maggie asked.

The Raynham tweed was a pattern designed by Thomas' great grandfather, the twenty-fifth baron, and only the current baron and his heir were permitted to wear it.

Thomas glanced at his sleeve.

"Yes."

He finished a final forkful of stew and stood.

"Some crumble? Mrs Cook…" Maggie began.

"No, thank you."

"David Attenborough?"

"No."

He ran an index finger down her cheek and Maggie flushed.

"If you're thinking of playing the footman and the housemaid, I'm afraid my wardrobe…" she began.

Thomas' mouth twitched.

"No."

"So?"

He pulled out her chair and took her arm

"I am going to enjoy letting you wonder about that. Come."

Chapter 42

Maggie had called Mrs Steeples and gotten an appointment to see Stephen at eleven o'clock about "an urgent private matter." Gina was going to meet Maggie in her rooms and they would go to see Stephen in the Master's Lodge together.

However, just before eleven, Maggie received a text from Mrs Steeples explaining that the Master was tied up. Could she come at two-thirty instead?

"Oh dear. Gina, can you stay?"

"Yes. As long as I'm back in London by tonight. I want to see what happens when he finds out about Gordon's Girls."

Maggie realised that Gina was still not convinced that the college would do anything about Ross' misconduct.

"Fine. In the meantime, I find I'm quite hungry. May I invite you to lunch?"

"All right."

Gina paused, then added, "Thanks."

Maggie took Gina to a nearby Indian restaurant. They were seated at a table by a window and Gina was telling Maggie about one of her cases when Maggie suddenly stiffened and said, "Oh dear."

"What's the matter?"

"It's… No, I'm only being… No, I'm not. It's…"

"Maggie, what is it?"

"Do you see those two women across the street? Wearing niqabs?"

Gina peered out the window.

"Yes. What about them?"

So Maggie explained about the Niqabis. And the stalking. And the book burnings. And the vandalism at Hereford Crescent. And the so-far fruitless attempt to discover who was involved in the harassment. And who was behind it.

Gina was irate.

"All this because of a book you wrote?"

"I tell myself I'm fortunate some mullah didn't issue a fatwa."

Gina scowled.

"All right. We'll see what happens when we leave."

Maggie paid the bill. Checked the street.

"I don't see them now. Maybe they gave up and went to their respective tutorials."

"Or maybe they're waiting out of sight. If they are, follow my lead and I'll see if we can't nab one of them."

"Are you sure…"

"Trust me. It could even be fun."

"Fun?"

"I've got some moves I want to try."

The women left the restaurant. They had not gotten ten steps from the door when Maggie turned and there were the Niqabis. Six of them.

All right, Eliot. Keep cool, she told herself

"They're behind us," she murmured to Gina.

"How many?"

"Six, I think."

"So here we go. Just make sure you keep up."

Gina began to walk at an increasingly fast pace. Without warning she pulled Maggie into an alley and waited out of sight in a doorway. They heard cries, then hurrying footsteps.

Gina thrust out a leg and tripped a niqab-shrouded figure, then used it again to sweep the legs out from under a second Niqabi, who fell on her back with a thud.

"Uh."

Not her back. His back. The voice was a masculine baritone.

The remaining Niqabis halted abruptly. Hesitated.

"You want some? You feeling lucky?" Gina snarled.

The Niqabi quartet turned and fled.

Maggie yanked the veil off of the first Niqabi. It was a young woman. Asian. Maggie thought she had seen her coming out of Chitta's rooms once or twice.

The girl was crying.

Gina knelt on the back of the Niqabi she had downed and pulled off his niqab. It was a young man. Also Asian.

"Get off me."

"Maggie, take their pictures," Gina ordered.

Maggie had already pulled out her mobile. She took photos of each, then called the special police number she had been given.

In what felt like to Maggie a very long time but was in fact less than five minutes, a police constable and a sergeant appeared.

"Lady Raynham?" asked the sergeant.

"Yes."

"You got two of your stalkers?"

"Yes. Here they are."

"And this is?" asked the sergeant, looking at Gina while the constable put handcuffs on the pair. The girl was still sobbing.

"Gina Burke. I'm a private investigator. I was assisting Lady Raynham on another matter when these two and four others threatened her. I was able to intervene."

"Hm. Well, we'll need a statement from you, Lady Raynham. And you too, Miss Burke. And we'll see about identifying these two. And what other information we might be able to get out of them."

"Thank you, Sergeant. However, Miss Burke and I are on our way to an important appointment with the Master of Merrion College. Would it be possible for us to give our statements after that?"

The sergeant thought.

"All right. These two'll keep. But as soon as possible, please. Here's my card."

"As soon as possible," the women assured him.

Maggie and Gina reached the Master's Lodge just in time.

Maggie introduced Gina to Mrs Steeples and explained that Gina also needed to be present at her meeting with the Master.

Mrs Steeples graciously indicated that they could enter Stephen's office.

Stephen was looking harassed.

"Tough day?" Maggie asked.

"You have no idea."

"I'm sorry. And I'm afraid it's not about to get better. But first let me introduce you to Gina Burke."

Hands were shaken.

"Sit down. Would you like some coffee? Tea?"

The women declined.

"So Mrs Steeples said this was urgent?"

"Yes. And there have been developments on the Niqabi front as well."

Maggie told Stephen about their capturing two of the Niqabis.

"The police have them in custody, I guess is the term. There was a man and a young woman. She looked vaguely familiar. I assume the police will find out just who they are. But meanwhile, I guess we should tell you why we asked to see you."

Maggie explained about Gordon's desperate request. And her enlisting Gina to help track down people who might have reasons to hate her colleague.

"I am assuming that Alastair drank the sherry with the cyanide by mistake. That it was meant either for Ross or for Deirdre although, like Alastair, there doesn't seem to be any reason why someone would want to kill Deirdre. Unless it was because of her relationship with Ross.

"So we were able to eliminate Ross' former colleagues from Glasgow. And Mrs Ross Number One and Mrs Ross Number Two. Neither were anywhere near Oxford. But in the course of our investigations, well, this is what is not going to make you happy, Stephen. We found out about 'Gordon's Girls.'"

"Gordon's Girls?"

"Yes. Apparently Gordon was swapping references and fellowships for, er, sex."

Stephen buried his face in his hands. Finally he looked up and managed, "Please tell me you don't mean…"

"I'm sorry Stephen. But Chitta found one of Gordon's doctoral students banging on his door after he'd been arrested and the whole sorry story came out. And it wasn't just Megan Thompson. There are seven other women we've found. Some are no longer at Merrion. And while none seem particularly eager to bring charges against Gordon or the college, that doesn't mean they mightn't feel vengeful."

"I'll need to tell the Vice Chancellor. And Merrion's legal counsel. And you say you know the names of the women Gordon... I can't believe Gordon would... He must have known... And he had Deirdre..."

"Yes. Who also, if you think about it, was a Gordon's Girl herself."

Stephen struggled to pull himself together.

"Right. Sorry. Did you say you could give me their names? And some contact information?"

Gina took out a list she had prepared and handed it to Stephen.

"And if you could let me know what's happening about this? I know Gina is convinced that this will all be swept under the carpet. That there won't be any real consequences for Gordon. Or that Gordon won't just get a position at another university and do the same thing all over again. And I know Chitta is also concerned."

"Let me assure you. Even if Ross isn't convicted of murder, you can be certain the man will never be able to get another academic position again,"

"Good. Which reminds me. It's about our last lead, if you will. Gordon has a son. Hamish Ross. His mother, Mrs Ross Number One, told us he's actually a student at Merrion. An undergraduate. Do you know him?"

"Hamish Ross? Can't say it rings any bells. Let me check."

Stephen rummaged through some folders, found the one he was looking for and opened it. He scanned some lists.

"No. No Hamish Ross. Are you sure he's at Merrion?"

"Well, his mother was certain he was at Oxford. She was less sure about which college. She remembered the name reminded her of someone from Robin Hood and we guessed Merrion because of Maid Marion. But I suppose it could be another college. St John's? Isn't Prince John in the story?"

Stephen shook his head.

"I'll have Mrs Steeples check the University enrolments."

"Yes. And then... Well, we didn't want to talk to Hamish without going through the proper channels. Given the sensitivities of the Zeitgeist. Which is why we came to you. As well as because of all this other stuff," Maggie explained.

"Mrs Banks, that's his mother, who was Mrs Ross Number One. She remarried. She said he had gotten a scholarship. Perhaps that will make it easier to track him down."

"If he's at Oxford, we'll find him," Stephen promised.

"Thank you, Stephen. While we like to call Ross pond scum, I want to be sure the right person gets punished for the deaths of Alastair and Deirdre."

"As do I."

They all stood.

"You'll let us know about young Master Ross?"

"Just as soon as I hear anything," Stephen assured her.

As the women walked back towards the quad, Maggie asked, "So I hope you felt that Stephen is not going to let the Gordon's Girls issue rest."

"No. You were right. He did seem outraged."

"Yes, he did."

The porter spied Maggie and signalled to her.

"Professor Eliot, you have a visitor. It's the Assistant Chief Constable. A Mr Rawlins."

Maggie glanced at Gina.

"Thank you."

Mr Rawlins was around forty, stocky and of medium height.

"Lady Raynham, the Chief Constable asked that I come and take your statement."

Maggie glanced at Gina.

"Mr Rawlins, this is Gina Burke. She was with me when we had the encounter with the Niqabis."

Hands were shaken.

"Please sit down. Would you like some coffee or tea?"

"No, thank you."

So Maggie told Rawlins about seeing the Niqabis while she and Gina were eating lunch. And being followed by the pack when they left the restaurant. And dashing around the corner and managing to catch two of them.

"Have you been able to identify either of the pair that were taken into custody?" Maggie asked.

"Yes. They were carrying ID."

Rawlins took a small notebook out of a jacket pocket and consulted some notes.

"The boy is Asim Jamali. A British subject. He works at Blackwell's bookstore. Accepting deliveries and seeing the shelves are stocked. He was also stealing the copies of your books that the group was burning."

Maggie wondered if the stolen volumes would still count towards her book sales.

"The girl is named Lina Armouti. From Jordan. And one of yours. Here. At Merrion."

"I thought I recognized her. I believe Professor Kazi, whose rooms are above mine, is her tutor."

"Miss Burke, do you have anything to add to what Lady Raynham has told us?"

"No. Except I assume you will review any CCTV footage from the area. That should confirm what we've told you."

"We have men working on it as we speak."

"And have Jamali and, er, Armouti told you anything? Like who is behind the stalking? And the book burnings? And the vandalism?" Maggie asked.

"No. All they've done is demand solicitors."

"I see."

They all shook hands and Rawlins left.

Chapter 43

Mrs Steeples called the next morning.

"Professor Eliot? The Master asked me to call and inform you that we checked and there is no student named Hamish Ross at Merrion. Or at Oxford. Neither at present nor in the past three years."

"Really? Well, thank you."

"Also, the Master asked if you can attend a meeting this afternoon at four o'clock. About the Jordanian girl."

"Four o'clock? All right."

"Professor Kazi will be there as well, as she is Lina Armouti's tutor."

Mrs Steeples ended the call. Maggie sighed and remembered a saying of her mother's. "It never rains but it pours." Bin Abdulaziz. Ross. The Niqabis. Armouti. And now Hamish. Did Fiona Banks really not know where her son was studying? Could she have meant Cambridge?

Maggie called a colleague with whom she had worked on a research project.

"Bert? It's Maggie Eliot. I wondered if you could do me a favour. Could you check your student register and find out if you have a student at Cambridge named Hamish Ross? He'd be an undergrad."

Professor Hopkins agreed and said he would email Maggie with what he could find out. Two hours later, Maggie received his reply. There was no Hamish Ross at Cambridge either.

Maggie was not prepared to check out other British universities. She reluctantly called a Birmingham number.

"Mrs Banks? It's Maggie Eliot. We met and talked about Gordon? And Hamish?"

"Yes. Yes. Of course I remember. How can I help you?"

She sounded impatient.

"It's about Hamish. You told us he is studying at Oxford. You thought at Merrion College. But we can find no records of a Hamish Ross enrolled here and I wondered…"

Maggie was interrupted by a throaty chuckle that was cut off by a phlegmy coughing spell.

"Sorry. I guess I forgot to tell you. I call him Hamish, but when George adopted the boy he insisted he change his name. Said he wasn't going to raise a son with another man's name. Hamish had just seen Mary Poppins, so he changed it to Michael. Michael Banks. You know? The banker and his son? George and Michael Banks?"

Fiona laughed again, then ended the call.

Maggie stared at her mobile for a moment, then searched in the Merrion directory and there he was. Michael Banks. First year student in PPE. Tutor Andrew Kittredge.

Chapter 44

There was a knock on Maggie's door. It was Chitta.

"Maggie? We've been summoned to the Master's Lodge. Are you coming?"

"Yes."

"Lina Armouti. I can't believe it. She's one of my brightest students. Her father is a Jordanian government minister and her mother is a professor. They're moderates. Well, they sent Lina to Oxford."

"This must be hard for you," Maggie sympathised.

Chitta shook her head.

Mrs Steeples greeted the women.

"Go right in. The Master is waiting. And the girl is here. With an escort."

Lina Armouti was sitting stiffly in a chair in front of Stephen's desk. She was dressed in the same jeans and pullover that she had been wearing when Maggie had removed her niqab the day before. She was pretty, with long dark hair and dark eyes that glared. Two PCs stood watchfully in a corner.

"Professor Eliot. Professor Kazi. Please sit here." Stephen motioned to two chairs positioned beside his desk, facing Armouti.

The women sat. Maggie glanced at Stephen, who made a small grimace, then began, "Miss Armouti. You were caught yesterday as part of a group that was stalking Professor Eliot. There is CCTV footage, photographic evidence and the statements of Professor Eliot and, er," he referred to a paper on his desk, "Miss Burke, so there is no possibility of your denying…"

"I do not deny I was following the infidel," Lina interrupted.

"You should know the University is taking a very strong stand against what you have been doing. The harassment of Professor Eliot. You can be expelled and, since you are a foreign student, your visa can be revoked and you could be sent home," Stephen cautioned.

Lina pressed her lips together.

Stephen continued.

"Perhaps if you would tell us who else is involved, who organised you…"

"I am no traitor!"

Chitta intervened.

"Lina, I don't understand. Would you tell us just why you have been stalking Professor Eliot?"

Lina stood and faced Maggie. The two PCs moved closer.

"Because you blasphemed the Prophet!"

Maggie also stood.

"Blasphemed the prophet? I have never done such a thing."

"Yes you did. In your book."

"My book?"

"Yes."

"But... I made no mention of the Prophet. Or the Quran. Or even Islam. In my book. Did you actually read my book?"

"No."

"Then why do you think..."

"I was told."

"Told by whom?"

"You're trying to trick me. I won't betray... You can't make me. I don't care what you do."

Chitta decided to intervene.

"But Lina, I have read both of Professor Eliot's books. And believe me, there is nothing about the Prophet in either. You have been misled."

"I'm sorry, Professor Kazi, but I don't trust you. You are her friend. And you are not a true believer."

"Lina..." Chitta protested.

"And as for you..."

Lina rushed at Maggie and, before the PCs could restrain her, spit in her face.

"Blasphemer! You should be put to death! Crucified!"

Maggie was stunned by the hatred in the girl's expression. Saliva dripped down her cheek. She fished in a pants pocket, found a tissue and wiped it away.

Stephen tried to hide his shock.

"Very well. Then I'm afraid you must face the consequences," he said quietly.

He nodded to the PCs. One, a woman, put Lina in handcuffs. Each took hold of an arm and they marched her out of the study. The door closed behind them.

"What will happen to her?" Chitta asked. She looked sad.

"I'm not sure. Her visa will certainly be withdrawn and she could be detained until she is deported. I doubt that they will take her to court for a single stalking incident. But they did search her room and they took her laptop. And her phone. I don't know what they may find. Emails. Web links. Text messages on her mobile. They may uncover some information about the Niqabis. Who else is involved. Even who is behind them. But it's out of my hands now. And I'm afraid the authorities will want to make Lina an example."

Chitta sighed.

"She was so bright. Her parents will be devastated."

Chitta glanced at her friend.

"Maggie, are you all right?"

"She really hates me. Because someone lied to her. About what I'd written. Why would someone do that? Who would do that?"

Stephen decided he would pretend the questions were rhetorical rather than mention the elephant in the room.

Chitta did it for him.

"Faisal bin Abdulaziz?" she asked.

Chapter 45

After a nearly sleepless night haunted by visions of Lina Armouti, Maggie was back at her desk at Merrion and attempting to edit the proof of Chitta's and her book.

There was a knock on her door and Gina entered. She was carrying a bulging briefcase and looked pleased with herself.

"Good morning," said Maggie as she rose and went to refill her mug with coffee.

"Coffee? Tea?"

"No, thank you. But wait until you see what I have," said Gina with a grin.

Maggie motioned Gina to sit down at the refectory table and took a place across from her.

"The friend I've been staying with in Summertown? She's a detective sergeant with Thames Valley. She hates Moss. Well, everyone does, according to her. He sucks up to the brass and got promoted to inspector by taking credit for another sergeant's work. Still takes credit for his own sergeant's work. Not that Bixby's any prize, according to Marcy. That's my friend.

"I told her what I was doing. About Ross. And how we haven't had much luck identifying another likely suspect. Not that I'm so anxious to get Ross off the hook. But I agree with you about making sure the right person pays for your murders.

"So she did me a favour. Because she'd like to see Moss with egg on his face. She copied the case files for me. Carrington's and Deirdre Ross'. At least the important bits. I stayed up all night going through them. And there's some interesting stuff here. I wanted you to see it. But this needs to be shredded as soon as possible. Marcy would lose her job if anyone found out we had this stuff."

"Wow. Well done, Gina. And thank you, Marcy. All right. Where do I start?"

"I guess with the most important thing. It's Banks."

"Banks?"

Maggie had texted Gina that Hamish Ross had become Michael Banks. And that he was indeed a Merrion student.

"He was interviewed by the police. Twice. He appears in both Carrington's and Deirdre Ross' files."

"Really? Why?"

"He was part of the catering staff at Carrington's party. According to his interview, he was out of the room washing up glasses when Carrington died. Did not notice anything. A colleague confirms what he was doing at the time.

"When Deirdre Ross died, Banks was with his girlfriend, an Emma Stone. They were interviewed because they both have rooms on this staircase. The police wanted to know if they saw or heard anything.

"Both say they heard Ross shouting and Deirdre scream. They came out of Emma's room to see what was happening and saw Ross sitting on the stairs and Deirdre's body lying on the landing in front of Kazi's door. They said you told them to return to their rooms, so they did."

"That boy? That was Banks?" asked Maggie, trying to remember. She had been so upset about Deirdre her recollection of anything else was blurred.

"Yes, it was. Both Banks and Stone say they didn't see or hear anyone except Ross and Deirdre. And you and Kazi. Marcy thinks they'll probably be called to testify to that at Ross' trial.

"The police interviewed everyone else who was there on your stairway. Which turned out to be only one other student. It's between terms so everyone else was away. The student—a Roger Barnet—was out. Studying in the library. The police confirmed that he was there.

"So in terms of Deirdre's death, it looks like Ross is the person with the best opportunity. The only opportunity. Banks has an alibi for that as well as for Carrington's murder. There were four catering staff. Two students and two townies. And a supervisor. None of them saw anything and again, Banks has an alibi."

"So it looks like it's Ross by default?" asked Maggie, while she wondered how she would break the news to her colleague.

"Looks like. Not that I'll be shedding any tears."

"Yes. I know. Pond scum."

Maggie thought.

"Do the police know Banks is Gordon's son?"

"I don't think so. Or at least it's not in the files. And technically, I guess he's the taxi guy's son. Since he was legally adopted. Do you think Michael knows Ross is his real father?"

"I don't know. He was around four when Ross left Fiona. And you heard Fiona say Ross wasn't much of a father."

"Yeah."

The women thought.

Finally Gina said, "Why don't you read through the files. See if I missed anything. You know all these people."

"All right."

"And I thought I'd go talk to Emma."

"Emma Stone?"

"Yes. Burke's detective agency is famous for its thoroughness. Leave no Stone unturned."

Maggie chuckled. Then asked, "Who will you say you are? What reason will you give? Emma's a student and with students these days it's kid gloves."

"Ha. I thought of that."

Gina was wearing a man-tailored dark grey pants suit. From an inner pocket she produced a small notebook and a ballpoint pen.

"What do I look like?"

Maggie took in Gina's sensible shoes, simple gold stud earrings, tidy hair and neutral lipstick.

"A WPC?"

"Exactly. I used Marcy as an image consultant."

"But isn't it illegal to impersonate…"

"Only if I say I am. I'm not responsible for what Emma assumes."

Maggie shook her head.

"All right. Just please be careful. Emma's room is on the fourth floor. The door on the right. And I'll look through these files."

Gina climbed up three flights of stairs and paused in front of Emma's door to catch her breath. She knocked and a soft voice said, "Come."

The detective entered a messy room that smelled unpleasantly stale. The bed was unmade, a heap of dirty laundry was piled in a corner, a desk held a jumble of papers and books and an open box on top of a dresser revealed a half-eaten pizza.

"Emma Stone?"

A skinny girl was curled up in a beanbag chair. She wore old jeans and an Oxford University t-shirt with stains on the front. Long lank hair would have benefited from a wash— and conditioner. A narrow face was sallow-skinned and unhappy and dark eyes had deep circles underneath.

"Yes. Who are you? What do you want?"

"Gina Burke. I'm following up your interview about Deirdre Ross' death."

"But I already told..."

"Just checking details. We're sticklers for details."

"Do I have to?"

"No. No, you don't have to. But it would helpful if I could just double-check. Woman-to-woman."

Emma sighed.

"All right."

Gina pulled out the desk chair and sat down. She took out her notebook and pen.

"So you reported that you and," she turned a page back and checked. "Michael Banks were in your room when you heard Gordon Ross yelling."

Emma sat silently. Then two tears rolled down her cheeks.

"Emma? Are you all right? What's the matter?" Gina was concerned.

Emma sniffed and Gina sensed that Emma needed to talk to someone.

"Can I help? You can tell me, you know."

Finally Emma said, "It's… It's about Mikey."

"Mikey. Michael Banks? Michael is your boyfriend, isn't he?"

"Was. Was my boyfriend."

"I'm sorry."

"So am I. Sorry. That I ever… Miss… Miss…"

"Burke. But you can call me Gina."

"Gina, that Mikey. He's a complete tosser. We met at the beginning of the year. We were in a seminar together. And we're both scholarship students and neither of us really fit in. Not with the posh, public school lot.

"It might have been okay if we were in computer science. They have lots of geeks there. But we're economics geeks. And in economics, you've got all these guys who are taking it because they think it will be helpful when they're appointed as a cabinet minister someday."

Gina nodded in sympathy.

"So Mikey and I... We started studying together. Then going out. Pubs. Movies. Then..."

"I know I'm nothing to look at. But he said he liked me..."

Emma sniffed again and blew her nose with a used tissue.

"Did he meet someone else?"

"No. No, I could understand that. I mean, look at me."

Gina did. Even with a good haircut and makeup, Emma would never be pretty.

"No. He just became really moody. Monosyllabic. We used to talk about everything. But he shut down. Stopped coming around. Didn't answer my texts. He just avoided me. And refused to talk about it. To give any reason..."

"When was this?"

"It was after Professor Ross' wife died. After he asked me... After I..."

Emma paused.

"After you what, Emma?" Gina asked gently.

"Miss Burke? Gina? How much trouble will I be in if what I told that police sergeant wasn't exactly true?"

Oh dear. Gina had no idea.

"It's better if you tell me what really happened now rather than have it come out later," Gina temporized.

"Well, Mikey asked me to lie." Emma was indignant.

"What did he want you to lie about?"

"That he was in my room when Mrs Ross screamed. He said it would save a lot of hassle with the police. But he wasn't here. He only came in after she fell down the stairs. I heard the yelling. And heard her scream and fall. Then Mikey rushed in and we both went to see what had happened."

Gina tried to keep her expression neutral.

"I can understand why he wanted me to say we were together. Who wants to be hassled? But as soon as we'd both told our stories, he just dropped me. And it wasn't only that I didn't tell the truth."

"No?"

"Even before that. He gave me a small wooden box and asked me to keep it for him but not look in it. He put it behind some books in my bookcase.

"Well, after a few days, of course I looked. What did he think? Who wouldn't? And inside, wrapped in some cotton wool, was a small bottle. A vial. With a cork. And it had some clear liquid in it. I didn't open it. I put it back and then, the next day, Mikey came and took it back."

Gina reflected that if the vial had contained cyanide, it was good that Emma had not opened it.

"Did you ever ask him about it?"

"No. Because I had promised him I wouldn't look. And then Mrs Ross died and Mikey started being so beastly and I forgot about it. But then I heard someone say the Master died of cyanide poisoning and I wondered…"

Emma chewed on her lower lip.

"Did Michael ever talk about his father?"

"The taxi guy? Once or twice. He said his father was not affectionate. But he was fair. And that his mother and father worked really hard. All the time. And his father made sure he studied and got high marks."

Emma paused.

"So how much trouble am I in?" Emma asked anxiously.

"I'll do my best to make sure you're not in any trouble. What you've told me has been very helpful. But for now, please don't mention our conversation to anyone else. Or share this information. About Mikey. Michael. And especially not to Michael. Please don't tell him that we talked. If you happen to see him. Were you planning on going out this afternoon?"

"No. I have some reading to do."

"Then give me two hours and I'll come back. And let me give you my mobile number. In case… Just in case you change your plans."

Gina gave her the number.

SUSAN ALEXANDER

Chapter 46

Gina burst into Maggie's room.

"Maggie! Emma Stone's alibi for Banks was false. He didn't get to her room until after Deirdre fell down the stairs."

"What?"

"We talked. She told me. And that Banks asked her to say they were together to avoid any hassles with the police. And that's not all."

Gina told Maggie about the mysterious box and its vial.

"Do you think that's the cyanide that they found in Ross' rooms?"

"I can't imagine what else it could be."

"So Banks is framing Ross?"

"He certainly had reason enough to hate the man."

"What about Carrington?"

"Well, he was there too. At the reception. So were you. What did you see? Do you remember?"

Maggie frowned. Concentrated.

"It was a bit fraught because of bin Abdulaziz. I was talking to my friend Anne. Thomas was... I think Thomas had gone to get drinks. Alastair came over to apologize for bin Abdulaziz's behaviour. I remember... I remember thinking Alastair looked like he had been enjoying his sherry. His face was flushed.

"Then... A waiter came by with a tray. Alastair's glass was empty. There was a glass of sherry on the tray. Alastair put his empty glass on the tray and took the full glass. That was the glass that had..."

Maggie stopped and remembered the Master's death throes.

"What about the waiter?"

"Um. I was not really paying attention. He went off, I guess. With his tray of glasses."

"Could it have been Banks?"

"I don't know. I've only seen Banks once that I know for sure. When Deirdre died. At the time... I was fairly distraught and wasn't paying attention to anything except Deirdre. The waiter, the one with the tray? He was young. Had dark hair. More than that?" Maggie shrugged.

"Could we look at the catering staff statements again?" Maggie asked.

"We could. But both Banks and his colleague—I think his name was Metcalf—were washing up. So they say."

"Do you think Metcalf could be lying for Banks? Like Emma?"

"We could try to talk to Metcalf. But you said Carrington took the sherry and the waiter left. So Banks probably was in the kitchen when Carrington actually died."

"Let me check something."

Maggie opened a folder and turned some pages. Read. Turned some more pages.

"You know, Gina. I don't see anything that says whose tray it was from which Alastair took the poisoned glass of sherry. Banks says it wasn't his. Metcalf says he served Alastair some sherry but thinks it was earlier. When the receiving line first broke up. The catering supervisor, a Mrs Dennis, says she remembers a tray of drinks on a side table. And that there was also a bar that served sherry. The barman says he poured out the sherry and put the glasses on the trays for the waiters. He was serving drinks when Carrington died."

Maggie leafed through some more reports.

"Oh look. Here's a photo of the box they found in Ross' room. And the vial. Do you think we could show it to Emma and see if she can identify it?"

Gina looked at the picture of a wooden box slightly larger than a deck of cards carved in a primitive pattern and the small, clear glass vial nested in some cotton wool.

"The problem is... That photo. We can't let anyone know we have this. We'll have to let one of the police show it to Emma. Which reminds me…

"Emma is a good kid. A female studying economics. A scholarship student. Feels like a fish out of water here. I don't want her to get into trouble when it comes out she lied to give Banks an alibi. And I'm also worried about what Banks would do if he thinks she might change her story. Since it seems he's already killed two people. She could be in danger. Any ideas?"

Maggie thought.

"We can talk to Stephen. Ask if he would be the one to tell the police what we've discovered and be present when they interview Emma. And make sure she isn't charged with… What would it be? Obstructing an investigation? The master of an Oxford college has a lot of clout."

"And protecting her from Banks?"

"Let's see how quickly we can get in to see Stephen," Maggie said and reached for her mobile.

They were in luck. Mrs Steeples had left for a rare lunch out and Stephen was eating a sandwich at his desk.

"Stephen? You remember Gina Burke. We have some new information. About the murders."

Stephen put down his sandwich.

"A student here at Merrion, Michael Banks, is actually Gordon Ross' son, Hamish Ross. He changed his name when his mother remarried and he was adopted by his stepfather."

"Really? I can't say I know him."

"He's a first year. In PPE. His tutor is Andrew Kittredge."

Maggie explained about Banks' being one of the catering staff at the reception when Alastair died and being on the scene when Deirdre fell.

"He convinced another student, Emma Stone, who was his girlfriend at the time, to give him an alibi. To say that he was in her room, when he wasn't. He also had her keep a box that contained a vial of clear liquid for him for a few days. We think it may have been the cyanide that was found in Gordon's rooms."

"We think Banks framed Ross for the murders," Gina stated flatly.

Stephen looked stunned.

"But why?" he finally asked.

"Gordon was an awful father. He refers to Michael as 'the little pissant' and calls his mother 'that fat cow Fiona.' I'm not surprised Michael hates him. Not that that's any excuse for what he did," Maggie said.

"And we're concerned about Emma Stone. We don't want her to get into trouble now that she's decided to tell the truth," added Gina.

"We hoped you could have the police talk to her when you were present and convince Moss he should be happy to get the truth and not charge the girl with interfering with an investigation or whatever it is when you lie to the police. She is a Merrion student and you are the Master," Maggie reminded Stephen.

Her colleague looked unhappy.

"I should probably call our counsel," he began.

"Who will be more interested in the college's position than poor Emma's," Maggie protested.

"And we're worried about Emma's safety. If Banks decides he can't trust her. He's already killed twice. The sooner she talks to the police, the better," Gina added.

Stephen thought.

"So what do you want me to do?"

"Call Moss. Find out when he can come. Then we'll bring Emma over," Maggie suggested.

He threw up his hands.

"All right. All right."

He rummaged in a desk draw, found a card and dialed a number.

"Detective Inspector Moss? It's Stephen Draycott, from Merrion College. I have some information relating to the murders of Alastair Carrington and Deirdre Ross I want to share with you. How soon can I see you? Here. At the college. At four o'clock? Fine."

Stephen checked his agenda. Sighed.

"I hope you appreciate this. I had a meeting with the Provost that will need to be rescheduled. Mrs Steeples will not be happy," he grumbled.

"We do appreciate this, Stephen. And don't you want all this settled? For the truth to come out?" Maggie demanded.

"I certainly don't want the truth about Gordon's Girls to come out," Stephen countered.

He saw the women's expressions.

"Don't worry. If Emma's testimony indicates that Banks is the killer and not Ross, you can be sure when he returns to Merrion it will be for the sole purpose of packing his things and clearing out."

Gina looked skeptical. "I hope that's the case. And, um, Emma will need an advocate. When she meets with Moss. I would come with her but I have an appointment."

Gina looked at Maggie, who understood why Gina could not be present when Moss was there.

"I'll come with Emma," Maggie said quickly.

"And another thing." Gina was on a roll.

"When I talked to Emma, she was a mess. I'm no psychiatrist, but she's obviously depressed. Don't you people have counsellors for students? Don't you notice these things? I assume you have some sort of responsibility of care."

"It's between terms. The dining hall is closed. So are student services." Stephen was defensive.

"Well, just so you know. Come on, Maggie."

Gina stood and the women left the room.

Susan Alexander

Chapter 47

Gina took Maggie to meet Emma. Even with her experience of how messy student rooms could get, Maggie was taken aback. The girl seemed seriously depressed. Between terms or not, she needed counseling. Someone to talk to.

Gina made the introductions.

"Emma, I assume you know Professor Eliot. A detective, Inspector Moss, is coming to see the Master at four o'clock. Professor Eliot will be there with you to act as your advocate. Both she and Professor Draycott are committed to ensuring there will be no negative consequences for your telling him what you told me."

Emma looked unhappy.

"Miss Burke, can't you be there?"

"I'm sorry, Emma. I have an important appointment that can't be changed."

"Come by my rooms at a little before four o'clock and we can walk over to the Master's Lodge together." Maggie tried to sound reassuring.

"All right."

Just before four o'clock there was a gentle tapping at Maggie's door. She found Emma, who had washed her hair and changed into grey slacks and a yellow turtleneck. She still looked forlorn.

Maggie was ready.

"Don't worry Emma. The Master and I are both on your side."

Moss and Bixby were already waiting in Stephen's study. Moss looked grumpy and Bixby's hair was stuck up even more firmly than when Maggie had seen it before.

Stephen indicated that Maggie and Emma should sit down in two chairs adjacent to his desk.

"Detective Inspector Moss, Miss Stone, who is a student of ours at Merrion, has some new information relating to Deirdre Ross' death. And Alastair Carrington's. However, before she shares it, I want you to make it clear that there will be no, er, repercussions, as it will mean revising her previous statement."

"I can't make any promises..." Moss began.

Stephen stood. "Then this meeting is terminated. Thank you, Professor Eliot and Miss Stone. I'm sorry you..."

"Wait a minute. Let's not be hasty," Moss raised his hand in a placatory gesture.

"Do I have your absolute assurance? If not, I am sure Professor Ross' attorney—his name is Burgess I believe—will be interested in what Miss Stone and Professor Eliot have to say."

Moss growled an assent.

"I will hold you to your word. Very well. First, you should know that we have discovered that one of our Merrion students is Gordon Ross' son. You interviewed him concerning both murders," Stephen stated.

Moss was flabbergasted.

"How do you…"

"We tracked down Ross' first wife. Fiona. They'd had a child. Hamish. When Fiona remarried, Hamish's stepfather, George Banks, adopted the boy. And changed his name to Michael Banks. Michael Banks was one of the catering staff at the reception when Carrington was killed. And his rooms are on the same staircase as Ross'. He was there when Deirdre Ross died.

Moss rounded on Bixby.

"How did you miss this?" he snarled.

The sergeant shrank away from his superior.

"We checked IDs. And whether anyone had form. We followed standard procedure. There was no reason to suspect Banks had any relationship to Ross," Bixby whined.

"And how did you not notice that he was interviewed for both murders?"

"I wasn't the one to question him. It was the PCs. You read all the interviews and you missed the connection."

Moss turned his back on his sergeant and glared at Stephen.

"So Banks is Ross' son. What else do you have to tell me?"

"That when Ross divorced his first wife, Fiona, he basically abandoned the child. Whom he charmingly calls 'the little pissant,'" Maggie spoke up.

"Right. So Ross is not up for a 'Father of the Year' award. A lot of men aren't," said Moss dismissively.

He pointed at Emma.

"So what do you have to tell me?"

Emma looked at Maggie for reassurance. Maggie smiled at her.

"Ignore the inspector's lack of manners and tell him, Emma," she said gently.

Emma took a deep breath.

"Well, when Mrs Ross fell down the stairs, I said that Mikey and I were in my room. And that we came out when we heard her scream. To see what had happened. I said that because Mikey asked me to. Because he didn't want any trouble with the police. But Mikey wasn't with me. When I heard the scream, I went to my door to see and Mikey had just gotten there. To my door. And he was out of breath."

"So Banks has no alibi," Bixby said.

"No. And neither do you," Moss said to Emma, who shrank back in her chair.

"But I was in my room," Emma said shakily.

"Alone."

"Yes, but…"

"Inspector Moss," said Stephen sharply.

"What?"

"I think Emma has more to tell you. And I am not prepared to have you bully her."

Moss glowered, then took a deep breath.

"Right. So. What more do you have to tell me," said Moss.

Emma wrung her hands.

"Before Mrs Ross' death, Mikey brought a small wooden box to my room. It was about the size of a deck of cards and was carved in a kind of aboriginal pattern. Mikey told me he needed me to keep it safe for a few days and he hid it behind some books in my bookcase. He made me promise not to open it."

"And did you open it?"

"Well, yes. After a couple of days. I looked inside. There was a small bottle. A vial, I guess you'd call it. Wrapped in cotton wool. Stopped with a cork. There was a clear liquid inside.

"I put it back really carefully so he wouldn't know I'd broken my promise. A few days later..."

"How many days?" Moss interrupted.

Emma shrugged.

"I don't know. It was after Mrs Ross died. He came and got it. Told me not to tell anyone and to forget about it."

"Humpf. What is your relationship with Banks?" Moss demanded,

"Nothing, now."

"Before?"

"We were friends. We were close."

"How close?"

"Close." Emma blushed.

"Were you having sex?" Moss demanded bluntly.

Emma hung her head and said in a small voice, "Yes."

"We need to talk to Banks," Moss told Stephen.

"Yes, I imagine you do. However, as he is a student here, either I should be present or he should have a solicitor," said Stephen firmly.

"Where is he? Is he in?"

"I will enquire."

Moss rounded on Emma.

"And you. You will need to give us another statement. And sign it. And see if the box Banks gave you and the one we found in Ross' room is the same. Come to the station tomorrow. Better late than never with the truth around here, huh?" Moss sneered.

Maggie stood.

"Are you finished with Miss Stone, Inspector?" she said coldly.

"For now."

"Then come with me, Emma. I think we could both use some coffee. Or tea."

Chapter 48

Maggie took Emma to a nearby teashop and bought her tea and scones. They talked about Emma's family in Manchester and her ambition to be an economist. Michael Banks was not mentioned. When they had finished, Emma announced she was going to the Bodleian. Maggie, who was feeling emotionally exhausted, said she would see Emma back at Merrion and try to find out what was happening.

Maggie was halfway across the quad on her way to the Master's Lodge when she saw a sullen Banks walking between two police constables, followed by a scowling Moss and an obviously chastened Bixby.

She stopped and watched the procession.

The group had reached the Porter's Lodge when suddenly Banks shoved one of the constables against the wall, then pushed the other so he fell backwards. Both the PC and Moss were sent sprawling. As the first constable began to recover, Banks gave him a vicious punch to the jaw. The PC careened into Bixby and they also went down.

Banks turned and sprinted through the portico and into the street. Maggie, who was running to help, heard blaring horns, a screech of brakes and screams. She helped Moss to his feet, then rushed out to see what had happened.

Traffic had stopped and a crowd had gathered. A white van with "Murphy's Meats" painted on the side was skewed across the road. The driver's side door was open and the driver, a stout, middle-aged man in a white uniform, was wringing his hands and repeating, "He just ran out. I couldn't stop. He just ran out."

Maggie saw a body lying face-down on the pavement. It was Banks, motionless, with his arms and legs splayed out. Blood was pooling beneath him.

Bixby was on his mobile while Moss felt Banks' neck for a pulse and the PCs moved the crowd back onto the sidewalk.

Stephen rushed out and saw Maggie.

"Bloody hell. What happened?"

Maggie swallowed.

"Banks. They were... Moss. Bixby. The PCs. They got to the Porter's Lodge and suddenly Banks shoved... They all fell down and Banks just dashed out into the street. He... The van couldn't stop in time."

"God. What a mess. I had better call the Vice Chancellor."

Maggie pushed back some curls that had escaped from her hairclip. Her hand shook and her face was chalk white. Stephen noticed.

"There's nothing we can do here. Come back to the lodge. You look like you could use a drink. I certainly could. The Vice Chancellor can wait a few minutes."

They were sitting in an elegant, formal drawing room that was still filled with the Carringtons' furniture. Late afternoon sun came through mullioned windows and warmed deep blue and pale gold brocade.

Stephen gulped his whisky while Maggie sipped some Vouvray.

"So what happened with Moss and Banks?" she asked as Stephen refilled his tumbler.

"Banks didn't even try to deny Moss' accusations. Mostly he ranted about Ross. About how abusive he had been to both his mother and himself. How he had come to Merrion hoping Ross might have changed and they could connect. But that Ross didn't even recognize him, his own son. Banks found out about Gordon's Girls—his room is on the same staircase as Ross' so that's not too surprising—and decided Ross was beyond redemption and had to go.

"Banks had meant the poisoned sherry for Ross. He said he had nothing against Carrington. Then he overheard the row between Gordon and Deirdre and seized the opportunity. He figured he could frame Ross for both murders and that Ross' spending his life in prison would be an even better revenge than killing him.

"Banks thought he could trust Emma. When he found out what she had told Moss, he called her 'that scrawny cow.' I sensed that if Moss hadn't arrested him, he would have gone after her next."

"It seems he was his father's son after all," Maggie commented sadly.

They drank in silence for some moments.

"And Ross?"

"I assume he'll be released. I already had our counsel draw up a letter terminating him immediately for cause. I told the Vice Chancellor, who was appalled and hoped it could all be kept quiet. I think he'd have preferred that Ross was tried for murder."

Maggie shook her head.

"And speaking of the Vice Chancellor, I had better make that call."

Chapter 49

Back in her rooms, Maggie called Gina.

"Gina? It's over. If you can you meet me for dinner, I'll tell you all about it. And if Marcy is off-duty, she is welcome to come too."

Marcy was free and they agreed that the women would pick up Maggie at Merrion and dine at the Cherwell Boathouse.

Marcy turned out to be tall and trim and wore her blonde hair pulled back in a French braid. Maggie thanked her for her help.

"As soon as Moss came in, he was told to report to the Chief Super's office. In addition to arresting the wrong man, losing a suspect is not a cool thing to do and the Chief didn't believe him when Moss tried to blame it on Bixby." Marcy was gleeful.

"So tell us. We know they arrested Banks. Well, tried to. How was Emma?" Gina demanded.

"Emma did well. Despite Moss' badgering. Stephen made Moss promise there would be no consequences for Emma if she told him what she told us. Oh. And Moss had apparently missed the fact that Banks was interviewed twice—after the deaths of both Alastair Carrington and Deirdre Ross. He was livid with poor Bixby."

"Moss is an asshole and Bixby's IQ approaches double digits. I don't know how he passed his sergeant's exam. They deserve each other," Marcy declared.

"So what about Ross?" Gina asked.

"Stephen Draycott has a letter of termination with cause ready and waiting. And he told the Vice Chancellor about 'Gordon's Girls.' Ross is out of Oxford and, academia being what it is, will have a hard time finding another position this side of Ulan Bator," Maggie assured her.

"Well, I won't say the case hasn't been interesting. But I'll be glad to get back to serving divorce papers and tracking down runaways and deadbeat dads," Gina concluded.

Back at Hereford Crescent, images of Alastair Carrington, Deirdre Ross, Lina Armouti, Emma Stone, Michael Banks and Gordon Ross went round and round in Maggie's mind like wooden horses on a carousel. She assumed his mother had been contacted about Michael by now and she imagined how the woman must be feeling. Was it her fault that Fiona's son was dead? Would it have been better to have left it alone and let Ross be convicted? Would he have been convicted?

Then Maggie remembered Alastair. And Deirdre. Innocent victims. Would Banks have stopped with them? There was Emma, who was a poor keeper of Michael's secrets. And Gordon himself. They were out of danger now.

She thought of all the fathers- and mothers-to-be that she knew. Surely they would be better parents than Gordon Ross. Certainly she would have been a better parent than Gordon, wouldn't she? Or would she? How much of the evil that Michael Banks had done was because of Ross? How much was innate? Then she reminded herself that Michael had chosen to act as he did. Other people had had bad fathers and did not murder.

It was all too much. Maggie's arm in its cast throbbed painfully. She took a painkiller and collapsed into bed.

Chapter 50

Maggie found she could not work. She went over and looked out of her window with its view of the Merrion quad. Between terms, it was empty and quiet. No Niqabis lurked in the shadows of the cloister. Instead, she saw a gardener removing weeds from a bed of vibrant red tulips.

Then she noticed Gordon Ross. He was scowling. His face was red, his shoulders were hunched up and his feet struck the path with unnecessary force.

Maggie was reminded of two lines from an old hymn she used to sing in church.

"Though every prospect pleases,
And only man is vile."

The song was about far-off, pagan lands, but could just as well be applied to Oxford. The university with its dreaming spires was certainly a pleasing prospect. And Gordon Ross was definitely a man who was vile.

She heard footsteps on the stairs. Then a fist pounded on her door.

She went to open it herself.

Ross brushed past and turned to face her.

"So thanks for nothing, Eliot. You may have gotten me out of prison, but you had to kill my son to do it. And you got me fired. You and your dyke girlfriend."

Maggie was speechless for a moment and then became angry. Really angry. She remembered Alastair's terror as he died. And Deirdre's clutching the picture from the sonogram.

"Ross, you may not be a murderer, but you're still pond scum. Get out of my room."

She grabbed Gordon's arm, thrust him through the door, slammed it shut and locked it. Then she cried.

When her tears had subsided, Maggie packed up her laptop and rummaged in her purse for her sunglasses. They would hide eyes that were red and swollen from crying.

She had received a text from Thomas. Traffic permitting, he would get to Hereford Crescent late in the afternoon. In time for an early dinner. She would surprise him and be there when he arrived.

Maggie was sitting in the library with an open bottle of Meursault and an untouched glass of wine when Thomas came in. He was surprised but pleased to see her. Then he noticed her expression.

"Maggie, what is it? More Niqabis?"

"No, although..."

She told him about Lina Armouti and her misguided hatred. Then she told him about the discovery that Ross had a son at Merrion. A son who hated his father, had killed Carrington by mistake and had pushed Deirdre to her death in the hope that his father would be blamed. That he had tried to escape the police and been hit by a van and killed. She did not tell him about her part in any of these events.

When she finished, tears were running down her cheeks.

Thomas held her.

"Mon pauvre paillon."

He pulled a perfectly pressed white cotton handkerchief from his pocket and handed it to his wife.

"Thank you."

Maggie buried her face in Thomas' tweed jacket. It smelled like Thomas and his citrusy-spicy aftershave.

"Thomas?" Her voice was muffled.

"Yes, my dear?"

"Take me home."

Thomas went still as trumpets sounded triumphant fanfares in his head.

"Home? To Boston?"

"No!"

"Home… to Beaumatin?"

He felt rather than saw Maggie's nod.

"Very well. We can leave right after dinner."

"Thomas, could we please leave… now?"

He tightened his hold.

"Of course. Just as you wish, my dear."

Maggie did not see his smile.

About the author

A native New Yorker, Susan Alexander lives in Luxembourg, where she writes and undertakes research on public policy and the social sciences.

She enjoys writing about women who have led complex and interesting lives, their relationships and the choices they have made. It frequently happens that there is some murder and mayhem involved in as well.

Read the beginning of the next Snowdrop Mystery

JERSEY JONES AND THE NEW WORLD ORDER

Available now through Amazon in print and Kindle formats.

SUSAN ALEXANDER

The New World Order

1. According to conspiracy theorists, the New World Order consists of a shadowy group of the ultra-rich and powerful who are plotting to take over the world, eliminate nation states and establish a global, totalitarian government controlled by themselves to their benefit. Political and, especially, financial events are interpreted as being orchestrated by this group and mainstream media reporting is assumed to be concealing the truth.

2. A reality TV show created by new media celebrity Jersey Jones. The half-hour show features Jersey and her crew travelling the by-ways of America and interviewing ordinary people about their daily lives. *Jersey Jones and the New World Order* airs weekly on cable's America's Home Entertainment Network.

Susan Alexander

Preface

"The world is going to hell in a handbasket," complained Lady Ainswick as she brandished a newspaper.

"As my father used to say," she added hurriedly.

Lady Ainswick came from a generation when ladies did not use bad language. And when bad language meant words like "hell" and "damn" and "ass." Stronger expressions, such as the "f" word, were not even part of her consciousness.

"*The Daily Post*?" Maggie laughed.

"Cedric gets it. He thinks it's funny."

Lady Ainswick—Beatrix to her friends—obviously did not share her husband's sense of humour. In her mid-sixties, the viscountess was wiry, of medium height and wore her greying hair pulled back in a bun. The light blue twin set she had on over a long grey skirt matched her eyes. Maggie was sitting in the kitchen of Rochford Manor, the Ainswick's home, and enjoying a coffee with her friend.

"The media have certainly lost any consideration for personal privacy," Maggie agreed.

Maggie and Beatrix stared at the front page. Under the headline "Kate's Baby Bump" was a picture of the Duchess of Cambridge, looking lovely in a stylish dress that revealed a slight bulge.

"Baby bump. What a horrid term, Can't the woman be allowed at least a semblance of privacy? And dignity?" Maggie agreed with her friend.

"I blame what they call those reality shows on television. And Facebook. And YouTube. And Twitter. Now that everyone wants to be a celebrity and is willing to share everything about themselves, whether it's nude photos or what they ate for breakfast or how their Uncle Fred molested them as a child, they think no one else deserves any privacy either."

"At least I don't need to worry. A video of someone sitting in front of a computer all day long would hardly attract many hits on YouTube. There is nothing less interesting than someone doing high level research. Unless, of course, one has a particular interest in that field," Maggie said thoughtfully.

Beatrix looked at her friend sceptically but refrained from sharing her thoughts. Which were that, as a controversial senior fellow at an Oxford college, in addition to being the wife of a peer from one of the oldest aristocratic families in England, the media would find Maggie very interesting indeed.

Chapter 1

Maggie and Thomas had been invited to lunch at Pemberley, a Cotswolds estate that had been bought and renovated by Stanley Einhorn, the American hi-tech venture capitalist and billionaire. He had funded the chair that Maggie currently held at Merrion College and had recently married Maggie's close friend and Oxford colleague, Chitta Kazi.

Thomas stopped his Land Rover at Pemberley's gate house, where a guard was posted.

"Raynham," he said.

"Raynham," repeated the guard, checking a clipboard.

"You're expected. Please drive through."

The gates opened and Thomas proceeded up a long driveway to a beautifully restored Georgian country house. Parked in front of the house was a shiny black van. On its side, in iridescent, Day-Glo pink letters, was written, "Jersey Jones and the New World Order."

"Jersey Jones and the New World Order? Does that mean anything to you?" asked Thomas.

"Nope. Haven't a clue," replied Maggie.

Thomas parked. He got out, came around, opened Maggie's door and helped her out of the car.

Maggie smiled. She wondered if she would ever take Thomas' perfect manners for granted. Probably not, she decided.

Stanley came out of the mansion's front door. In his early forties, he was of medium height and had thinning brown hair. His most unusual feature were his eyes, which were nearly colourless. He was casually dressed in tan slacks and a red Ralph Lauren polo shirt.

"Maggie! Thomas!" he beamed.

Three people emerged behind Stanley.

The first was a woman. She was gorgeous. In her mid-twenties, she had honey blonde hair that fell in a luxuriant curtain down her back. Perfectly shaped brows arched over sky blue eyes that were framed in lashes thick with mascara. A fine, straight nose did not distract from full lips that were coloured a luscious rosy pink.

Tight designer jeans showed off a derrière Jennifer Lopez might envy, while a skin-tight pink t-shirt showcased an equally enviable bosom. She wore matching pink platform sneakers and a dozen golden bangle bracelets snaked up one arm. She carried a microphone.

"My goodness. Who can this be?" wondered Maggie.

Behind the woman was a man holding a professional-looking video camera on one shoulder. He was also in his twenties and, from biceps that bulged beneath a New York Mets baseball shirt, obviously worked out. He was handsome, in a young Marlon Brando sort of way, with tousled dark hair and bedroom eyes. Or eye, as only one was visible, with the other glued to the camera's viewfinder. His posture shouted, "Attitude!"

The third person was another woman, who stood further back and was hesitating inside the front door. Also in her twenties, she had long, limp strawberry blonde hair whose split ends suggested the need for a haircut. She wore no makeup to cover her freckles and pale green eyes squinted in the sunlight. She was skinny and her well-worn jeans into which were tucked a grey t-shirt lettered with "Stanford" in red made it obvious that she lacked any of the curves of her companion. Long, pale fingers with bitten nails played with a lank strand of hair.

The first woman pranced up to Thomas. She spoke clearly into the microphone. "So Jersey Junkies, guess who's coming to dinner?"

The man moved in and pointed his camera at Thomas.

Thomas frowned. He put one hand over the microphone and with the other pushed the video camera away. He looked at Maggie and his look said, "Did you know about this?"

Maggie shook her head.

"Stanley?" asked Thomas in arctic tones.

"Lighten up, Thomas. This is Jersey Jones. Surely you've heard of Jersey Jones and the New World Order?"

"No, Stanley. I have not." Thomas' tone was discouraging.

"Really? Oh. Well, this is Jersey. And her cameraman, Mike Martinelli. And that's Cressida. Cressida Figg. She's called Cressie," he waved towards the front door where Cressie still hovered. "She's the, um, editor. The video editor," he clarified.

"Jersey's a celebrity. She has over twenty-two million followers on Twitter. Her TV series, Jersey Jones and the New World Order, is viral. And she's here to interview me for a show about my life that will be aired on ACEN— America's Cable Entertainment Network," Stanley continued.

Well, that explains the van, Maggie thought.

Stanley turned to Jersey. "Jersey? This is Thomas…"

He noticed Thomas' expression.

"Or perhaps I should introduce him as Lord Raynham."

Jersey appraised Thomas. Tall and thin, with greying brown hair and bright blue eyes, he had handsome, chiselled features and stood straight in his impeccably tailored country tweeds. Despite his sixty-one years, Jersey was immediately interested. She glanced at Mike, who mouthed "Money."

"Lord? Is he really a lord? Or is that just a name? Like Duke Ellington. Or the Artist Formerly Known as Prince. Or…"

"No. He's a baron."

"Like Sacha Baron Cohen? You know. Borat? Ali G?"

Seeing Thomas' look of confusion, Maggie decided perhaps she should help.

"No, a baron is a peer. Like a duke. Or an earl…"

"Hey. Like Duke of Earl?" interjected Mike in an accent that broadcast his Brooklyn origins. He was ignored.

"So why aren't you Baron Ray… Ray…"

"Raynham. Because a baron is addressed as lord," said Thomas, drawn in despite himself.

"So you're not Baron, but Lord Thomas Raynham?"

"Er, no. Just Lord Raynham."

Now it was Jersey's turn to look confused. But she smiled a kittenish smile, put her microphone back in place and gestured to Mike, who continued filming.

"So Jersey Junkies, it looks like the New World Order is meeting the Old World Order."

She turned to Maggie.

"And you are…"

"Maggie," she said hurriedly. She extended her hand and tried to keep out of the range of Mike's camera, as well as Thomas' scowl because his wife was avoiding using her title. As usual.

"Maggie," repeated Jersey, shaking hands with the woman who had long, unruly auburn curls that were trying to escape from a hairclip and deep green eyes. Equally thin and nearly as tall as her husband but some half dozen years younger, she was casually dressed in navy blue slacks and an oversized fisherman's sweater.

"Maggie is Lady Raynham. Although she's also Professor Eliot. She's the Weingarten Fellow at Merrion College, Oxford. It's a chair I funded. Named after my mother," Stanley explained.

"You're Baron's wife? As well as some university brainiac?"

"Um, yes I'm Thom… Lord Raynham's, er, wife. And a professor at Oxford."

"Cool. You get that, Jersey Junkies? But hey. You don't sound English. Your accent. Are you American?"

Maggie hesitated, then admitted, "Yes."

"Knew it. Where from?"

"Um, Boston."

"From Boston. I'm a Jersey girl, myself, but I won't hold it against you. Let me know what you think, all you Jersey Junkies from New England."

Maggie smiled weakly.

Chitta appeared in the doorway. She frowned when she saw Jersey with her microphone and Mike with his camera, then tried to replace it with a smile.

"Hi, Maggie. Hi, Thomas. Why don't you come in?"

Lunch was informal. Mrs Peters, the Pemberley housekeeper, served a vegetable soup, ham, cheese, bread and salad. Dessert was fruit and pound cake.

Maggie sat next to Chitta, a stunningly beautiful Bangladeshi. In her late thirties, she was four months' pregnant. She was also a vegetarian, so she skipped the ham. Maggie noticed Cressida only ate salad and some fruit.

Chitta followed Maggie's glance.

"Cressie's a vegan," she murmured.

"Oh dear," was Maggie's reaction.

Jersey was entertaining the table.

"We were filming the New World Order in Oklahoma. A really small town in the boonies. Tornado central. It was lunchtime and we saw this Chinese joint. It had a big sign in the window. 'Now serving sushi.' So we figured we'd check it out."

Maggie glanced at Thomas. While she and Chitta and Stanley loved sushi, Thomas was not a fan.

"So we go in and the décor is pretty much what you'd expect. Formica and linoleum and these plastic golden cats that wave their paws and are supposed to attract money. There were maybe a dozen cats waving away but the place was empty so I'm not sure they were particularly effective. Anyhow, we asked about the sushi and this young Chinese woman says yes, they have sushi. There is a sushi platter. So Mike and I say that's what we'll have while Cressie asks for vegetable fried rice.

"About fifteen minutes later out comes this big plate filled with sushi. It looks like tekka maki. You know, those rolls with tuna in the middle that are wrapped with seaweed? And it has little dishes for soy sauce and blobs of green wasabi and small piles of pink pickled ginger.

"Mike and I take our chop sticks and each pick up a piece but then look more closely. Something doesn't seem right. So we deconstruct one and find it's not tuna at all but Spam! Can you believe it? They'd served us sushi made out of Spam!"

Everyone laughed except Thomas and Cressie.

"So that's what we mean when we talk about Oklahoma sushi," Jersey finished.

As lunch was ending, Chitta murmured to Maggie, "Do you have a moment?" Then said more loudly, "I must show you what we're doing with the baby's nursery."

The group stood. Stanley turned to Thomas. "Thomas? I have a question. My study?"

Thomas followed Stanley and Maggie went upstairs with Chitta.

Maggie admired the large, sun-filled room with light pink walls and curtains in a gay floral pattern.

"Pink?" she asked Chitta. She knew the baby was going to be a girl.

"It seems Stanley's very traditional that way," Chitta smiled.

She plopped down in an arm chair.

"Maggie, I need your help," she said seriously.

"Of course. Anything I can do."

"That woman. I've got to get her out of here."

"Woman? Oh. You mean Jersey."

"Yes. Jersey. She's been here for a week and I don't think I can stand it much longer."

"What's…"

"She and that microphone. And camera. They're everywhere. We have no privacy except when we're locked in our bedroom. Or the bathroom. Stanley was thrilled when he learned the network wanted her to do a programme about his life. Apparently she's quite famous although I'd never heard of her. Had you?"

Maggie shook her head.

"And Stanley? He's like a puppy dog. He's happy to have her follow him around."

"You don't think…" Maggie was concerned.

"Oh no. No, Stanley would never... But she's so pretty. And perky. And young. And I feel so fat. And ugly. I don't recognise myself when I look in a mirror. And Jersey just makes my condition seem more obvious. At least to me. And it's not like Stanley and I have that much time together anyhow with me at Oxford and Stanley still trying to take over what's left of the world that he doesn't already own..."

Chitta looked like she was about to cry.

"I'm sorry. It's my hormones. They're out of control." Chitta sniffed.

"Oh dear." Maggie could empathise. She took her replacement hormones religiously every day to avoid just that.

"Is there anything I can do?" she asked.

"Make her go away, Mommy," Chitta tried to joke.

"Surely Jersey must have finished interviewing Stanley. Won't she move on?"

"The interviews are done as far as I know. Cressie is editing the files—it's all digital these days. But Jersey thinks England is quaint and she's had this inspiration about doing some shows on The New World Order meets the Old World Order. She wants to stick around. And Jersey can be really relentless."

"She certainly can't think Stanley is part of the Old World Order," Maggie pointed out.

"No. But..."

Maggie had an intuitive flash.

"You mean that's why Stanley invited Thomas to lunch? I thought that was out of character."

Chitta looked embarrassed.

"I'm well aware of how much I owe Stanley. And you know I'd do anything I possibly could for you. But getting Thomas to agree to being interviewed by Jersey? And filmed? He hates publicity. I think he'd rather be torn apart by a pack of badgers. Or wouldn't see much difference between that and being the subject of a Jersey episode."

Maggie thought. "Perhaps she could be diverted to Oxford. That should certainly be quaint enough for her. And she must have fans among the undergrads."

"Yes. Well, it's good to think we have a Plan B. But you know Stanley."

Maggie did know Stanley.

"The irresistible force is about to meet the immovable object, then," she concluded.

Chitta nodded and both women laughed.

Chapter 2

Thomas followed Stanley to his study. The large room was panelled in dark wood. One wall held bookshelves. Another looked like mission control, with an assortment of built-in monitors showing news channels and other media feeds and financial market reporting. Additional screens displayed what looked like spreadsheets with numbers blinking in green and red. A massive carved oak desk held a laptop and phone set, but nothing else.

Stanley indicated one of a pair of leather club chairs that framed a fireplace.

"Sit down, Thomas. Would you like some more coffee?"

"No, thank you. So, how can I help you?" he asked politely.

Thomas did not like Stanley. He resented the man's close friendship with his wife, even though he knew it was platonic. And although the Raynhams had considerable wealth, he was acutely aware that it was dwarfed by Stanley's billions. And that he lacked the power those billions gave the man. Whom he knew could be ruthless.

Thomas also knew he had Stanley to thank for Maggie's fellowship, which allowed her to spend less time at Oxford and more with him at home at Beaumatin, the Raynham ancestral estate. And that he had conspired with Stanley to bring this about. Which was something he hoped that Maggie would never discover.

Stanley sat down behind his desk in a modern, ergonomic chair at odds with its Georgian surroundings.

"So Thomas. I have a problem and I'm hoping you can help me out."

He who dances must pay the piper, Thomas reminded himself grimly.

"You've met Jersey. She's awesome, isn't she? Smart. Pretty. Successful. A darling of the cyber set. In fact, I'm probably going to make a big investment in her company. But that's beside the point."

Stanley twirled around to look at a screen that was flashing green, then turned back to Thomas.

"But Jersey is making Chitta unhappy. Chitta hasn't said anything and doesn't know that I'm aware of how she feels. But as you can imagine, I would do anything, absolutely anything, to keep Chitta from being unhappy. Especially in her current condition. So I need you to do something for me."

"Yes?" Thomas' tone was not encouraging.

"Jersey's come up with this idea. I think it's great. But if she follows through with it, it would mean her staying longer at Pemberley and that's not an option. So here's what I wondered.

"Jersey has a show. Jersey Jones and the New World Order. And she thinks it would be cool to do a short series she wants to call Jersey Jones and the Old World Order. About your quaint olde, merrie olde England. And as there's no one I know who is more Old World Order than you, the twenty-eighth baron, I would like you to agree to let her come to Beaumatin to film part of it."

Thomas looked pained.

"Couldn't she film some Morris dancers? Ride with the Beaufort Hunt? Attend a meeting of the Bullingdon Club? From what you've said, they must be fans."

"No. That's not what she does. She does interviews. Captures people's lives. Their hopes and dreams contrasted with the reality of their daily existence. It's quite compelling stuff. Despite the pop packaging."

Thomas made a restless gesture.

"Invite her to come to Beaumatin. Put her up. Let her follow you around. Visit the sheep. Ride. And Maggie still shoots, doesn't she? Jersey needn't include shots of your Constable. Or your Rossetti. That would not be a smart idea, not with your dodgy security. But the baronial portrait gallery would certainly be a hit. And what's the name of those friends of yours? The viscount and his wife?"

"The Ainswicks?"

"They're the ones. They'd also be perfect for what she has in mind."

Thomas thought of how Beatrix would react if he suggested she be interviewed by Jersey. He almost smiled.

"And what about Maggie? I can't imagine she'd want to do this anymore than I..."

"Ah, Maggie. Maggie will do whatever you want. She always does, doesn't she? When it comes right down to it. Like her resigning the Appleton chair to accept the Weingarten fellowship. So she could spend more time at Beaumatin. With you."

There it was. The blackmail.

And what did he know? Maggie might even enjoy being in a Jersey episode, he rationalised.

"All right, Stanley. You've made your point. I'll invite Jersey. Does that crew of hers come along as well?"

Stanley nodded.

"When can I expect them?"

"How about tomorrow. Say, after lunch?"

Stanley noticed Thomas' expression.

"Man up, Thomas. What's that expression you Brits have? Close your eyes and think of England."

"So what you're saying, Stanley, is that I'm about to be buggered."

Stanley laughed.

AND ONLY MAN IS VILE

Susan Alexander